THE MAN

IN THE

BOAT

Other Fiction
by Cheryl B. Dale

Romantic Suspense

Intimate Portraits
Set Up

Paranormal/Gothic Romance

Treacherous Beauties
The Warwicks of Slumber Mountain

Light Mystery

Taxed to the Max
Overtaxed and Underappreciated

Vintage Mystery

Losing David

This book was previously published in 2012 by MuseItUp Publishing.

Copyright Information
Copyright 2012-2014 by Cheryl Dale
Published by J&H Press
Previously Published by MuseItUp Publishing
Cover Art by J&H Press
Edited by: B.L. Wilson
Copyedited by: Greta Gunselman

ISBN: 978-0-9908695-3-5

www.cherylbdale.com
cherylbdale.blogspot.com
cherylbdale@hotmail.com

THE MAN

IN THE

BOAT

by

Cheryl B. Dale

J&H Press

PROLOGUE

THE HOUSE CAN'T be far.

The man in the boat squinted at the water out of the good eye not swollen by the beating. Breathing hurt.

God, please help me find it soon.

Emily would fix the whole stinking mess. If he didn't believe that, he might as well give up.

Too many years since he'd been on the lake. Maybe he'd forgotten what the point looked like. What if he missed the way?

I'll never make it. God help me, I'll never make it.

At that moment, his bass boat rounded an island. Before him lay the rocky promontory marking the familiar lake finger.

There!

He sobbed. Somehow he got the wheel turned toward the rocks.

He would make it, he would. He'd escaped and now the bastards would pay. For the beatings. For everything.

Emily would see to it they paid.

He looked over his shoulder. Nothing there.

A fishing boat anchored to the side. A wet-suited skier cutting a boat's wake. A sailboat, sheets slack.

No sign of them, but any minute the big cruiser might roar into view.

Everything seemed dark. Was it clouding up?

No, the sun shone, but boathouses looked like cottages, floating brush like boats. His sight . . .

He could hardly see.

Would he recognize the cove?

He had to. He couldn't fail. Not now. Not so close.

The small boat jounced over the wave crests. He clung to its wheel.

There it was! The channel.

Toward its end, a cove lay ringed by stands of wild cherry, pine, and dogwoods. In the cedar house high on the hill with its tubs of geraniums and petunias, Emily waited.

Emily would make sense of what had happened.

Renewed strength swept through the man in the boat.

I'm going to make it.

CHAPTER ONE

A BOAT HUMMED in the distance.

In tankini and sunscreen, I should have been enjoying the sun beaming down on the swim dock at Lake Lanier.

Instead, I brooded over a life-changing decision.

Marrying Mark had been a mistake. Everyone had warned me, but I hadn't listened.

I'd thought I could handle his abrupt and unexpected departures as well as the weeks or months of separations his job required. Surely, my love would break down his reserve.

Wrong. All my hopes. All my beliefs. Everything.

As I sat cross-legged amid glistening lake waters and blue skies, the same sad facts led me to the same sad conclusion.

Divorce.

My mind said it was necessary, but my heart broke.

Biting a lip, I put my name over one side of a legal pad and Mark's name on the other.

Go on. Do it. Set out what has to be divided.

How could I tell everyone? What would I say?

Fee, level-headed older sister and confidante, knew about our problems. She'd been the one to urge, "Come up to Alexandria and stay with us, Steve. Or go up to the lake cottage for a few days. Divorce is so final. Make sure what you want before you do anything you'll regret."

Fee was right. Three days alone had cleared my head.

Still . . .

Once set down in black and white, the words couldn't be rescinded.

Do it.

SUV, I wrote firmly under Mark's name.

Coupe, went in my column.

From the lake channel, the boat's drone increased.

Sweet Rowdy raised her head and whimpered.

A gift from Mark in better times, the mutt masquerading as part Sheltie was my sole companion.

Methodical waves slapped the sides of the swim dock tied to the boathouse, making Mark's boats rock against their moorings. From woods rimming the lake, a raucous jay scolded. Three ducks, beady eyes looking for a handout, swooped down to float on the swells in front of the swim dock.

"Sorry, guys. No bread today."

Late April in Georgia was too early for swimming but perfect for lazing in the sun. Too glorious a day to end a marriage.

I'd call Fiona first, tell her Mark and I are through. Tell her we don't talk, don't have sex.

He never cared about our baby. He couldn't have.

I would see a lawyer as soon as I got back to Decatur.

Eyes teared up, but I swiped them impatiently.

A cloud inundated the brilliant sun. In the sudden shadow, the boat whine intruded.

Concentrate on the list.

Bank accounts. Mark's went under his name, mine under my name. The joint account went in the middle alongside furniture and stocks to be evenly divided. That was fair.

The sun emerged.

The boat reached the mouth of our cove.

Too bad I couldn't stay here forever, cocooned in the protective tranquility of the lake. But the forty-year-old bungalow belonged to Mark. Before our marriage, he'd purchased it from a friend's grandmother. The time we'd spent renovating it had cemented our relationship, but the lake house remained his.

I put it under his name.

We'd bought the Decatur house because it was convenient to Emory University and my work, so the old house in Atlanta's suburb went under my name.

An equitable division of property.

Mark wouldn't protest. He was never unreasonable.

Sweet Rowdy growled. She sprang up and ran from the shade of the boathouse into sunshine that turned her coat radiant as an angel's halo.

"Rowdy. Calm down."

Angel she wasn't, but she was near enough despite her chasing squirrels, terrifying strangers, threatening delivery men and, when she escaped from her fence, retrieving peculiar garbage from neighboring cans.

She'd been a lifeline during the past terrible months.

Now she danced and bared her teeth at the encroaching noise. As she let out an experimental woof, she cocked one eye toward me, seeking approval.

"Hush, Rowdy-gal."

The offender came into sight.

A small bass boat, low and narrow and built for speed.

Not unusual. Anglers often trolled the cove before heading back toward the riverbed where bigger fish lurked.

Rowdy began to bark in earnest.

"Come on, Sweet Rowdy. It's just a fishing boat. Mind your manners."

Back to the list.

I chewed my pen.

Furniture could be a problem. We both loved the antique icebox purchased on our honeymoon. And the old dish cabinet picked up at a yard sale . . .

The boat sped into the cove. Sweet Rowdy pranced and yapped.

"It's okay, Rowdy-gal. I'll protect you. Sit."

She whined but sat as the motor got louder.

Great. My last peaceful afternoon, ruined by an obnoxious fisherman.

I had to go home tomorrow. Mark's agent bragged that the sculpture for the Dream Sugar Corporation, the largest commission he'd ever wangled, would lead to bigger things for Mark. I'd reluctantly promised to attend the unveiling.

No need to spoil his night. I'd keep my word and wait till afterward to tell him I wanted a divorce. Mark shouldn't be surprised, but if so, he'd never show it.

He'd met my announcement that I was going up to the lake to think about our marriage with the same noncommittal air as he met everything. Anger and joy equally contained, all true emotion hidden behind those cursed laughing eyes and charming smile that revealed nothing.

I'd admired his composure before we married, but even then I'd suspected he would be a hard man to learn, a hard man to understand.

Not hard to love. He'd never been hard to love.

Stop it! Don't you cry.

I blinked hard.

Mark never lowered his guard, not even with me. Only in his studio did he give vent to whatever passions his amiable mask confined. There, his talented hands breathed life into wood and stone and metal as he created wondrous animals and plants and fairies.

And babies.

Two weeks ago I had found the finished marble cherub with glowing face and waving hands and feet, looking for all the world like a real infant encased in stone for eternity.

Mark, drying his hands after washing off clay, had caught me staring. "Good, isn't it? Maybe the best thing I've ever done."

I almost lost it.

That's when I realized Mark was incapable of real grief, which in turn meant he was incapable of love.

Real love. The kind of love I needed. The kind that joined two people so they could laugh at jokes no one else understood and finish each other's thoughts before the words were spoken. The kind of love that shared everything.

Hopes. Fears. Heartbreak.

In the bright sun, my heart twisted remembering the lifelike statue. The tiny fingers partly curved into fists, the sweet mouth parted and turned up as if crowing.

No! No use thinking of the sculpture that had meant the real end of our marriage. *Put it away.*

Bzzzzzzzzzzzzz.

"For pity's sake." Why didn't the stupid boat slow down or go away?

Sweet Rowdy, obediently sitting but desperate to jump up, yipped.

The boat veered toward our dock.

Probably one of the reckless kids who buzzed swimmers and cut in front of skiers. A cocky, inexperienced teenager pushing the family boat to its limit.

No way to concentrate with so much noise and misery. Time to go up.

I stacked legal pad and pen under the eReader beside my cell and then stood up on the rough planks and shrugged into a terry cover-up. Bare feet slid into canvas clogs.

The boat didn't slow down. I glanced around.

My jaw dropped.

That idiot kid was about to run into a dock and smash his father's boat to smithereens. Serve him right, too. Still, he should be obeying the No Wake sign.

I waved. "Hey."

He didn't see me.

I jumped across to the walkway winding through the boat slips, ran to the end, and waved both arms. "Hey!"

The driver didn't notice.

"Are you crazy? Slow that thing down!"

The boat got so close I could see orange-red hair whipped by the wind. A haggard face.

Teeth bared in defiance.

No kid. A man.

"Slow down," I screamed at the top of my lungs.

He lay over the wheel, as still as a dead person except for the one eye, wide and staring behind billowing carrot-colored tendrils.

Then the boat zoomed by. It missed by inches the swim dock vacated moments earlier.

The prow embedded itself into the bank. The crunch reverberated round the cove. The motor shut off.

The abrupt silence, the cessation of all sound except the churning water, left a vacuum.

The boathouse pitched wildly. So did Mark's two boats it sheltered and the swim dock tied alongside. Thrown off-balance, I clung to the rail to keep from falling into the lake.

My original surprise morphed into outrage. Outrage faded to dismay.

What kind of nut would run a boat up on the bank? He had to be drunk. Maybe a druggie.

And I was by myself.

Was I safe? Sweet Rowdy, racing back and forth between me and the boat, offered little protection.

As soon as the deck stopped its wild rocking, I snatched her up in the middle of a boisterous round and tucked her squirming body under my arm. "Shut up, Sweet Rowdy."

Offense is the best defense.

I marched off the dock to the end of the ramp near where the bass boat lay on the grass.

"What do you think you're doing? You nearly—"

The man stayed slumped over the wheel.

Sweet Rowdy slid out of my suddenly limp arms and ran barking toward the boat.

I took a hesitant step. "Hey." The man didn't stir. Had he suffered a heart attack? "Hey, mister, are you okay?"

Slowly, very slowly, as if the slightest movement pained him, the man lifted his head.

He was alive.

Bright hair fell away from the white face.

When part of his chest became visible, I gasped and raised my sunglasses.

No need to verify. The dark lenses hadn't distorted.

A long gash, brownish and clotting, covered the left side of his forehead. His other features were puffy and swollen where his face had rammed the windshield. Freckles, stark against the pasty skin, popped out.

But his face didn't trigger my gasp. Nor did the bottom lip, gnawed bloody.

The thing that caught me, the thing I couldn't take my eyes off, spotted the front of his once-white dress shirt.

Bright red on the edges, deep red in the middle, enlarging slowly outward.

My heart lurched. "You're bleeding."

I started toward him before stopping. He didn't need clumsy hands causing more pain.

The man mumbled something unintelligible. One eye was swollen shut. The other, maybe once blue but now a glazed, indeterminate gray, stared.

He reached out to me. I bent as close as possible to the moving lips without touching him. I didn't want to touch him.

I might hurt him, I rationalized. "I'm sorry, I'm sorry, I'm so sorry. I can't understand you."

"Em-i-ly." He rasped out each syllable.

A boating accident. Several years ago a boat's gas tanks had exploded on the lake, killing a man and hurting several others.

No, this boat was intact. Only the man was hurt. Something had happened to him, not the boat.

Emily. Who was Emily?

Calm down. Focus on what's important.

"You need help." I ran back to the rocking swim dock for my cellphone. Everything, even the eReader, had been dumped into the rough waters.

Damn.

I rushed back to the boat and the unmoving man. "Listen, my cell fell into the lake. I'll have to go up to the house and call for help, okay?" *Steady, steady. Don't sound like a wimp. Show some confidence.* "I won't be long. I'll come right back."

Bloody fingers, stopping me when I would have run away, caught the pocket of my cover-up. "Tell Emily . . . Don't give them . . . Don't—"

A gurgle came from his throat. He fell forward, still clutching my cover-up.

Was he bleeding inside? No time to waste. He needed help. I gingerly pried the terrycloth loose, trying not to flinch. "I have to go up to the house to call."

He offered no further resistance. "Tell Emily . . ." His good eye clouded.

"Yes. I will. I'll be right back." I started to say he should wait there, realized how absurd the words would sound, and repeated encouragingly, "I'll be back with help. I promise."

He groaned.

Sweet Rowdy barked as she caught my sense of urgency, but the coward in me was glad at the excuse to run away, to flee so I needn't look at the spreading stains.

As I turned, his flat sigh of despair floated past my shoulder. "Em-i-leee . . ."

The Army Corps of Engineers preserves the property adjoining the lake in its natural state. I sprinted over it, Sweet Rowdy on my heels. Across a grassy strip into the woods we ran, beneath trees where birds had chirped not five minutes ago. There we flung through undergrowth, hitting the worn path scattered with blown dogwood petals. They stood out stark and fragile against the brown humus and pine needles.

I catalogued the creamy dollops with one side of my mind as Rowdy and I flew through the glade. The demise of the dogwood blossoms became entwined to the plight of the unknown man.

Hurry, hurry. He could die, too.

The interior of the pines was dark and tangy, cool after the sun's warmth. A few minutes ago my only concern had been a divorce. Now . . .

I panted, ignoring the stitch in my side.

Another, different motor came from the lake. Low in pitch and muffled.

A large boat. An inboard.

I couldn't see it for the woods, but I could hear it plainly.

Maybe its driver would stop and wait with the injured man. If he had a cell, he would call for help.

My lungs burned.

By the time I barreled through the woods and passed the brilliant azaleas Mark had planted beside the walk, I could barely navigate the steep set of wooden stairs.

On the deck by the flowerboxes, my legs faltered. I gulped for air and scanned the normal panorama of blue waters ringed by mountains for the boat I'd heard.

There. A big cruiser with several passengers.

One of them pointed past our dock toward the man in the boat. The prow turned. They'd seen him.

They'll help him.

Energized, I ran through the screened porch.

A woman answered the emergency line, and I gasped out the situation. "And he's hurt really bad."

"What do you mean by hurt?" The woman sounded as unruffled as Mark.

"He's bleeding. And he's barely conscious." Something jabbed at my hip wedged against the counter. Reflexive fingers felt the pocket. "There's a lot of blood. Too much blood."

"Is Fence Rose Trace Circle just off Rose Garden Path?"

"Yes." Shuddering at the touch of the stiff terrycloth, I fished out the offending ballpoint and dropped it into the pencil jar. The action distracted, calmed me. I slipped back into my normal guise.

"Okay, I have it. You're Mrs. Early?"

"Yes. I'm Steve. Stephanie Early."

Stephanie Pool Early, twenty-eight, married six years. Assistant professor of American History at Emory University, working on a doctorate but now on medical leave after a near-fatal miscarriage. Competent, intelligent, valued as an employee, as an educator, as a woman, as a wife.

The truth chose that untimely moment to attack.

A failure as a wife, a failure as a mother.

Just as I had been unable to understand my husband, I had been unable to give my baby life.

The ambush of reality was hastily denied and relegated to the depths of my heart.

It wasn't my fault I'd failed with Mark and couldn't keep our marriage intact, not my fault our baby had died.

Not my fault . . .

"Ma'am, can you describe how he's hurt?"

No time for this painful self-analysis. Time to be professional, like the woman on the phone.

I could pull myself together, and I did.

Afterward, the impersonal voice paused for an interminable second before saying, "An emergency team's been dispatched. I want you to stay on the phone with me so—"

"No, I'm going back to him. If help doesn't get here soon, he may die. He could be dead right this very minute."

She kept speaking. I slammed the phone down.

On the deck steps, I remembered the blood. I needed something to stanch it.

Towels would do.

I turned around, scrounged up some.

At the end of the stairs, overgrown azaleas lined the foundation and walkway in a wall of flame. I hurtled past to the shady trees. Squirrels scampered out of my way, but Sweet Rowdy ignored them to run beside me.

Almost there.

When I came out of the woods onto the grassy plain beside the lake, sunlight jumped out and dazzled me.

My sunglasses. I'd left them on the kitchen counter.

Never mind them. Get to the boat.

Sweet Rowdy bumped into my calf when I stopped abruptly.

Where was the man, the boat?

There was some mistake. I was looking at the wrong spot. My eyes weren't adjusted to the sun.

I started forward uncertainly, Sweet Rowdy beside me.

Wasn't it here that the boat had slammed against the shore? Yes, this place with the ugly slash in the grass, right beside the dock.

A motor droned beyond the bend of our cove, heading toward the main lake body. Behind me a single loon called. Sundrenched water lapped at the shore. A bee buzzed in a patch of wildflowers to my left.

As the hum from the boat faded, the natural noises around the lake took its place until everything seemed as before.

I stared at the bank where the bass boat had lain, and wished, for one craven moment, that my husband with his unflappable logic stood beside me.

Because there was no redheaded man, nor anything else in sight.

Not a small bass boat on the grass, not a large inboard cruiser in the water.

Only the sun rippling on the waves.

From a distance came the wail of a siren.

Help for a man who no longer needed it.

* * * *

"I DIDN'T DREAM him," I told the polite sheriff's deputy after the disgusted EMTs, upon finding no victim, had picked up their bags and left.

"No, ma'am. I can see that." The deputy, young but reassuring with his neat uniform and earnest features, pointed to the shore. "Something or other raked the bank there. You can tell by the red clay dug up through the grass."

Relief came, quick and dizzying. I'd been halfway afraid no one would believe my story. I wasn't sure I believed it myself.

Silly. Of course the boat had come flying into the shore. Of course there was a bloodied man driving it.

I might be depressed, but my nerves hadn't degenerated to where I imagined things. Not yet.

"If that wasn't enough," the nice deputy added, "there's your jacket."

His finger pointed to the dried blood on the terry pocket.

I shuddered. "He reached out to me. He wanted me to help him."

"I'm sure you did your best, ma'am. Did he speak to you at all?"

I tried not to think about the fingers I'd disentangled from my cover-up. "No. Well, he asked for someone named Emily."

"Do you know an Emily?"

"I had a childhood friend named Emily, but I've not heard from her in years. And I've had several students named Emily. But they wouldn't have any connection up here. Maybe the Rachinoffs next door know her. They live here all the time, but this is our weekend place. We're from Decatur."

"How long have you owned the cottage?"

"My husband bought it before we married six years ago."

"Would your husband know who Emily is?"

"Mark's never mentioned an Emily." I snuffled. "The man was pitiful. He looked so . . . He seemed so anxious to find her, but he was bleeding and could barely get her name out. Where do you suppose he went? And how did he go?"

"I wouldn't know, ma'am. It's possible he wasn't hurt as bad as you thought."

I opened my mouth to object but he went on, "I reckon you might know about the drug bust a few weeks ago. The house in the next cove over?"

"Drug bust? No, I hadn't heard." What did that have to do with the man in the boat? "You think this is connected to drugs?"

"It's strange. Out of all the docks on the lake, the man came here. Out of hundreds to go to, why choose your dock?"

I had no answer.

"Then to take off like that when you called us." The young deputy shook his head.

"He didn't look like he'd be able to take off at all," I said. "I don't even know how he got the boat back in the water. He was in really bad shape and you can see the boat ran clear up on the bank."

The deputy shrugged. "Maybe he had a reason not to wait around for us. Fear makes people do desperate things." He looked back at the mark in the mud. "Strange. Real strange."

After a half hour or so of filling out paperwork, he left me to brood over what he had said.

And not said. The deputy had come very close to hinting Mark or I might be involved in something illegal, like drugs.

No, I read too much into his words. The deputy might suspect the man in the boat maybe, but not us.

When I went back to the dock, Sweet Rowdy trailed behind. She whimpered and nuzzled my leg so I picked her up and petted her. "It's okay, girl."

But it wasn't. The redheaded man had been slumped over the wheel like a dead man. He'd seemed so dazed. And the bloodstain on his shirt had kept spreading.

Don't think of him.

I checked the swim dock in case something hadn't fallen into the water.

Nope, none of my things had survived. No eReader, no phone, no writing pad. Nothing.

I'd have to get another cellphone. And I'd have to start another list. I'd need it to go over with Mark before I spoke to a lawyer. I would be fair in dividing our property, and he would be agreeable. Mark was always agreeable. It was compassion he lacked, else he could never have fashioned a joyous marble cherub with our own baby not dead six months.

I wouldn't think about the statue either.

The sun's red edge touched the mountains across the lake. Its warmth had fled. Dusk's shadows crept toward my feet at the edge of the woods.

Sunset. That explained why I felt so chilled.

"Come on, Rowdy-gal. Let's go have supper."

For not the first time, I blessed the little dog's company.

CHAPTER TWO

AS THE EVENING faded, so did the afternoon's horror.

Who the redheaded man was and why he'd ended up at our dock remained an enigma, but I might never learn anything more and so I tried to put him out of my mind.

Sweet Rowdy and I ate. The homely tasks of loading dishes and wiping down counters let me return to mulling a future without Mark. By the time the kitchen was spic and span, I'd mentally worked out compromises for our joint possessions.

The lake cottage didn't possess a computer or TV to distract me so an hour's work produced a new list dividing our things. Then I picked up a magazine, but thumbed through it aimlessly. I kept remembering the man in the boat and playing the deputy's words over in my head. Then I moved to worrying how to tell Mark my decision and wondering how he would react.

I tried not to think of our baby.

After yawning for the umpteenth time, I gave up on the magazine and got a doggy biscuit to wave at Rowdy. "Okay, Rowdy-gal, ready for a bedtime treat?"

She pranced and wagged her tail.

I had to laugh. "You sweet girl." I put her out, brushed my teeth, and slipped on ragged boxers and a tee.

By then she had done her business and waited at the door. Swaggering in, she grinned hopefully and licked her lips.

"You can't be hungry. You just had your snack."

She wagged her tail and licked her lips again. She pointedly shifted her gaze to the box of dog biscuits on top of the counter. Then shifted it back to me.

"Sorry, you know the rule. One's the limit. We girls have to watch our figures. Come on, let's go to bed." Her doggy grin drooped, but she dutifully followed. As I slid between the sheets, she lay down on the braided rug by the bed. Her breathing soon settled into a regular rhythm.

I tried but couldn't follow her example. The warm April night rendered the room unbearably stuffy. Even the revolving ceiling fan didn't help.

First I kicked off the tangled sheet. Then, after tossing and turning, I picked up pillow and quilt.

Sound sleeper that she was, Sweet Rowdy snored on as I moved past her.

Mark had given her to me our first Christmas together. She'd run amok through gaily wrapped packages and kept us awake at night with pitiful cries. "Is she too rowdy for you, love?" Mark asked after a morning rife with chewed up newspapers, strewn ribbons, and overturned water bowls. "Good grief, she's managed to get herself stuck behind the fridge. Is she too much? Shall I take her back to the Humane Society and swap her for a quieter pup?"

"I don't think you'll find one, babe. All puppies are pretty rowdy. Besides," I called his attention to her expression as he rescued her, "how can you think about giving up a dog who looks as sweet as that? Now really."

"Rowdy but sweet, eh? Well, she seems deficient to me, but if you think she's normal . . ."

"Of course she's normal!"

She had been a godsend the past months. After I came out of the hospital and Fee flew back to Virginia, Sweet Rowdy became my solace. She kept watch over me with anxious eyes, licked my hand when I cried, and sat at my feet for hours at a time.

I probably owed her my sanity.

Leaving her to happy dreams of bones and squirrels, I stole through the cottage to a wide hammock strung up at the far end of the screened porch. The night air was cool and fresh.

Spreading out the quilt, I climbed into the swaying bed and stared out at the stars.

Mark and I used to curl up in this hammock together and watch the night skies. We had touched each other with tenderness and passion. He had pushed back my hair and looked into my eyes and whispered, "I love you."

In the moon-washed dark, I pulled the quilt over my head. Better not think of Mark.

I would plan my future. In the Decatur house, I would paint the bedroom apple green and fill it with cherry furniture and hang chintz curtains.

Mark disliked apple green walls and cherry furniture and chintz in any form, shape, or color.

When at last I fell asleep, I dreamed of a man with orange-red hair and a knife in his chest. In my dream, he ran from me and shouted "Emily" at a woman with her back to us who glided off into the mist.

* * * *

A DOG STARTED to bark, abruptly stopped.

I opened groggy eyes, heart thudding after a nightmare reliving the afternoon.

Then I relaxed.

No man. No boat. No blood.

My pulse slowed.

Sweet Rowdy must have discovered me missing. Any minute now she would wander out to the screened porch searching for me.

A sleepy glance toward open sliding doors revealed no little dog. The click of her nails should come any time when she hit the hardwood floors. I listened, smiling a bit.

The hammock lay in shadow, but moonlight filled the other half of the porch. Its rays cast a luminous sheen on the glass table and the chaise lounge in the far corner. Its pale fingers touched a rattan cabinet full of beach towels and drew an intricate pattern of light and dark on its front.

Moonlight also flooded the sliding doors and highlighted a silhouette directly inside the living area of the house.

A man's profile glided away toward the hall. The ebony shadows swallowed his form.

A man.

My eyes snapped wide. Blood drummed in my ears.

A man. Inside the cottage.

I was dreaming. I must be dreaming.

No. No dream.

Mark. It's Mark.

No. That had not been my husband's profile. The jutting nose and receding forehead belonged to no one I recognized, to no one who should have been in this house.

I came wide awake. I had to get away, out of this delicately illuminated porch that had turned into a trap.

Slowly, silently, eyes riveted on the sliding doors, I eased off the hammock.

A board underfoot creaked.

Don't let him hear. Please don't let him hear.

The screen door leading onto the deck lay across from me, at the end of a path bathed in moonlight. Other than going through the house, the moonlit path provided the only escape.

I took it, lifted the latch on the screened door, and pushed.

"She's out there," said a gruff voice from inside.

The intruder wasn't alone. He had another person with him, maybe more than one.

And he had seen me.

I burst through the screened door.

Rather than descend the steps to the deck and cobbled walk in a circular route, I climbed over the railing and dropped on hands and knees to the ground among the azaleas.

Pine mulch stung my feet.

I stumbled on a cobblestone.

The scent of crushed daffodils rose as I flew across the patch of grass.

If I could reach the sycamores separating our lot from the Rachinoffs' lawn . . .

Behind me, a heavy body thumped on the ground.

Feet crunched mulch.

Branches slapped against flesh.

A deep voice swore.

In the distance, a dog bayed.

I kept low, dodging willow limbs.

Sticks and pine cones cut into bare feet. Bushes tore at boxers, briars flailed skin.

Bursting from the sycamores, I darted round a gazebo Trina Rachinoff had bullied her husband into constructing last summer.

The Rachinoffs' two dogs, an Irish setter and a German shepherd, met me at the rhododendrons. My throat, useless until now, poured out a wail.

The vigilant dogs must have recognized me at the same moment they discovered my pursuer.

They dashed past me into the night. Their threatening growls erupted into furious barks.

Snarling and curses followed, but I kept running. "Evan, Trina, help! Help me!"

At the Rachinoffs' porch steps, powerful floodlights flicked on. Their harsh light revealed the lawn and everything around the house. Behind me, canine snarls accompanied human yells.

I rushed up the steps.

"Let me in!" While the dogs faced their quarry, I beat on the door. "Trina, Evan, help me! Let me in!"

The door took an eternity to open.

Evan Rachinoff stood framed there, an incongruous pot-bellied figure clad in plaid flannel pants and nothing else, but his shotgun at the ready.

His wife Trina came up behind him, heavy-eyed with sleep, pulling together housecoat lapels.

"Steve," they said in unison with mouths dropping open.

I fell sobbing into Trina's arms and looked behind me.

There was no one in sight except the dogs, trotting back toward us and looking thoroughly pleased with themselves.

* * * *

EVAN RACHINOFF CALLED the authorities and went with them to our cottage.

He was the one who disclosed, as we stood in the great room lined with shelves displaying Trina's plate collection, "Someone was in your house all right, Steve."

The somber tone alerted me. "Did they trash it?"

"Not the house." He looked away. "Your little dog."

I fingered the lace on the robe Trina had given me to cover my tee and boxers. "Rowdy?"

"I'm sorry. Rowdy's—She's dead."

Ice formed in my stomach, spread through veins. Tiny black spots flickered.

I started to slump.

Trina's hands steadied me, led me to a chair.

"Evan, you clod," she snapped in her strong Michigan accent. "Don't you have any sensitivity at all? You can't—"

No sensitivity. Like Mark.

My baby. Now Sweet Rowdy. How could I bear losing her, too?

* * * *

SWEET ROWDY'S THROAT had been cut.

Two uniformed deputies questioned me about the intruders, about the man in the boat, about what I thought the men were doing in my house, about whether I knew anything about a meth lab over in the next cove.

They were disinterested and formal, unlike their friendly colleague of the afternoon.

I told them several times that I didn't know anything.

They asked about Mark. "Where is he?"

"At home. We live in Decatur." I gave them the address and phone number.

"Do you want us to call him for you?"

"No. It's the middle of the night. I'll talk to him tomorrow. I'm going home then anyway."

"What kind of business is he in?"

"He works for an auditing firm based in Virginia."

No need to mention his sculpting. These men would immediately connect an artist to a wild lifestyle that included drugs. Which didn't describe Mark at all.

"Could he have some kind of enemies?"

"Mark?" I laughed, or tried to. "No. Not Mark."

My husband was the type of person everyone liked at first sight. Laid back and a good listener with a warm personality, Mark didn't make enemies. He didn't let his guard down long enough.

"Is it possible he's involved in activities that might explain what's happened here? Like maybe he knows the man in the boat. And maybe the man in the boat had something to do with your intruders tonight."

"I don't think so. We haven't been up here since last fall. And the man in the boat asked for Emily, not Mark."

They kept on. It was all I could do to fend them off.

After what seemed like hours they left me to spend the remainder of the night with the Rachinoffs. I lay awake on their spare bed that smelled of faintly musty potpourri and grieved for Sweet Rowdy.

The seeds planted by the investigators germinated.

What did I know of Mark's background?

He'd been an MP in the army before graduating from a small college in Virginia and going to work with the Foundation for the Institute of Fiduciary Auditing. His job as contract auditor for FIFA seemed irregular to outsiders, with the sudden departures and absences it entailed, but it allowed him to spend much of his time on sculpting, his real interest.

As for his family, his father and mother had died when he was twelve.

His grandparents raised him but they were dead now, too. He didn't talk about them so I didn't probe.

He did have an aunt in Virginia. She'd come to our wedding, and I liked her as well as you can like anyone seen once or twice a year. We sent her and her husband Christmas cards and received cards in return, but otherwise had little interaction.

They lived their life and we lived ours. She and Mark seemed satisfied at the amiable estrangement.

From occasional remarks, I inferred his parents had been cold and demanding. A dysfunctional early life could damage people, but Mark seemed unscathed.

Except for his abnormal poise.

At least his character was above reproach.

I might abhor his impenetrability, but there was no need to worry about his involvement with drugs or anything else illegal.

No need at all.

I yielded to my heartache over Sweet Rowdy and cried into my pillow so as not to bother the Rachinoffs.

* * * *

WHEN SUNSHINE LIT the edges of the window shade, someone started moving around in the house.

Good. I'd awakened before five but lain quietly, unwilling to rouse the Rachinoffs.

The bathroom mirror reflected my misery.

Below thick brows, weary eyes stared out. Circles underneath them emphasized gaunt cheeks. The bowed mouth and straight nose were mine, but they were changed, too. Coarse, almost sullen. Dark hair, straight and thick, fell to the shoulders, but a small briar twig stuck out from the top.

A souvenir of my dash through the woods.

I shivered and plucked it out, then rinsed my mouth, washed my face, and finger-combed my hair. I didn't feel much better, but how could I? A frilly housecoat four sizes too big swamped me. A yucky taste in my mouth begged for a toothbrush.

This apparition mocked the neat, efficient woman I claimed to be.

Freshly brewed coffee drew me to the kitchen. As an under-cabinet radio played, Trina toasted bread and fried thick patties of sausage.

"Evan's gone to take care of poor Rowdy." She handed me the spatula. "Watch the sausage, would you? We thought we could bury her behind the honeysuckle if that's okay with you. She always liked to roll in the mulch there."

"Yes, she did." My voice trembled, but I turned the sausage. "I appreciate him doing it, Trina. I don't think I can handle it. Not right now."

I'd not been able to handle my baby being buried either; Fiona had arranged the funeral while I was still in the hospital.

She patted my shoulder. "Don't you worry, hon. Evan will see to her."

The music on the radio faded, and a cheery DJ gave out morning news. Another murder in Atlanta, fire at a Gwinnett apartment building, flooding in Europe, famine in Africa, and rumblings of higher oil prices due to recent spills and well sabotage in the Middle East.

The usual things one listened to every day.

Except an injured man had disappeared and my house had been broken into and Sweet Rowdy was dead.

As Trina and I sat down with toast, eggs, and sausage I didn't want, and a cup of coffee that I did, Evan appeared in the kitchen door.

He puffed from running but said between gasps, "Call the sheriff, Trina. Looks like Steve's burglars came back and ransacked the place. It's the biggest mess you ever saw."

* * * *

THE LAKE COTTAGE looked like a band of malicious children had gone through it. And on top of that, I had to endure a third round of questioning by the county authorities.

They were not sympathetic or disinterested this time. They were harsh, almost hostile. What I underwent was a grilling.

By the time they finished digging about me and Mark and our occupations and finances, they'd made me angry and upset and late leaving the lake.

I went straight home, not even stopping to replace my lost cellphone. Thanks to the dragged-out interrogation, it was mid-afternoon when I finally reached our old two-story near Emory University.

Half-timbered with fieldstone, the small house boasted intricate and varied roof angles. It, like the others in the older middle-class neighborhood, expressed an individual character that appealed to Mark and me. The long and narrow lot on a winding street stretched back, providing ample space in the rear for gardens and patios and outbuildings.

A small red convertible blocked our driveway. Its bright color and fast design was out of place on a street which favored green hybrid vehicles or minivans.

The sporty car belonged to Candy something-or-other, a model Mark had been using lately.

I didn't want to ask her to move it—interrupting them would mean meeting Mark—so I parked by the curb and carried my suitcase in by the front door.

Built during the nineteen twenties, the house featured high ceilings and spacious rooms. At the moment, they were mercifully empty, their dim coolness extending refuge from the outside glare.

Mark and the sexy Candy would be in the rear garage. He'd converted it into a studio and worked there four to ten hours a day when FIFA left him in town.

Candy would be posing. He would be stroking and molding and coaxing his vision of her into reality. I could almost see his proficient hands, almost follow their deliberate movements when he forced the wet clay to conform to his version of her body.

Thank God Candy was with him. I was still too shaken to face him.

Sweet Rowdy's death and the man with orange-red hair haunted me. On the way back to Decatur, I had worried over the deputies' pointed questions about my husband, but here, safe at home, concern faded.

Mark's innermost thoughts might always remain closed to even his wife, but he would never do anything criminal.

I called Trina to let her know I'd arrived safely.

"What did Mark say about the break-in?" she asked.

"I've not told him yet. He's worked hard for a chance like this Dream Sugar commission, Trina. Tonight's his night, and I won't spoil it."

Nor would I expose my personal problems for Trina to exclaim over and talk about. I'd made up my mind to divorce Mark. No need to look for anyone's approval or advice.

Upstairs, the mauve and blue bedroom with its rosewood furniture allowed no respite.

I laid my suitcase on the padded cedar chest at the foot of the modern wall bed. It had a recessed mirror in the headboard. A long shelf stretched across the top of the mattress and formed nightstands on either side. Several of Mark's smaller works adorned the polished shelf. A carved wooden druid next to a jade mermaid, a bronze Athena beside an iron caveman.

In the middle of unpacking, I saw he had added another after I went up to the lake.

This figurine normally stayed on his chest of drawers. Mark had done the statue, about four inches high and of heavy ceramic over an iron core, right after we married and long before my pregnancy.

I'd sat for him on a cushion, one ankle over a knee, a brush held up to my hair. My arm started aching before he got through with the preliminary sketches.

"Push your chin up," he prodded. "Like that. Yes, good. Do you know you look a little like Jeanne Crain?"

"That old actress? The dead one?" I already regretted my agreement to pose. "Don't you think I have a few years to go yet?"

He laughed, lashes drawing together. He looked carefree and mischievous. "A young Jeanne Crain."

His wavy hair, tied back, threw his face into sharp focus. I remember thinking what a nice face he had. A broad forehead and high cheekbones surrounded smiling eyes that said he loved life. He loved me.

Staying still made me restive.

"No, don't move. Keep your chin up. You're so gorgeous it's all I can do not to come over and kiss you. Oh, hell, why do I fight it?"

So he came over and seized me and kissed me and the kiss led to other things which meant that no little time passed before I went back to my uncomfortable position, breathless and content and terribly in love.

That had been the one and only occasion I'd posed for him. It was too hard to be still. Most of his models were college students needing extra money, but when it came to his art, Mark made use of anyone who came to hand.

Including our baby. He had used our pathetic baby first by imagining him fat and healthy and laughing, and then by freezing him that way forever in stone.

I could have forgiven Mark anything.

Anything except changing my lifeless baby into a plump and happy infant I'd never know, could never hold. He'd taken a private grief and incorporated it into his art.

He should have realized how I'd feel when I saw it.

I would never understand him. Never.

I shook my head to clear it, but nothing in the room could clear away my misery. Like the lake cottage and the small bits of sculpture scattered around me, Mark had created this bedroom, too. He had chosen the contemporary furnishings and fabrics. He'd forged the tranquil ambience, made it a place to hide from the world.

Once we'd used it with warmth and passion and love. Now I finished unpacking and despised it.

If only I hadn't promised him I'd attend the Dream Sugar opening with him.

But I had. I'd rest, dredge up enough strength to get through the night.

Falling on the bed, I closed my eyes and tried not to dwell on the emptiness without Sweet Rowdy curled nearby. Evan had assured me she hadn't suffered. Maybe it was true.

My sleepless night made me doze and dream.

A man with freckles and orange-red hair held a small blonde dog in his arms. Bloody droplets came from beneath his shirt and fell across Sweet Rowdy's fur until the pinkish-brown stains spread over all of her. She howled mournfully. An eerie cry trailed in the air.

"Em-i-leeee . . ."

I awoke to silence, the name ringing in my ears.

Who was Emily? Why had the redheaded man chosen our boat dock? Was I really so certain Mark knew nothing about the man or the burglars?

Or Emily?

I yawned, rubbed my eyes. The afternoon had all but fled. Through the miniblinds, the light slanted over the bed to the bureau and held the peculiar vagueness of sunshine fading before the onslaught of dusk.

Shaking off the numbness caused by deep sleep, I rolled over and looked at the clock. After six.

"Oh, no." I should have already showered by this time, should have been applying makeup, putting on clothes. If Sweet Rowdy were here, she would have roused me.

Pain rocketed through me.

Her death was too fresh. Its hurt would linger.

I gritted my teeth and dragged out a robe. When I started for the bathroom between the two upstairs bedrooms, voices drifted up the stairwell.

Candy's, sulky and pleading at the same time: "You'd enjoy it more if I went with you tonight."

And Mark's ready answer: "Hey, there's no doubt you'd increase the enjoyment quota a thousand percent. But Steve's coming with me."

"I could make you forget Steve if I wanted to." Candy's voice softened, became low and throaty. "What's more, you know I could." A breathless giggle floated up. Then there came a pithy silence, the kind where two people were passionately kissing.

I sighed, beyond jealousy. Candy might not even be the first lover Mark had taken during the past months. He possessed too earthy a nature to deal with abstinence for any length of time.

And I couldn't bear for him to touch me.

Seemed like I'd have to attend the Dream Sugar opening whether I wanted to or not. Mark would hold me to my promise despite Candy's pleas.

Escorting a girlfriend while living with a wife would be a serious mistake for a promising sculptor. It might not matter in big cities like New York and Los Angeles, but here in Atlanta, it could mean professional suicide. People were conservative, even in the large corporations that commission pricey art.

Mark and Candy would be under the impression they were alone. So as not to embarrass us all if they unsuspectingly tripped upstairs to use the bed, I hurried into the bathroom.

Turning the taps on full blast should let them know I was back.

Before I could, Mark spoke, totally unfazed by whatever had occurred in the previous silence. "Anybody but a complete idiot would take you up on your offer, Candy, but I've never been smart. Be a good little girl and run along home. I'll see you at nine Tuesday morning."

He sounded as he always sounded. Pleasant, calm, amused.

So damned unperturbed, taking everything in stride.

He wouldn't show the slightest surprise or distress when he heard about the bloody man in the boat and Sweet Rowdy's cut throat.

Our baby's loss had meant so little that he could use it to create a cold statue.

What kind of man had I married?

CHAPTER THREE

WHEN I EMERGED from my shower, Mark, in stained T-shirt and jeans, stood brushing off his tuxedo.

At thirty-four, my husband had a deceptive, lanky six foot frame that failed to hint at the strength capable of lifting huge chunks of wood and stone. Nor did anything else in his appearance coincide with most people's idea of an artist.

He wasn't a wild-eyed visionary. He didn't wear a stud in his nostril or ear. He boasted no tattoos. His mild temperament made him the sort of man other men and women gravitated toward.

Except for his beautiful mane of chestnut hair, he might have been another face in the crowd.

When I stopped in the bedroom door, he looked up from his task but made no move to touch me. A tacit agreement had evolved between us following the one unsuccessful attempt at sex after the miscarriage.

But ultra-thick lashes narrowed as the corners of his eyes wrinkled in a welcoming smile.

"Hi. When did you get back?"

"About three."

"I didn't hear you drive up."

"Candy's car was in the way so I parked out front. Gosh, look at the time. I'll have to hurry." Busying myself as an excuse to refrain from conversation, I got out a new pair of panty hose, chose earrings with rhinestones gaily dangling from pearls, found my good strand of pearls with the diamond clip, and picked out silver evening shoes.

The navy two-piece suit? No, the silver dress looked more festive and matched the shoes. I took it into the bathroom to change.

After I dressed and sat down on the cedar chest opposite the dressing mirror, the state of his tuxedo finally satisfied Mark. Putting up my hair in a knot let me ignore him.

He came over to the corner of the bench and squatted down on the floor beside me. I couldn't avoid his mirrored image.

"How are you feeling?"

"Fine." Using a clasp made of faux pearls, I secured the knot. "It's late. You need to get cleaned up."

"I'm practically ready. Are you really fine? Did the time to yourself help?"

Help.

My stomach began to burn. I put away my brush and looked at him squarely. "I want a divorce."

The words fell on the air, bald and irretrievable.

He blinked.

I hadn't intended telling him like that. I'd meant to wait until after the celebration, after his sculpture had been unveiled and christened and applauded. Tonight should be Mark's night, the culmination of all he'd worked so hard to achieve. I hadn't wanted to spoil it for him.

Or had I?

Perhaps my subconscious had intended all along to sabotage his evening and make him suffer. Perhaps I really was mean-spirited.

No, don't go there.

But if childish spite motivated me, it failed.

Mark didn't exclaim or tear his hair or beg me to reconsider. He remained as unruffled as always, though the lines around his eyes deepened. He always seemed to be laughing at some joke heard by his ears alone. "A divorce?"

The wheels turning around his head were obvious as he decided the best way to handle the situation.

The best way to handle me.

Something inside exploded.

"Yes, dammit. I said I want a divorce. Why can't you say 'Oh, no!' or 'Go to hell,' or 'Fine,' or whatever it is you feel? Why's everything always a joke to you? Isn't there anything that can pierce that armor-plated rock you call a heart?"

He stiffened, incredulous.

Equally horrified by the harpy I'd become, I covered my mouth with both hands.

Too late to hold back words better left locked away.

I'd wiped the amiability from Mark's face, but at the cost of my self-respect.

"I'm sorry," I whispered, putting out a hand in appeal for forgiveness.

"So am I." His astonishment faded. He ignored my hand, rose and dusted off the seat of his jeans. "I want you to be happy, Steve. Believe it or not, that's all I've ever wanted."

He turned away to get into a drawer of his chest.

His words underscored my guilt for such an unprovoked attack.

I took a quivery breath. "We can't go on like this. You know we can't. A divorce will make things easier," I said to his back. I needed to persuade him, to persuade myself. I wanted to make up for spoiling his night. "I couldn't help hearing Candy a while ago. If you want to take her to this Dream Sugar thing, I don't mind."

He yanked out underwear and slammed the drawer shut.

I jumped.

Mark never slammed drawers.

His level look bore no signs of humor. "The last person I want to take anywhere is Candy, thank you very much. You promised you'd go with me to the unveiling. I assume you'll keep that promise, even if you are so set on breaking another."

Stung, I turned back to the glass.

A stranger stared back, a woman of brittle porcelain, with blue eyes made enormous by shadows and patrician lips colored too red. "No. No, of course I'll go. I just thought you might enjoy it more with someone who, someone more, more . . ."

My silly explanation floundered.

I felt his presence before I saw his reflection. His rangy form came up from the side in one springy step. He put one hand on my shoulder and used the other to push back my head. Bending over, he grazed his lips against my exposed neck.

I cringed as though branded by a hot iron.

Mark released me instantly. The mirror revealed a tight smile that left the rest of his face untouched. "It's impossible to get on with our life when you refuse to let go of what's done and past."

He had never looked quite so bleak, but the fascinating air of assurance clung to him still.

For all his easygoing ways, no one could manipulate or coerce Mark. I didn't like being at odds with him.

When no response came, he pivoted and left. I heard the shower start up and exhaled, hard. My complexion looked waxy. My breaths came in irregular bursts. The place on my neck his lips had touched felt fiery hot, but my reflection, as I straightened the knot he'd disarranged, showed no trace of his kiss.

Calm down. What could Mark do even if he decided to fight a divorce? No matter what happened, I would get one. It might take longer if he contested it, but eventually it would happen.

Silly to let his determination disturb me.

If only I had never met him, never loved him.

While Mark finished his shower, I went downstairs and collected myself. Then I moved my car to its usual parking spot beside the house and came back inside.

Mark descended the stairs, coat folded over one arm, both hands working on his tie.

He had always been self-sufficient, both in his business and personal affairs. In the same way he balanced his own checkbook and packed his own suitcase, he tied his own ties, business or black, with intrinsic dexterity. He never asked for help.

When his long form, debonair in the starched white shirt and gray cummerbund, reached the bottom of the stairway, he paused at the mirror over the hall desk and gave the bow one last tweak.

As I waited at the front door, he ambled toward the kitchen. "I'll set the alarm."

We had put in a security alarm when we first bought the house, an expensive system I argued was unnecessary.

Mark had pointed to the crime rate in our Atlanta suburb and insisted that his work and our renovated house needed protection. From vandals or worse. In the end, he got his way and installed the alarm system.

Before we married, he'd put in a security system at the lake cottage, too. Had I used it, Sweet Rowdy might be alive.

One more failure on my part.

While Mark set the controls, I went outside to his car, an older SUV. He soon followed. "I didn't see Rowdy anywhere. Do we need to check on her or did you put her out?"

Tears pricked. I blinked a few times, turned my beaded evening bag around and around, but still couldn't keep my voice from breaking. "She's dead. Evan buried her behind the wild honeysuckle bush in the woods."

As expected, he emitted no exclamation of shock, no word of distress. He slid in, pulled the car door shut, and turned his steady gaze on me. "What happened?"

Any other man would have displayed some emotion on learning of a beloved pet's death, reacted with surprise or at least concern. Mark showed nothing.

Surely, he couldn't be so uncaring. I gave him one last chance. "What made you so cold, Mark? Why can't you feel anything? What turned you into this mechanical robot that walks and talks and acts like a man?"

Level eyes held mine. "Is that what you think of me?"

"Yes."

"One thing I love about you, Steve, is that you're so unmercifully honest. At least about most things." He turned and cranked the car. "What happened to Sweet Rowdy?"

I fastened my seat belt. "She got in someone's way."

"What do you mean?"

As he drove, I began with the man in the boat and then hit on the high points of the past two days.

Mark made an excellent listener, absorbing everything with occasional prompts. All the time he listened, he noted red lights, used turn signals, kept the correct distance from the car ahead, and drove like the good driver he was.

His driving pretty much summed up Mark. He never did anything unexpected, never did anything without considering every aspect, every possible result.

That was why I found it so hard to forgive him for the adorable baby he had chiseled from marble.

This was going to be a long evening.

* * * *

DRIVING TO MIDTOWN took longer than usual. After my terse story, Mark withdrew into himself, and I reflected on my failed marriage.

There'd been no way to know it would end like this.

Mark and I had got on well from the start, when, as a groomsman in my sister's wedding, he was a last-minute substitute to pick me up at Dulles Airport. We had stood shoulder to shoulder at the luggage claim, me waiting for Fee who'd promised she or Dan would be there to meet me, and Mark searching in vain for a male rider.

Both of us kept surreptitiously eyeing the other.

He looked like a graduate student because of his ragged jeans and the thick chestnut waves falling down to his shoulders. He said later he pegged me for a newly elected politico's daughter or niece, coming to the Capital for the first time.

Except for his wavy mane of hair—some women would have killed to possess such hair—he wouldn't have commanded a second look.

When all the luggage disappeared except for two suitcases and a hanger bag on the carousel that kept revolving, he approached me. I innocently took his apologetic air for shyness. "Waiting for someone?" he asked.

I never encourage strangers, especially long-haired, unkempt strangers. But he seemed harmless enough and his dark eyes were those of a friendly spaniel. "Yes." I unbent enough to add, "But I think I've been stood up."

"Me, too. I hope those bags going round and round don't belong to the guy I'm supposed to pick up. If they do, I guess he's missed his plane."

I atypically confided, "If my sister's forgotten me, I'm going to catch a cab and make her foot the bill before I murder her. Slowly and painfully."

Lines radiating from his eyes had been caused either from squinting into the sun or smiling a lot. "Without hearing her excuse? She might have a good one."

"It would have to be better than good to save her."

"You don't suppose there's any chance your sister's run away with my passenger, do you?"

I laughed aloud at the idea of sensible Fee running off with anyone. A satisfied expression flitted over his face. A lazy grin spread, turning up one corner of his wide mouth and then the other. I remember being startled and a little apprehensive at how his entire countenance sprang to life.

From someone nondescript, he suddenly became a man who deserved a closer look.

The chestnut curls sprang back from a widow's peak which pointed downward to prominent cheekbones and a nose threatening to tilt. Thick black eyelashes ringed eyes alight with good humor. At first I thought them brown, but closer inspection noted black specks that darkened pale gray-green irises.

Unsettled, I was slow to detect the understated confidence that lay over his lank form like an invisible mantel.

This man might appear to be engagingly shy, but underneath lay a controlled individual capable of standing up for himself.

All that went through my mind in a flash, to be discarded as quickly.

I didn't know the man. I would never see him again. I had no reason to be wary, no reason not to enjoy our brief exchange.

He added, still looking at me with that wonderful, and by that time, alarming smile, "Now be honest. Can you swear positively your sister's not the type to make off with some poor unsuspecting fellow she may have taken a fancy to? Like my rider for instance?"

"Certainly not." His twinkle caught me off-balance and made me grin back. "My sister was expecting me, and your rider was expecting you, I'm sure. Why would either go off with someone else?"

Naturally, I was Mark's passenger.

He apologized profusely. "It's the kind of haphazard planning that drives me crazy." He hefted up my large bags with deceptive ease, in a sweeping fluid gesture of such grace as defied description and caused a peculiar flutter at the bottom of my stomach. "Chuck, Dan's best man, called and said Dan was supposed to pick up a Steve Pool at the airport but couldn't. So he drafted Chuck. Then something came up so Chuck couldn't get away. I, obliging soul that I am, agreed to meet Steve Pool at the baggage claims. No one said anything about you being a woman. Honest. I figured you were Fee's brother or uncle or cousin or something."

I assured him the mistake was perfectly understandable. "How could you have known Steve was really Stephanie?"

Once I coaxed him out of his embarrassment—which later I realized he'd exaggerated to draw me out of my shell—the confusion gave us cause for hilarity on the way to Fee's apartment as Mark cut between cars with an aplomb that left me, who always ground my teeth when at the wheel, envious.

Fee, noting my high spirits, warned me as soon as Mark left. "He's cute, sweetie, but he's got a live-in."

"Why should I care?" Her knowing look put me on the defensive. "I only just met him, Fee. Stop matchmaking."

At the wedding rehearsal, our camaraderie resumed. Since I'd been warned about Mark's love life, I knew where things stood. Still, it was nice to find someone who shared my sense of the ridiculous as we went through the motions of the ritual. Someone to exchange laughing glances with when the best man showed up in snakeskin boots, sleeveless tee, and cowboy hat.

Someone to wink at when the minister kept referring to Dad as Mr. Pond.

"Monopolizing my new sister, Mark?" Fiona's groom interrupted our flirtation and took me aside to issue a plain warning. "Don't get in over your head, kid. Mark's not—" Dan, big, bluff, and good-natured, looked over his shoulder to make sure no one overheard. "You don't need to get your pretty little self mixed up with Mark."

"Didn't you choose him to be one of your ushers? I thought he was a friend of yours."

Dan tugged at his collar. "Well, yeah. We've lived in the same neighborhood for years. Mark's okay. No one better in a crunch. But he's a sculptor, and you know what they say about artists."

"No. I don't. Tell me."

"They're hard as hell to live with, but harder than that to get rid of. No, you want someone steady, Steve. Not Mark."

Under cover of wedding party chatter, I stuck out my tongue. "I understand he's taken, Mr. Guardian Angel, so no need for you to obsess. I'm just talking to him."

"Sure you are. And I'd hate to see it go any further." He stopped me again as I took a step toward the others. "Look, Steve, here's the thing. Mark hangs out with women who can take care of themselves."

"What? You think I can't?"

Dan guffawed and squeezed my waist. "Oh, honey, Mark would

run over you like a Mack truck. Believe me, he's not your type, kid. Not your type at all."

I had one semester before getting my BA in History, but I still knew everything. Naturally, Fee's warning and Dan's well-intentioned advice made Mark Loren Early that much more enticing.

And girlfriend or not, Mark spent most of that evening and a portion of the next day's reception talking with me. I nearly forgot he was taken until Fee stole a moment to pull me aside.

"Mark's live-in I told you about," she muttered, giving a slight head jerk toward a sophisticate in designer dress and mink jacket. "Her name's Cora Cinnamon or Cora Lemon or something like that. No, I remember. It's Cora Vanilla. Looks expensive, doesn't she?"

My heart sank. The gorgeous brunette laughing up at Dan's best man was everything I'd never be. Glamorous, chic, and absolutely sure of herself. No way could I compete with such a ravishing creature.

I put thoughts of Mark Early aside and went home.

Then a few weeks later he called out of the blue. He had moved from Virginia to a small town north of Atlanta, and would I be interested in showing him around the city?

Six months later, right after I graduated from North Georgia College, we had married.

As the old memories threatened to overwhelm me, I deliberately blanked them out.

Mark and I were two different people now.

I should have listened to Fee and Dan.

* * * *

"GOOD GRIEF," SAID MARK. The SUV idled, stalled in a long line of cars waiting to get into the parking deck of the new Dream Sugar headquarters building. "Look at the people. Where do they all come from?"

"The suburbs."

Hundreds had been invited to the opening, and we spent twenty minutes waiting to get into the deck. Inside, Mark stalked a parking spot as groups of laughing and chatting people in formal attire swarmed toward the elevators. One couple strolled unheeding, the man's arm around the woman's waist and her head snuggled against his shoulder.

Their affection emphasized my own unhappiness.

But my heartbroken rage had expended itself in the inexcusable outburst at Mark. I could get through this night and I would.

Undoing my seat belt, I opened the door.

Mark took my arm.

I jerked involuntarily at this second violation of our unspoken no-contact pact.

He didn't apologize nor did he retreat. His fingers rested on my arm, light but persistent. "Before we go in, I'd like you to tell me again what happened up at the lake."

Though shadows hid his face, I sensed his eyes were narrowed. "I've told you."

"Tell me one more time," he drawled in his old manner. "I'm a slow listener, don't you remember?"

I slipped from his grip and held up my wristwatch. "It's twenty past seven."

The last thing I wanted to do was repeat the story.

I was sick and tired of talking about the boat and driver, of remembering Sweet Rowdy and imagining her death at the hands of the intruders. I needed to forget yesterday and last night. "You're going to be late."

When I slid out and started toward the elevators, he called to me. I quickened my pace.

If only this dinner and unveiling were over. If only my marriage was over. Maybe then I could turn back into the person I used to be, the person I had been before Mark.

His car door opened and closed. Behind the quick tap of my heels, leather soles whispered against smooth concrete.

He came up and without warning took my arm in a viselike grip that dragged me off balance. "You don't think you're going to tell me this bizarre story and then run away, do you?"

The lulling cadence next to my ear lied. A threat lurked beneath the words.

For one terrible moment, his eyes looked out at me, fierce and accusing. "You can pull your head in like a turtle about some things, Steve. But not about this. You can't shrug off a dying man like he's a piece of driftwood. Come back here and tell me exactly what happened."

"I'm not pulling my head in and I'm not shrugging anything off." The anger at his contempt may have been contrived so I wouldn't have to admit that the man in the boat might have been dying.

So I wouldn't have to admit that Mark's aggression frightened me. "You don't know he was dying."

"You don't know he wasn't."

"We'll be late."

His fingers cut into my arm.

"You're hurting me."

"I'm beginning to doubt anything's capable of hurting you," he said brutally. "Come back to the car."

Never during our entire courtship and marriage had Mark treated me with anything but lighthearted solicitude bordering on old-fashioned chivalry. This man beside me was a stranger. I didn't know whether to be angry or affronted.

Or—insane thought—afraid.

Laughter rang out in the sterile parking deck. Amid the high spirits of the convening crowd, Mark lifted my elbow in a determined hold. If I didn't submit, he'd drag me away beneath the amazed eyes of the crowd.

I made a half-hearted attempt to wrench away. "Let me go."

His grip didn't relent. "Come back to the car."

A group of people approached. I almost screamed out, but I disliked scenes as much as Mark. I gave in.

He guided me back to the car and threw open my door. "Get in."

The unaccustomed grimness, coming on the heels of the other uncharacteristic behavior, flustered me. I let him press me into the SUV, protesting when he shoved me further in. He slid in, too, so that we both ended up in the passenger seat. The console hindered me from moving to the driver's side, but I drew as far away from him as I could.

Not that it helped. His thigh pressed hard against mine.

Damn him. He knew quite well how I felt about him touching me. Up until this afternoon, he'd respected my need for distance between us.

I scowled at his face shoved within an inch of mine.

He paid no attention.

I tossed my head.

He paid no attention to that either. "I want you to start over and tell me everything you remember about the man in the boat."

I might have been some incompetent student he was assigning a task.

No, I was mistaken. A teacher wasn't what he reminded me of. He reminded me of the skeptical investigators at the lake this morning, the ones who had bombarded me with unpleasant questions.

"Tell me," he said again.

"You—" I sought in vain for words to describe what I thought of his highhanded manner.

"Tell me exactly what the man in the boat looked like. Exactly what he said. Exactly what happened last night."

Surrendering, I repeated the whole story, including a detailed description of the bloodied man I'd wanted to forget. I related how orange-red hair had fallen around his battered face, how glazed eyes had stared out at me, how he had asked for Emily. "I told the authorities we don't know an Emily?"

He ignored the implied question. "That's all he said? Just Emily?"

"Yes."

Unlike the detectives at the lake, he waited. What more did he want me to tell him?

Tell him . . . Tell Emily . . .

"He said 'Emily. Tell Emily. Don't give them.'"

"Give them what?"

"I don't know. That's all he said. I just now remembered it. But that really is all. Mostly he kept repeating her name. Emily."

Mark asked about the second boat. "You didn't see it stop?"

"I got a glimpse of it as it turned toward the bank." Mark would have said if he had recognized the name Emily, I told myself, but the assurance rang hollow. I was no longer sure of anything about Mark. "I looked back when I reached the deck. It went past the trees toward our dock. I assumed the people on it had seen the man and were going to help him."

"Could you see any of the people or the boat close enough to describe?"

"No. The boat looked like one of those large cruisers. A white one with a dark stripe. And all I could see were three or four fishermen on it."

"Fishermen. Did they have rods?"

"I don't know." I tried to remember. "Maybe not. But what else could they have been doing there if not fishing?" Under his accusing silence, I broke. "Besides, what difference does it make?" I was wild to be done with his questioning and disturbing presence. "They couldn't have made the man and his boat vanish."

Mark didn't reply.

The clutching hand. The pitiful plea. Perhaps the man had been begging me to stay. "Could they?"

Mark opened the door.

No. Of course not. The people in the second boat had nothing to do with the injured man who had rammed his boat into the bank. If so, if the second boat was somehow related to the redheaded man's disappearance, then I had abandoned him to . . .

What?

CHAPTER FOUR

MARK STOPPED AT the restrooms inside the entrance of Dream Sugar's brand new thirty-five story building in the heart of Midtown Atlanta.

"Go wash your face." He sounded composed, laidback, kind. Normal. "Your eyes are puffy, and you look like you've been drinking."

"I'm close to crying." I held out my arm. "You hurt me."

He barely glanced down, clearly disinterested as to whether or not he'd injured my arm. "It isn't bruised."

This from a man who wouldn't let me spank Sweet Rowdy for wetting the hardwood floor.

"I don't have to be b-bruised to hurt."

His voice softened. "Go wash your face, Steve." His eyes crinkled. He looked like himself again. The awful intensity of fifteen minutes past dissipated, the genial mask firmly back in place.

Mark was the same man he'd always been.

The cold water on my face calmed me.

Hearing I wanted a divorce made him seem so different, so daunting. That and finding out about Sweet Rowdy.

Mark was no callous stranger.

I dried my hands and repaired my makeup.

He hadn't denied knowing an Emily. I should ask him straight out, but could I? I might not care for the answer.

When I came out of the ladies room, Mark paced beside the water fountains, talking on his cellphone. "If that's the case, they've lost him. He must have been—" He saw me. "I'll talk to you later."

I leaned down to drink from the fountain.

He didn't hang up but listened to someone on the other end. Then, "Yes, I realize it isn't my affair." He listened again. "I won't promise anything. My battery's low. I have to go. Let me know when you hear."

He closed his cell without goodbyes.

"Who were you talking to?"

It could have been Candy or someone like her. But I didn't think so.

"Abner."

I should have known. Abner Crowley. Mark's boss at FIFA and

my nemesis. I'd never met him, but early in my marriage I had learned to recognize and dread his voice.

It never failed. Abner Crowley called and Mark left.

Once, during a weeklong visit by my sister and her husband, we were dressing for a Falcons' game when Mark's cell rang. I knew it was Abner before Mark told me. Pulling out the small bag that he always kept packed, he disappeared for nearly a month. The rest of us had continued to the stadium where I sat beside Mark's empty seat and silently cursed Abner Crowley.

Another time we were readying for a long-anticipated vacation cruise when Abner called.

Mark hung up, turned to where I was stacking shorts, and made a face. "Got an assignment. What can I do? Sorry, love." He put away his cruise clothes, pulled out the work bag, and left.

It's his job, I told myself as I slung clothes back into drawers. He can't help it.

I had rebooked our trip and tried not to be angry with Mark.

It was easier to be angry with Abner Crowley.

From the beginning, Abner was connected to that inaccessible portion of Mark. I needed someone to blame for the unseen wall between my husband and me, and Abner was handy.

Abner and FIFA were responsible for Mark's reserve.

FIFA, the Foundation for the Institute of Fiduciary Auditing, was a huge financial planning and auditing firm with a clientele that included, besides diverse businesses, countries and governments. Mark lived always on call, but FIFA paid him a retainer generous by any standards, considering he worked a total of four or five months a year and had the rest of his time free for sculpting.

Because of the job's advantages, I accepted abrupt departures and last minute cancellations of long-scheduled outings. I didn't nag about not hearing from him for periods of two days to two months during his assignments to godforsaken places no one had never heard of.

I was a supportive, compliant wife.

Until I lost my baby, and Mark was absent in one of those faraway places where Abner Crowley had sent him.

That explained why, in the Dream Sugar building about to be dedicated that night, bile rose at Abner's name. Fair or not, he got the blame for my being alone when I most needed a husband.

Had Abner not called that week, Mark would have been there to trim the bushes and rake the leaves and drag the heavy bags to the curb. I wouldn't have worked myself to exhaustion under the hot October sun.

The doctor had said those exertions hadn't caused me to miscarry, but I didn't believe her. If Mark had been home, I would have done light chores and carried my baby to term.

As far as I was concerned, the flowers Abner and FIFA sent to the hospital and to my son's funeral were empty gestures.

So when Mark admitted he had been speaking to Abner Crowley, I didn't hide my disdain.

"Your lord and master? What travel arrangements has he made for you this week? Shall we go home so you can get your bag?"

Mark's grin flashed. "Stick to pleasantries, love. Cynicism doesn't become you." Taking my unwilling arm like the most affectionate of husbands, he led me toward the main lobby and the unveiling ceremonies.

I could drive my elbow into his side. I could haul off and hit . . .

Fantasies. There was no way I could hurt Mark. I was not a violent person.

All right. I would play my part one more time. I would be the faithful handmaid to Atlanta's newest artistic lion. I would put on my company manners and make social chitchat and hope the unveiling portended as big a success as everyone predicted. Once Mark was entrenched on the ladder to prosperity and renown, he wouldn't fight my leaving him.

At least I hoped he wouldn't.

I shivered, recalling his implacable demeanor in the parking deck. *Face it. You don't know what Mark will do.*

I'd thought I understood my husband inside and out, down to that one inner spot he forever barred to me and everyone else. But tonight I'd seen a side of him I didn't know existed.

He must give me a divorce. He has to.

We couldn't go on this way.

* * * *

MARK GAVE A low whistle. "Wow, look at this."

When I would have passed the threshold into the midst of the festivities, he held me back and waved at the atrium. "What's the rush? Let's look the place over."

"We're late." My words were automatic. I wanted to go in, get the night over with. Forget what had happened in the car.

"Affairs like this never get started on time." The surroundings enthralled him. "We won't be missed. Look at the aviary, the way its bars curve against the inside atrium. Almost makes me wish I'd taken up architecture."

Another time I might be impressed by the design and the exotic birds and the soaring atrium, but not tonight.

"Come on, Steve." His voice softened. "This place is beautiful. Look at it."

Recalling his earlier obstinacy, I wavered. Unwilling to confront that stranger again, I complied.

Open for five stories up, the lobby furnished a worthy showcase for my husband's most ambitious and important project to date. The admired aviary encompassed the entire left corner. Fine latticed bars curved up over two stories and back to form a giant cage housing a flurry of colorful birds.

The fountain stood in the corresponding position on our right.

"They use a computer to control the water," Mark said of the dancing streams. They rose as high as the aviary roof and then diminished to a gurgle. Colored lights played on the spray. "They can make each stream spout to a different height. Wouldn't it be neat to have one of those beside our patio?"

"Um."

"There's *Dreaming*." Mark steered me toward the enormous draped mound in the center of the lobby. "Takes up a lot of room, doesn't it? Good thing they don't charge me rent." His fingers continued to grip my arm, giving me no choice but to follow where he led.

Aware of my turmoil, he murmured against my ear, "Come on. Let's try to enjoy the party. Okay?"

Not much of a peace offering, but it was probably all I would get. "Sure." I tried to concentrate on the giant carving rather than the shoulder pressing mine.

Hidden beneath draperies of fuchsia, ecru, and teal, Dream Sugar's corporate colors, the sculpture soared for fully thirty feet to dominate the spacious lobby area and the small teal covered tables scattered around its base. After working on the project for over two years, last week Mark had shipped the four marble sections comprising the massive sculpture to the Dream Sugar building for assembly.

I supposed he delighted in his achievement. Any normal man would, but that was another of the things about him I would never know for sure. Pride, frustration, anger—his breezy casualness covered everything.

"Mark, Steve." A blue-haired matron, one of Mark's early patrons indirectly responsible for him landing the Dream Sugar commission, came toward us with fluttering hands.

"Hello, Gretchen. How's my favorite angel?" He released me to kiss the cheek she proffered.

I murmured greetings—heartfelt greetings since she had freed me from that invidious clasp—and took my turn at brushing a cheek against her overly rouged one.

"My dear, I can't wait to see it." The gestures of her hands set the rows of bangles and chains lining each plump arm a-jingle. "I spoke with your agent, and he's so pleased. As is Foster, of course. And I'm so proud to have had a part in this."

I stood aside while they talked, glad to be ignored, taking the chance to recover from exposure to Mark's unsuspected dark side.

Did I dare slip away?

Mark saw me edge backward and slid an inconspicuous hand around my waist. I managed not to grimace when he excused us to Gretchen.

As a live collage of people filled the lobby, the mass of perfumes, the hum of voices, and the occasional trills of laughter frayed my nerves.

Black seemed to be The Color for women as well as for men this year. The occasional rich purple or royal blue stood out as did my silver dress.

I should have worn the navy two-piece.

Many local celebrities were there. Politicians, sports figures, television and radio personalities mingled with Dream Sugar executives and other dignitaries. Some sat and conversed as others stood with drinks in hand. The majority hovered over sumptuous food presentations.

Serving tables ringed the lobby. We went by some loaded with pineapple, melons, and other fruit and skirted others that held salads, fresh as well as egg and potato. Pasta with varied sauces including beef Wellington and marinara stood by tables where chefs carved meats. One table held different cheeses, soft, chunks, and balls. Roast beef and lobster skewers sat beside boiled shrimp and grouper in champagne sauce.

Everywhere, we saw food.

"Do you want something to drink?" Mark was perfect in his role of attentive escort.

"Yes. Please." Anything to take him away.

"The champagne's free," an unabashed eavesdropper put in, holding up his fluted glass. "Not too bad, either."

As Mark pushed our way through the crowd, his hand grasped my elbow as though I were a show poodle on parade. We passed the dessert table. Sundry pastries on a tiered tray sat on a table filled with cheesecake, key lime pie, carrot cake, alongside my favorite: huge fresh strawberries dipped first in white chocolate and then in dark.

Mark towed me by. "Time for sweets later. Do you want champagne or something else?"

"Champagne's good."

"Champagne it is, then. Come along, love, and don't get lost in the crowd."

As if we were still a couple. As if our marriage was still normal.

Anxiety faded. His threatening aura in the parking deck had been a delusion. It must have been.

He led me past the head table near the podium where name tags marked each place. Set with napkins and silverware and crystal, it bore, as did the serving tables, an ice sculpture shaped like a contemporary tree of some sort.

Dream Sugar's trademark was a tree, but the ice tree centerpieces were ugly. I didn't point out the lamentable carvings mass produced from a mold, but it wasn't necessary.

Mark noticed, made a face, and deliberately turned our backs to them. He had definite ideas about tasteless art.

Once we would have exchanged laughing winces at the ragged ices. Tonight we avoided looking at each other.

"Mark." A portly man with thin gray hair and glasses rushed up, followed by a small entourage. "Where have you been? Paula has been frantic."

"Sorry, Foster." For the second time, Mark was forced to release me as he shook hands with Dream Sugar's CEO. "Traffic was unbelievable. Especially right outside the building."

The man beamed. "Wonderful, isn't it? Everyone wants to be here. They didn't expect anywhere near this kind of turnout. Paula and her group are worth every penny."

"Don't forget Gretchen knows a lot of people, too. She did a marvelous job spreading the word," Mark murmured.

"Oh my, yes, you're right about that. She's fabulous, isn't she? Even if her voice is a little shrill."

No longer frightened, I smiled politely, stepped into the background with the people following Foster, and kept my mouth shut.

Why had Mark dragged me back to the car for a second recital of my tale? For the first time since our altercation in the parking deck, I wondered.

Could he have an idea as to the identity of the man in the boat? Going one step further, might he also know who Emily was?

No, the idea was ridiculous. He would have said.

Wouldn't he?

Unconsciously massaging my arm, I surveyed him from beneath

my lashes. His face, as he chatted with Dream Sugar's CEO, displayed the same lines as always, with no hint of anything except geniality.

One never realized how engaging Mark could be until he decided to make you notice. I knew that from experience.

He spotted me rubbing my arm but the only sign was a subtle tensing of his jaw. Putting a hand on my waist, he urged me forward. "This is my wife, Stephanie. Steve, this is Foster Cardwell, the CEO who had the good taste to choose Dreaming from the other sculptures recommended by his committee." Mark exuded relaxed bonhomie. "Naturally, Foster's one of my favorite people."

Murmuring my 'how-do-you-do's', I tried to shrink back into oblivion, away from the fingers that burned through the thin fabric of my dress and threw me into disorder. Mark knew I hated having him touch me, but he refused to loose me. His hand on my back slid further around my waist, and his arm became a band securing me to him. Heat rose throughout me, either from anger or fear.

I wanted only to be somewhere else. With someone else.

An image of the stranger in the parking garage materialized, only to be quickly banished.

I wouldn't think about that other Mark. Not now.

The Mark by my side ignored my attempts at escape. "I see Paula at the bar. We need to be heading her way."

Foster Cardwell looked over and beamed, rubbing his hands together. "Good, good. I'm really anxious to get things underway and I know Paula is, too."

From behind the fountain, a small orchestra, its members in tuxes and long skirts, played classical music as Mark introduced me to Dream Sugar's public relations head.

Paula, a spare woman in her forties, exhibited the chic hardness some women acquire. I wondered if at twenty-eight I already possessed it, whether my draped silver silk softened my expression any better than her severe black sheath softened hers.

With a perfunctory nod in my direction, Paula set about disengaging Mark.

Mark balked. "I don't like leaving Steve alone."

Paula didn't know that agreeable smile meant he was about to dig in his heels. I did. He would listen but tactfully deflect requests he wouldn't agree to.

His manners had been one of the first things I'd admired about Mark before I realized what they were. One more layer of a barrier to keep the world at bay.

Including me.

His arm settled snugly around my waist, making me dizzy.

I might faint if he didn't let go.

Adrenaline rushed. I wanted out but not by making a scene.

"Go on with Paula. I don't mind. I'll be fine. I'm sure I can find someone to talk to."

He laughed. "No way. You aren't going to abandon me when I need you most, are you? I'd be lost without you."

He was mocking me. He must be mocking me. "You'll be fine."

"Of course he will, and so will your wife, Mark." Paula proved to be a woman of resource.

Before I finished speaking, she'd summoned an underling with a flick of a finger. "See to Mark's wife, Dave. Make sure she gets a drink and whatever she wants to eat." Then to Mark, "Don't you worry about being abandoned. I'm going to stick like glue to you until this dedication is over. It's going to go off as smoothly as oil on satin."

Mark tightened his grip as he started to object. "I can't leave—"

Desperate, I caught hold of his pinkie in a move learned from a long ago self-defense class.

Using my purse to shield my actions from Paula, I pulled back. Hard.

His flinch as he let go gave me no small satisfaction. In the split second of freedom, I stepped out of his reach and took Dave's arm, smiling victoriously, if breathlessly. "I'll be fine with Dave. Do go on, Mark, and don't worry about me."

I thought for a moment he would refuse, but then his mouth curved, acknowledging the success of my gambit, and he shrugged. "Okay, love. If you insist."

He switched his attention to Paula's flunky. "I'll have my eye on you, kid. Don't put your hand on her butt and don't get her drunk. She likes to climb on tables and take off her clothes when she's drunk. Oh, and don't let her get into those chocolate strawberries, either. She'll be sick on the way home."

Dave recoiled before he decided Mark was teasing. "Oh." He laughed uncertainly. "Sure thing. Don't worry. I'll look out for her."

"You'd better." Mark's eyes, their corners crinkled in amusement but their depths unfathomable, returned to me. "See you later." He lingered, nursing his finger until Paula bore him away.

I was left with Dave for company. "You don't have to worry," I informed him. "I never drink enough to make me climb on tables and take off my clothes. I do like strawberries, however, and I'll eat as many as I want."

CHAPTER FIVE

DAVE, YOUNG AND not long out of college, itched to advance his career. Being pleasant to me was part of his job, but I didn't care what his motives were so long as he helped me get through the next few hours.

As the head table filled, he tried to herd me toward the podium. "There's a place for you beside your husband. You need to be there when ceremonies start."

"I like it better here." Mark could come up with an excuse for my absence if anyone noticed.

Poor Dave proved no match for a woman determined to stay as far away from her husband as possible. By the time the speeches began, he and I were settled near the terrace, our plates filled with buffet delicacies. At the head table, the mayor and Dream Sugar's CEO ate with their respective wives.

Paula had abandoned her chair to slide into the empty seat beside Mark. Sandwiched between her and Foster Cardwell, Mark gave her his undivided attention.

No skin off my nose. She was welcome to him. For good, as far as I was concerned. Hard-nosed female and hard-shelled male, the perfect match.

They spotted us.

Paula looked annoyed and said something to Mark. He raised his brows at me and shrugged at her.

No one came to haul me away.

Dipping our lobster kabobs into drawn butter, Dave and I listened with equal stoicism to the CEO's explanation of why Dream Sugar, an international corporation, had elected to consolidate its headquarters in Atlanta, and how the building site and design had been chosen. By the time he came to the part about corporate responsibility to Georgia's art community, twenty minutes had passed. Dave and I had finished fresh key lime pie and tackled a plate of dipped strawberries.

Mark noticed and frowned at me. I picked up the biggest and held it so he could get a good gander, then took a slow bite.

Finally, the CEO got around to ceding the podium to the mayor who gave a brief but gracious welcome to Dream Sugar. Next came the Governor, overlooked by me till now, who in the course of his speech, dropped several hints that he would be running for national office when his term ended.

Then one of Georgia's Senators spoke, lauding his committee's success in energy regulation, already campaigning to replace the exiting Governor.

"—and with the recent success of a genetically engineered microorganism able to convert wastes of trees, cotton, sugar cane, and other natural fibers into ethanol," he bragged, "we will soon have a new and endless source of energy for our great country. When that happens, then, my friends, never again—never again!—" he thundered, waving his fist in the air like an old-fashioned brimstone and hellfire preacher, "will the American public be cowed and pushed to the brink of depression by greedy oil interests banding together to extort money from this great country."

"How much more of this do we have to listen to?" I asked Dave under cover of applause.

Dave sighed, as bored as I. "The home stretch is coming up. Paula's on next and then your husband."

We had long since folded our napkins and sat back in our uncomfortable chairs.

At nearly ten o'clock, other people besides us were squirming in their seats around the teal-topped tables. By the time Paula took the microphone, her frown failed to squash the low hum of conversation, and she was forced to call for quiet.

After reciting details of Mark's education and study, she quoted critics, some names I recognized and others were unfamiliar, who had lavished praise on his earlier pieces.

"She's done her homework," I whispered to Dave.

Dave's four glasses of champagne made him honest. "No, she hasn't. I've done her homework."

"Did you have to put that in about him being the most talented young sculptor in the eastern and possibly the entire United States? He's conceited enough as it is."

Dave displayed unexpected diplomacy. "Paula wrote her own introduction."

At last Mark's lean figure, cavalier and very much at ease, strolled up to the podium. He ignored the buzz of voices.

"Thank you, Paula, for those kind remarks," he opened inauspiciously, "but I doubt my credentials sold Foster and his board on the piece we're about to view. Nor did my talent, great though my talent might be. Nor did Foster's enthusiasm in acquiring a fine work of art for Dream Sugar. No, I'm afraid a much more prosaic emotion hooked Foster on this piece. Put bluntly, it was sex."

The whispers died. Mark waited, one beat, and then another. "No, no, clean up your minds, people." He wagged one finger in admonishment. "I don't mean that I pimped for Foster."

Another beat passed with a few titters here and there. An impish grin flashed as Mark dropped his voice to a confidential level. "Although I might have if he'd asked. You'd be surprised how desperate we starving artists get."

Chuckles began and spread. Mark had their attention.

"When I say sex hooked Foster, I mean the sculpture itself is pretty erotic. But there's a reason. Foster asked for a tribute to that part of the human spirit that lets people dream when all else is gone. And we all have our impossible dreams, right? Remember Suzy Frigglethorpe, guys, head cheerleader in the ninth grade, who took your flowers but never remembered your name? Or Joe Pectulus, gals, the football captain in the eleventh grade, who copied your English notes but who took Suzy Frigglethorpe to the prom?"

Again, the relaxed hand acknowledged the chuckles. "So. Taking sex as a main drive of the human spirit, it seemed logical to incorporate it into the kind of statement Dream Sugar wanted to make. I figured the best way would be to strip a man and woman of all pretensions—and incidentally, for you more prurient souls, all clothing—to emphasize the invincibility of the human spirit. And I thought it might be appropriate to try to incorporate in the work, a hint of how people fulfill those dreams that the spirit yearns for."

He took a sip of water before resuming. "Everyone dreams. I dream, you dream, those people outside in the streets dream. But without some sort of outside help, say financial aid, emotional satisfaction, mental stimulation, physical assistance—without help of some kind from somewhere, it can be hard to turn dreams into reality. That's what brought Dream Sugar to Atlanta. That cooperation between state and city and company. And it's the same spirit of cooperation among ordinary people like you and me that's so necessary in making dreams come true. So that's what I've tried to depict. I hope I've succeeded."

He turned toward Paula. "Ready?" At her nod, he turned back. Lights dimmed except for spotlights darting across the tall veiled sculpture. A vigilant drummer set up a drum roll. "On behalf of Dream Sugar, I give you Vision of Dreaming."

His words were a signal. Ropes were pulled, draperies of fuchsia, ecru, and teal floated down. The rat-a-tat of the snare drum climaxed in a ringing clash of cymbals as the entire piece stood revealed.

Throughout the lobby, before, behind, and around me, came "oohs" and "aahs" of admiration.

Next to me, I heard Dave's startled, "Cool!"

The small orchestra behind the fountain had regrouped to strike up, of all things, Schumann's *Traumerei*. Daydream, reverie.

A year ago, I'd have looked toward Mark, knowing the orchestra's idea of appropriate musical accompaniment meant he'd be grinning at me.

But it wasn't a year ago, and tonight I looked at his work instead of my husband.

I'd seen Vision of Dreaming in its sectional phases, but when the completed sculpture rose before me, I marveled, as awestruck as everyone else in the large lobby.

Mark had composed a tree with its branches growing up toward the heavens.

Except that closer inspection proved the tree was in reality a woman, and the two branches were her arms lifting a long, flowing scarf that billowed like a screen of windstruck leaves.

Staring harder, one could make out her face, wistful, eager, anxious to try, to experience reaching for something.

Perhaps the stars.

A still closer look revealed the man supporting her. One of his hands held a buttock while the other rested beneath her breast so that he could lift her up toward the heights to which she aspired.

She stood on tiptoes on his knee and stretched upward toward her unseen star, but he was conscious of nothing but her. His eyes dwelt on her face as she craned her neck to look up, always up.

Resignation, pride, love, joy. All were written on his features as he formed the brace that sustained her.

A spontaneous clapping spread, until the entire lobby rang with applause that drowned out the small orchestra.

I applauded, too, unable to tamp my enthusiasm.

"That's some pile of stone," Dave leaned over to my ear. "To think I was scared we were going to be stuck walking past some gawd-awful thing with circles and triangles and cubes every morning on our way to work. Your husband's really good, isn't he?"

Mark certainly was good. I'd known he had talent, but I'd never realized how brilliant he was until that sculpture was revealed.

Yes, it was sex. A nude man and woman always imply sex. But the statue stood for much more.

The woman with her hands reaching skyward did so as openly as a child, confident of her partner's support. The man sustaining her mirrored the wonder on her face as he held her up. No one viewing them had a doubt that, together, they would reach the stars and fulfill their dreams.

Mark was saying something about Dream Sugar, and his words were followed by someone else's closing remarks. But I was lost, as were most of the people around me, in the magic of Mark's work.

"Look at that expression on her face," a woman behind me gushed. "However did he capture that?"

"She's obviously just got up from a roll in the hay," a jaded man to the side answered.

"If that's what it is, he looks even more satisfied than she does," she said, miffed.

The more I studied it, the more the piece bothered me.

I'd accepted that Mark kept his innermost self private. Seeing the passion in his sculpture after the unsettling experience in the parking deck made me certain that he possessed deeper, more complex emotions beneath his casual facade.

It didn't matter. What did I care?

It's too late. Tears stung my eyes to be hastily blinked back.

When Dave started a light flirtation with a pretty woman, I strolled through the crowd and viewed Vision of Dreaming from each angle.

It was easy to see how the ancients could worship statues of this magnitude. There was a presence about the immense couple that demanded respect.

Every detail was meticulously crafted. A casual glance would take the sculpted scarf, with its ripples and wafted ends, as a mass of windblown leaves. A closer examination made it look like an actual length of sheer silk lay over the woman's hands to float against her budded breasts. The workmanship was flawless.

As I admired the man's massive leg—the muscles in the thigh and calf seemed to tremble from the effort of lifting the woman—I glimpsed in the opening between his thigh and her calf Mark's neat ponytail across the lobby. In the midst of a group of laughing men and women whose aura exuded old Atlanta money, he swiveled his head.

Someone had called to him.

A woman approached, a dark exotic woman whose bright red dress made her stand out like a flame from the sober colors around her. She reached up with the ease of an old friend, kissing Mark on the mouth before putting her arm through his and drawing him to the side, away from the group whose homage failed to keep him.

I hadn't noticed her earlier but couldn't have missed that blazing dress. She'd either been hiding or had just arrived.

Her name was Coral Varelli, not Cora Vanilla as Fee had thought at her wedding reception when she pointed out Mark's girlfriend.

Had Mark invited her to this unveiling? Had she come down

from Virginia specifically for it? Had she and Mark kept in contact after our marriage?

I wondered, but not because I was jealous. Since I had told him I wanted a divorce, Mark could see or not see whomever he pleased.

I turned away from the statue.

Later when, despite my protests, Dave returned to babysit me, Coral showed up again. Several couples had begun to dance in the area between fountain and aviary, and Dave and I joined them.

As we became a part of the shuffling crowd, I looked over his shoulder in time to see Mark saunter toward the exit corridor. Coral's red dress pressed against his black tuxedo, and she clung to him as tightly as he had clung to me earlier.

Except there would be no coercion from Coral. Mark would be quite willing to go wherever Coral chose to lead him.

Maybe Coral was the reason he hadn't wanted Candy to come in my place.

My heart had no business giving a little twist, but it did.

Mark's agent saw me dancing with Dave and crossed the room to share his exultation. He was smashed, as much from excitement as from champagne, and talking of high six, maybe seven figure commissions in the future.

"Didn't I tell you?" He seized my hand and pumped it. "Mark and I were here two nights, till three this morning, setting up. But it was worth losing sleep over. Everybody's talking about Dreaming."

When he left to corner another unfortunate soul, Dave grinned at me. "He'll be floating for days."

"So will Mark, I'm sure."

But Mark showed no signs of euphoria when he rejoined Dave and me. Nor was there any indication of Coral's presence. He didn't say what he'd done with her, and I didn't ask.

When he thanked Dave for looking after me and dismissed him politely, my husband seemed the same as always. No threats, as I had imagined in the parking deck, nor elation from the accolades thrown his way all evening.

No guilt from a tryst with an old lover.

"Did you make out all right with Dave?" he asked.

"I made out fine. Not as good as you, but good enough." I mentally kicked myself for sounding like a scorned wife.

He thought I meant the applause. "I'm glad everything went off okay. Sorry Paula dragged me away."

"Don't worry about it. I was fine."

"Yeah, I figured you were when I saw the kid feeding you. Ready to go home?"

I blinked. "I thought we were going to Foster Cardwell's party."

"I begged off. I didn't get much sleep last night or the night before with setting up and all. I'm pretty beat. I may be coming down with a cold."

"All right." Mark didn't catch colds, but nothing suited me better than to leave.

He never mentioned Coral to me on the way home, nor did I bring her up. In fact, neither of us said anything during the thirty minute drive back to Decatur. He seemed preoccupied.

Maybe his preoccupation had something to do with Coral.

Not until we'd gone upstairs did we speak. I came out from the bathroom after changing into my pajamas and met him leaving our bedroom. He had discarded his coat and tie and shoes and socks, but still wore his starched shirt and formal pants and carried his pillow.

I checked in mid-step.

The lines around the corners of his eyes deepened. They deepened whenever he was immersed in thought, but their presence always made it seem he laughed at some unexplained joke.

I had realized, after the first few months of being married to Mark, that humor made an effective shield for his true feelings. It didn't matter back then.

He patted the pillow he held. "I figured I'd move into the spare room before you threw me out."

"I can sleep in there." I was anxious to be fair. "I don't mind."

"No, I'll go."

"You'll need sheets."

"I'll put them on. I know how to change a bed." He disappeared into the blackness of the spare room.

"I know you do," I muttered. "Self-sufficient SOB."

He should have let me protest further. He hadn't so much as told me good night.

Grow up.

This annoyance came from guilt. I had spoiled his triumphant evening by broaching the subject of divorce prematurely.

In the room that had been ours, I climbed into the bed we had shared.

Sleep did not come immediately. Moonlight sifting through the blinds made patterns on the ceiling, and Mark's odor, a subtle blend of clay and metal and pine soap and body oils uniquely his, permeated the bed linen.

I would wash the sheets the next day.

Mark seemed reconciled to a divorce. I should have been happy, but melancholy loomed heavier than ever. I would be starting a new life, but it would be a life without Mark, without Sweet Rowdy, and without the longed-for baby. I would be alone as never before.

Instead of the anticipated relief at the prospect, I felt curiously empty.

No wonder. An injured stranger bursting into my life. Losing Sweet Rowdy in such a violent and senseless way. The hateful deputies . . . Enough to traumatize anyone. And then, before the reception, Mark's unsuspected temper display. And that's what it was.

He'd been angry.

I didn't know him, I had never known him.

The way he'd looked when he accused me of abandoning a dying man . . . I wouldn't think of that, or my own fear. Everything would be better in the morning. Had to be better in the morning.

Sometime during my attempts to rationalize my immature behavior and convince myself that tomorrow would be better, I fell asleep.

* * * *

I DREAMED OF the man in the boat again, blood pouring from his back as he tried to pull the captive Sweet Rowdy from an adversary with a crooked nose and receding forehead.

In my dream, I tried to run toward the bleeding man, but my body stayed frozen.

Nor could I cry for help. Some sort of encumbrance trapped my voice in my throat.

"Mrs. Early," the redheaded man whispered. "Mrs. Early."

No, that wasn't right. He should have been whispering something else.

Emily. He should have been calling for Emily.

"Mrs. Early."

Mrs. Early . . .

I struggled to open heavy eyes.

A cold sharp object pricked the base of my throat. My arms were immobilized.

A dark figure, his craggy profile plainly outlined against the glimmer of light from the hall window, stood in the doorway.

I opened my mouth, and the sharp point pressed hard against my skin. A whisper, terrifying against the silence of the house, heated my ear. "Shut up, Mrs. Early. If you make a sound, I'll slice your neck like I did your little dog. You don't want that, do you?"

A man leaned over the bed, pinning me down, threatening me.

There were two men in the house, inside my bedroom.

A scream swelled, was stifled.

"Where's your husband?" The same deadly whisper delivered the question.

I couldn't answer. It took all my concentration to hold the scream inside.

The point of the knife pricked at my throat once, twice, and made me whimper.

I came close to losing the scream.

Warmth traced down the sides of my neck.

Blood. The warmth was my blood.

"Where is he?"

From near the door, the man with the crooked nose levitated to the foot of the bed. As his companion held the knife against me, he leaned over.

"Better tell, Mrs. Early." His whisper, toneless and disinterested and businesslike, frightened me more than the other. "He likes to cut people."

The wet at my throat dripped down onto the pillow and my tee. "I d-don't—"

"Shut up!" The hiss along with the knife cut off my words. "Speak quietly."

I had to wet my lips before managing a coherent whisper. "I don't know." I wasn't being heroic. My mind had gone blank.

As soon as I said the words, I remembered, but by then, the man with the knife had muttered, "Find him."

His companion with the jutting nose turned without a word and disappeared into the darkness.

I ought to cry out, to warn Mark.

A ragged moan emerged before the knife cut into my throat and extinguished the sound abruptly.

I lay on my side, facing my captor, with my right hand and shoulder under my pillow, the way I generally settled before falling asleep. The left arm was free of the sheet but held down by my assailant. My other arm, stretched out toward the headboard, was beneath the pillow. Too frightened to move, I shrugged my shoulder to relieve the uncomfortable pressure.

The knife blade dug in.

I froze.

The next few minutes seemed like hours. The man with the crooked nose didn't come back.

The man holding me captive kept turning his head to glance toward the door. He didn't release me or allow me to move.

Blam!

Someone had run into a piece of furniture and knocked it over in the room across the hall where Mark slept.

The man hovering over me jumped.

I took advantage of the blade's momentary withdrawal to move my arm and shift the weight off the trapped shoulder. Fingers touched, closed over one of Mark's small figures on the bed shelf.

Complete silence followed the noise in the other room. The knife returned to graze my neck.

I held onto my statue the way I held onto the arms of the dentist's chair.

The man beside me waited a long minute but must have decided stealth was useless after the previous commotion. "Did you find him?"

No answer.

The man's breathing quickened. He cursed. The blade wavered at my throat. He cursed again and grabbed my shoulder.

"Get up," he said, no longer trying to whisper.

A rank odor came from his mouth.

The odor of fear. An idiotic observation when the knife's tip was piercing my skin.

He's as scared as me, but he has the knife.

His voice boomed in the dark. "I have your wife, Early. If you don't want her hurt, you'd better come in now."

As he spoke he yanked me up. The blade slipped away from my neck. His head turned slightly to watch the door.

Terrified, I let my arm swing around as he jerked me to my feet.

My hand clutching the heavy statuette arced up and back down of its own accord. It lined up to connect with the side of his head.

I didn't pull the blow, but struck with all my strength.

The thud as the solid figure hit his temple sickened me.

The shock of the impact ran all the way up my arm to my shoulder.

His hold relaxed. He staggered to his knees.

A moan came. From me or him, I couldn't tell.

It floated in the air as I jumped across him.

At the door, the screams belonged to me and me alone.

Two hands reached out and caught at me, pulled me into a tight grip I couldn't break.

CHAPTER SIX

SCREAMING AT THE top of my lungs, I flailed out blindly.

One wild swing caught my new captor on his shoulder and another on his face before my wrists were forced down and his arms tightened around me.

I screamed again, struggling with all my might before I heard Mark's voice calling my name and realized who held me.

"Steve, Steve. Hush, Steve, it's me. It's all right, it's me, Steve."

I collapsed against him.

His hand reached past me to the light switch. At the dazzling whiteness, I hid my eyes against his shoulder and began to shake.

"It's all right," he said again, but his attention, after he made sure I was unharmed, switched toward the man I'd hit. "It's fine, Steve. You're okay."

He set me, despite my vehement objections, gently but firmly aside to approach the figure huddled like a pile of old rags beside the bed.

"Mark, don't leave me."

"You're safe." He focused on the man.

The man I'd struck. Where was the other one?

"There's another man in the house." I couldn't stop trembling, could barely keep from sobbing. "He was—"

"I know, love. I found him." Mark knelt beside the figure on the floor. "It's all right."

He wore a dark long-sleeved pullover and jeans. Except for socks and shoes, he was fully dressed. He usually slept in his undershorts, but his attire didn't matter.

"Mark, the other man!"

"He's tied up in the other room, love. He can't hurt you."

"Oh." Relief whooshed out.

Mark caught my attacker's hair and turned the head. "Hit this guy kind of hard, didn't you?"

He sounded as self-possessed as he had been throughout our marriage. Tonight that composure was comforting.

I went to where he squatted on the floor.

The skin of the heavyset man, above the bushy black beard, was grayish. Similar in build to the other intruder, he had a round face and a broad, squashed nose.

"Do you know him?" Mark asked.

I had never seen him before. "No. Is he dead? Did I kill him?"

Mark gave a little laugh as he rolled back an eyelid and studied the eye. "I'd say not. He may have a concussion but hey, it couldn't happen to a nicer guy, could it? Hand me a couple of ties from the closet, will you? The narrow one your mother gave me that I don't wear, and the Texas shoestring one you think is so funny."

I did as he instructed, choking back the sobs. Mark, with the quick and efficient motions that were his trademark, tied the man's ankles to the bed frame. Once he finished, he pulled a drawer out of the heavy chest that sat beside the bed.

"What in the world did you hit this guy with?" Mark could have been discussing the weather.

I still clutched the figurine, the one he had done of me brushing my hair. Not trusting myself to speak, I held it out. The heavy clay ceramic had cracked to reveal its iron core.

Mark glanced down at the chipped piece, annoyance flitting over normally dispassionate features.

He bent over again and bound the man's wrists to the frame of the chest where he'd removed the drawer. Only then, after standing erect in a motion of pure dark liquidity that somehow enhanced the proficiency of his previous actions, did he come back to me. He put his hands, warm and substantial, on my shoulders while I covered my mouth and tried not to throw up.

"You can stop shaking," he said. "Everything's fine. Are you going to be sick? Did you stuff yourself on those damned strawberries tonight?"

His matter-of-fact tone comforted me, but my body would not stop jerking. "I only had six." Dammed-up tears stung. "And no, I'm not going to be sick."

"Good. Then you're all right. Everything's fine now." His fingers clenched and unclenched on my shoulders. He might have been wondering whether or not to take me in his arms. In the end, he drew away and took the cracked figure from my fist.

Then he saw my neck. His shoulders tightened, his jaw clenched. His free hand went to my throat, nestling round it and lingering before sliding down and pulling back the collar of my tee.

Craning my neck, I found the stream of caked blood leading behind my shirt and down my breasts. Brown spots marred the cotton. I shuddered, remembering the knife at my throat, and looked up to an expression on my husband's face I'd never once seen in all the years we'd been married.

He looked like a criminal himself. Far more threatening than the countenance in the parking deck, this face with its ugly mouth and flared nostrils and narrowed eyes turned my blood cold, frightened me almost as much as had the unknown attackers.

I hoped wildly that the fury depicted in every line, every motion, was not aimed toward me. "H-he had a knife. He cut m-me." I started to shake again, afraid of the memory of the men, afraid of this husband I didn't know.

"I see he did. He won't do it again." The terrifying expression dissolved. With a quick motion, he caught me to him. I didn't return his embrace nor did I resist, but in the back of my mind flickered the barest modicum of shame.

Common sense, common decency, said I shouldn't be here in his arms, not after the past months of armed truce, not after I'd told him I wanted a divorce.

I ignored sense and decency. Mark was strong where I wasn't, certain where I wasn't. For these few moments, I needed to be held. Mark, somehow aware of my need, held me.

Eventually, the confidence of his body seeped through mine, and the shudders racking me stopped. I lay against him, dry-eyed and enervated, cradling my head against his shoulder as he threaded his fingers through my hair. The muscles in his chest and stomach rippled. His steady heartbeat quieted me. After a bit, he stopped stroking my hair and took his hand away from my waist. Glancing up, I saw him looking at something he held behind my back, something beyond my range of vision.

I shifted to see.

The broken figure.

"I'm sorry." It was one of his favorites. "I didn't think. I didn't mean to hurt it."

"I'm glad it was there," he said briefly. The small figure might have meant nothing to him. "Split right down the middle, didn't it? Maybe I can mend it, since there's no hope in hell I'll ever get you to sit for me again." The air of resignation about him played at odds with his previous protective stance.

My mind filled with intruders waving knives and pinning me down. "What if there's more of them, Mark? Those men, I mean?"

"There aren't."

I threw a glance over my shoulder, toward the bound figure on the floor. "How do you know?"

He put the fractured piece on the dresser and drew a reassuring hand down my cheek. "I'll check the house if it'll make you feel better. You wait here, okay?"

"No!" The thought of him leaving me alone was enough to make me hysterical. In the end, I put on a robe and we went downstairs together to search. A window glass had been cut in a back window, but as he had predicted, there were no more invaders.

Returning to the foot of the stairs, he stopped. "The phones are dead, and I must have left my cell in the car. I'll get it in a few minutes to call the police. Can you make some coffee, Steve? I'm sure we'll need it before the night's over."

"Is it safe for you to go outside?" He could be hit over the head or knifed.

"Oh, I think so. And yes, dear, I'll be careful though you haven't got around to that part of the script yet."

His airy reply would have infuriated me a few hours before. Now it calmed me and gave me a false sense of security.

He softened his tone. "I wish you'd put on that coffee. I want to go back and check on those men. Then I'll see about the cell."

I got to the kitchen door before something else occurred to me and I turned. "Mark."

Halfway up the stairs, he didn't pause. "What?"

Fleeting curiosity as to why he would check on the men faded before a more urgent question. "Why didn't the alarm go off?"

He stopped in mid-step. A marked hesitation preceded his answer. His back stiffened, and I could sense, almost see, the old reticence cover him like a cloak. "Don't hit me, ma'am. Mea culpa. I was so tired after all the whoop-ti-do and excitement of the reception, I guess I forgot to set it."

He climbed up the stairs.

Mark never forgot anything. He was a creature of habit. Methodical, plodding, dependable.

Strange that the first time he had forgotten to set the alarm, someone had broken in.

In the kitchen, Rowdy's empty dish invoked a fresh threat of tears that had to be squelched.

Then, while putting in the filter and measuring out coffee, I pondered Mark's manner. The slight hesitation before his answer had sent the same signals that had contributed to the demise of our marriage. The nebulous suspicions held since the first year we married returned.

Mark was holding something back.

By the time the coffee had dripped, Mark still had not come down, and I was becoming more and more uneasy.

Nothing seemed right. I had been hysterical, nearly out of my mind, but Mark . . .

Mark had been dressed except for socks and shoes.

Had he been expecting the two men?

No, I scoffed while pacing back and forth in the tiny kitchen. I was crazy for thinking such a thing. How would he have known? He couldn't have.

Still, the idea once formed wouldn't go away.

Could tonight have something to do with the events at the lake? What a stupid question. The same man was involved. No one could mistake that profile. I needed to tell Mark.

Why had the man come here? How did he know where I lived?

Another stupid question. He'd found my address in my purse during the ransacking of the lake house.

I found myself wringing my hands.

To keep them busy, I poured out a mug of coffee and sat down at the kitchen table. The silence was oppressive. What was keeping Mark? I ought to check. Or maybe not. Maybe I should stay here with my coffee.

No. Check on him. What if one of those men got loose?

Almost to the top of the stairs, I stopped. My eyes were on a level with the bathroom, and the open door allowed the view of a man, hands bound behind him, kneeling in front of the toilet. Mark, back half to me, perched on the edge of the tub. He held the man by the neck.

Deceptively unpretentious shoulder muscles bulged, revealing the hidden strength as my husband pushed the man's face into the toilet with one hand and flushed it with the other.

My mouth opened but no sound came out. I clung to the banister and watched while the water roared and died away.

After long seconds, Mark fished out the choking man. "Nothing personal, you know, but I've got to make sure," my husband said with perfect aplomb, "that you've told me everything you know."

The man sputtered incoherently. "I don't know any more! I swear—"

"Let's try once more. Just to be sure."

My world crumbled around me as the toilet flushed again.

I turned and went blindly back down the stairs, but my legs wouldn't take me as far as the kitchen. I drew out a chair from the writing desk in the hall and sat down, spending long moments controlling runaway emotions.

On the wall before me, a mirror hung. It reflected my white face. To its side a framed photograph displayed Mark and me on his sailboat the year we married, when we were still happy, still in love.

That glowing girl seemed decades younger than the woman in the mirror.

The antique clock chimed the hour. I folded my hands on the desk and waited for Mark.

Mark. My husband. Funny, easygoing, confident Mark, who never made enemies, who never forgot to set alarms, who never did anything before thorough review and consideration.

The man I knew and loved couldn't be the man glimpsed in the bathroom.

They were incompatible. Unless the man upstairs was that inner man I had sought for six years without finding. Could this aberrant, and abhorrent, behavior explain why Mark had taken such care never to disclose his true self?

Strangely enough, I did not tremble when I imagined what was happening upstairs in my house. My hands lay perfectly steady and unmoving, stacked one on top of the other.

Another of Mark's figurines stood nearby.

I picked it up, rubbing the smooth curves of the bronze dolphin with my thumb, brushing across the bottom and his initials that were Mark's signature. How could the same man create this beautiful work of art and then do something so uncivilized?

How could a man create a beautiful laughing baby in stone after losing his child?

The dolphin slipped from my nerveless fingers and fell to the desk top, scratching the finish of the wood and denting one of the bronze fins.

"You've nearly destroyed my favorite piece already. Trying for another? Then what? My whole collection?"

Mark's cheerful voice hit me like icy water. He strolled downstairs as though he was coming down to breakfast and hadn't been shoving a man's face into a flushing toilet minutes before.

The chair overturned in my haste to get up.

He knew at once. The amused expression fled. His eyelids narrowed, his lips tightened. A place in his jaw pulsed as he became the man I didn't know, had never known.

From the living room, the ticking of the clock that had been my great-grandmother's marked off the seconds as we stood like wary animals. In the narrow confines of the hallway, the overhead lamp threw a yellow glow that changed his brown hair to deep gold.

Neither of us made a move toward the other.

I ended the impasse. "Are you going to call the police?"

For once I could read his mind.

He was wondering if I was still upset over being attacked in my bed. Or if I had observed something I ought not have.

I was positive he could explain everything that had happened and why it had happened, beginning with the man in the boat and ending with tonight's intruders. I wanted to ask, but I was too afraid of what he might say. I compromised. "Mark, you aren't involved in anything illegal, are you?"

His brows rose in surprise, as if this were the last question he would have expected. "Not unless you count my monthly poker game." Humor returned, lengthening his mouth, crinkling his eyes. "Are you?"

"You know the answer to that." But I didn't know whether to believe him. I didn't think I could believe him. "Are you going to call the police?" I asked again.

The clock from the living room continued its loud ticking.

"I'll go out to the car for my cell phone right now," he said at last. "Pour us a cup of coffee, would you?"

I went toward the kitchen, careful not to touch him as I passed.

* * * *

THE MAN WITH the jagged profile, the man I had seen being pushed into the toilet, had escaped by the time the police arrived.

I was frantic. "What if he comes back?"

Mark laughed at my fears. "Come on, Steve. Would you stick around a place where your accomplice had got a concussion and the police were on their way?"

I bit my lip and kept my terror to myself.

The emergency technician assured us that the unconscious man was in no danger of dying from my blow, despite having to be transported out on a stretcher. That relieved one worry, but another one appeared in the person of the Dekalb County investigator.

A courteous African-American with a small mustache, his jaded expression said nothing could surprise him. As Mark and I gave our versions of the night, he wrote in a small notebook. Though he listened to my tale of the man in the boat and the lake break-in, it was my husband he questioned when I finished.

I didn't think he was chauvinistic. I thought he suspected my husband possessed the answers.

"Why do you think your wife's been attacked like this?"

The direct challenge didn't faze Mark. "I don't know."

The same thing I'd responded to the authorities at the lake.

I really hadn't known anything then and still didn't. But now I had doubts about Mark and worried about what he wasn't revealing.

My husband smiled blandly.

The detective, equally unperturbed, waited.

"I would imagine," Mark said, "that everything goes back to the man in the boat. Perhaps our intruders, whoever they are, think he told something to Steve before he disappeared."

The mustache quivered in my direction like a dog's nose. "What do you say, Mrs. Early? Was there something said, or exchanged between you and this missing man? Something that might have slipped your mind?"

I didn't like the way the detective surveyed me. I was sick of insinuations. "The man could hardly talk."

My words came out sounding flat and unfeeling. Sounding like Mark sometimes sounded. Had Mark been hiding his own confusion and concerns all this time with his nonchalant, couldn't-care-less air?

I pushed aside the fancy. Perhaps if I'd had time to follow it up, I might have come closer to understanding my husband that night, but the detective waited, and the opportunity evaporated.

"Emily. That's all he said to me. I don't know an Emily and I didn't know the man in the boat. If he had anything he wanted to give Emily or anybody else, it was in the boat and left with him."

"So after all this, you still don't know anything."

It was not a question, and I did not answer.

The detective slapped his notebook shut. "Thank you for your cooperation, Mrs. Early," he said without irony. "If you remember anything else, please let me know right away."

"She's told you everything she knows," Mark intervened.

"Yes, I've told you everything I know," I repeated. Which wasn't true. I hadn't told of my suspicions that Mark knew the identity of the man in the boat. Nor had I told what I'd witnessed in the bathroom.

I met the detective's eyes and tried not to tremble.

* * * *

BY FOUR O'CLOCK in the morning, Mark and I had ushered the detective out.

"Always good to see our tax dollars in action," Mark said when the door finally closed and he locked it. "With as much time as the nice man spent with us, makes me feel we're getting our money's worth. Doesn't it you?"

"This is serious. Mark—"

"Go up to bed. You're exhausted."

He was right. Questions could wait till the next day. What difference would it possibly make?

Coward. I was afraid to ask him about what he'd done in the bathroom, afraid of what he'd tell me.

I started toward the steps, but my feet lagged. I didn't want to go upstairs by myself because I didn't want to be alone.

Mark didn't follow me. He had started toward the back of the house.

"Aren't you coming?"

"Later. Go on to bed, Steve. See if you can get some sleep. Lord knows we both need it."

A heavy weight descended at the thought of going up the stairs alone. I leaned on the writing desk.

I'm depressed because I'm so tired.

Being tired explained why I felt like weeping, too.

"How can I sleep?"

At my plaintive cry, he turned in the doorway of the kitchen. "Steve."

"I saw you, Mark. I saw what you were doing to that man in the bathroom."

He nodded, unsmiling lips out of place with the laugh lines around his eyes. "I thought you might have."

Wild imaginings took hold of my fevered brain. "He, he isn't dead, is he? You didn't—"

"Good lord, no." Mark seemed genuinely shocked that I would ask such a thing. "What do you think I am?"

I didn't know. I had never known. I didn't probe further about the intruder's whereabouts for fear of what I would discover.

One large tear threatened to overflow, and I swiped at it. "What are you involved in?"

"Nothing. I have no idea what this is about."

His words sounded truthful, but I no longer trusted him.

"Mark." I couldn't continue because I didn't know what I wanted to say. I was afraid, afraid of what was happening and afraid of what else he might reveal. Afraid he might tell me things I didn't want to hear.

For the second time that night I picked up the bronze dolphin for comfort, caressing and turning its smooth body so that the bottom exposed the neat initials. Again I ran my fingers over the entwined initials.

Mark Loren Early.

"Go upstairs," Mark said from across the hallway. He sounded very far away.

I stared at the M., L., and E, seeing the letters come in and out of focus beneath the yellow illumination.

M. L. E.

Em. El. Ee.

The truth burst like a brilliant light. The threat of tears vanished. "Emily!"

He started toward me. "Steve."

I whirled on him. "You're Emily, aren't you?"

He stopped in his tracks, stricken.

"You knew all the time that man wanted you. Why didn't you tell me? Why did you lie?"

More things slipped together. Grinding mental gears adjusted so that the opposing cogs melded smoothly. I swayed over the desk, caught its corner to steady myself. "You knew those men would come here tonight, didn't you? Like you knew the man in the boat was looking for you. You know who he is, don't you?"

"Yes, I knew the man in the boat was looking for me. And yes, I know who he is." The stricken look vanished. The time when he might have revealed himself came and went. His caution was too ingrained, his detachment too much a part of him. "But no, I didn't know those men would come here. I thought it possible. If not tonight, then another night. Possible, but not probable. I didn't know. Not for sure."

"But you left off the alarm just in case. You let them come into our home. Let them attack me." I wanted him to deny it, waited for him to deny it. All the while knowing he wouldn't.

"It seemed," he said reluctantly, "the easiest way. I didn't expect them to get in without me hearing them, but I was so damned tired. I was awake all last night and the night before setting up Dreaming for the opening. I dozed off and they came." He ran his fingers through his hair in a gesture of futility. He wouldn't meet my eyes. "It was my fault you were hurt. I'm sorry."

"Sorry!" I bit back the invective. Anger turned to cold fear when he didn't explain further. "What's happening? What are you involved in?"

His lips pressed into a line. "This is nothing to concern you."

"Will you stop it?" I hurled the bronze dolphin across the foyer. It thudded against the wall, scarring the sheet rock and slapping a framed painting lopsided before bouncing onto the carpet.

Mark's eyes widened in disbelief.

"Will you stop keeping everything to yourself, never giving anyone a hint as to what's going on inside you? I'm sick of being on the outside, Mark. I'm sick of trying to figure out what you want from me."

The words weren't planned. They burst out of nowhere.

After a moment, he went over and lifted the dolphin off the floor where it had landed.

Running his hands over the bronze back, he avoided my eyes. "Harris Orville Ogden. That's his name. We trained at FIFA together. He calls me Emily and I call him Hoo. He works for another section of FIFA."

My outburst had reaped unexpected rewards. The tension subsided.

"When I transferred to Atlanta, Hoo's grandmother had gone into a nursing home and I bought her lake house. That's why Hoo knew to go there."

Mark had known the identity of the man in the boat all along. I ought to be surprised. "Why didn't you tell me?"

He looked at me finally. One brow lifted. "Why didn't you tell the nice detective what you saw me doing to that creep in the bathroom?"

I had no answer. "You should have told me."

He waited a moment before giving a mirthless chuckle. The corners of his eyes were wrinkled in their old manner, but the eyes themselves were opaque and unreadable. "We've not confided in each other for half a year. You were the one who never bothered to tell me about Hoo till we were on our way to the reception tonight. Last night, I mean," he corrected himself as if it mattered.

"You've never confided in me. Never."

His mouth parted to deny my words. Emotions, so fleeting and flimsy that I might have imagined them, transformed his expression from anger to hurt to bewilderment and finally to stoicism. He shrugged. "Have it your way."

My chest ached as though I were drowning. I swayed against the desk. "Why didn't you tell that investigator about your friend?"

"Because Hoo *is* my friend. I happen to trust my friends and I try to be loyal to them."

I shrank back at the dig.

"So till I know what's going on, what Hoo's mixed up in, I'm not giving the police anything they might use against him. Can you understand that?"

We remained locked in our adversarial positions. The yards separating us across the room could have been miles.

Could I believe Mark? Was he telling me everything he knew? Was Hoo, or both Hoo and Mark, involved in something illicit, something bad?

I dragged myself up the stairs like an old woman.

At the top, I looked down to see Mark's back disappear from the hall leading to the kitchen.

CHAPTER SEVEN

REMOVING THE BLOOD-STAINED tee, I patted alcohol on my neck. The cuts were too minor to have produced so much blood.

There'd been a lot of blood on Hoo Ogden, too. Where could he be? Was someone looking after his wounds? Was he all right?

I stumbled to the bed, the adrenaline rush long since gone.

The crumpled sheets looked okay, but blood stained the pillow. I wouldn't worry about the case now. Just turn it over and get on clean jammies. The first ones at hand, a delicate set Mark had given me as an anniversary present, I usually saved for special occasions.

What did it matter? Mark wouldn't know or care what I wore. I pulled the silk camisole over my head and stepped into the loose taps.

In bed, despite my weariness, I couldn't close my eyes without seeing the tormented face of the redheaded Hoo or the hooked nose of the intruder.

What if he came back?

Even exhaustion wouldn't make me sleep. After a half hour of wakefulness, of thrashing my pillow and listening in vain for Mark's footsteps in the spare room, I put on my robe and went back downstairs.

The smell of fresh coffee met me at the bottom of the steps. A lamp in the living room made a dim luminous circle by the sofa. Mark sprawled out there, studying a mug.

He looked up and saw me. "What's wrong? Can't sleep?"

"Are you going to sit up the rest of the night?" My mouth dried with a new fear. "Are you waiting up to see if that man comes back?"

"He won't be back."

"You've done something with him, haven't you?"

He tilted his head. "You have a vivid imagination. What would I have done?" He took a sip from the mug, gauging my reaction over the rim.

I wanted to believe him, but I couldn't. "Then why are you so sure he isn't coming back?" I went over to him. "Don't lie to me."

He set the mug down on a side table. "I've never lied to you. I've always thought lies between a husband and wife were out of place." Leaning forward, he reached out with both hands and caught the ends of my robe to pull them together. The process of his snugging the belt around my waist brought me one step closer to him, and then another.

He cupped my hips with his hands and pulled me deeper between his spread knees so that I could feel his heat. "You used to think that, too." He slid his hands down my hips, down my thighs, and back up.

The lamp stood behind me. My shadow darkened his face, leaving his features inscrutable.

I ignored his murmured words, ignored his possessive clasp, ignored the subtle intimate link he wove. Diversions, all of them. "What did you do with that man?"

"He's gone. He wanted to go." His soothing tone pacified. He used it to reassure and deflect questions he didn't want to answer. "He won't be back." His hands stopped on my hips. "Go up to bed."

Had he touched me this way a week ago, I would have cringed and run away. Earlier in our marriage, I would have let him reassure and evade my questions, let him persuade me to withdraw, let him make love to me.

I had changed in the past few hours. I stepped back out of his grasp, ignoring the intensity around us. "Tell me what you did to him, Mark."

Perhaps Mark saw something in my face that warned him I wouldn't be shunted aside. Perhaps he decided I could handle the truth. Perhaps he remembered my earlier words when I had accused him of shutting me out.

Whatever the reason, his hands did not follow my retreat.

"I made a deal with him." He picked up his mug and swished around its half-drunk contents. A half-smile mocked me, but his voice was flat. "I made sure that he knows you don't have anything to do with whatever's going on with Hoo. That you don't know anything, period." His legs encased in the dark jeans shifted, one stretching out, the other remaining bent. He rested the mug on his stomach, holding it there with both hands. "When I was sure he understood you weren't involved, I let him go."

"You let him go? Deliberately?"

"Yes. He knows you don't have Hoo's papers, that you aren't hiding anything. He'll take that information back to whoever hired him." He looked up at the ceiling. "I showed him the door personally. You shouldn't be bothered any more. No more midnight visitors, no more tete-a-tetes with suave police detectives."

I dropped into a chair. "I don't believe it."

"That's your problem, not mine. Now you know it all." His mouth twitched. "All that I know, anyway. We may never learn what Hoo has gotten into, but you're out of it. That ought to make you feel better."

It didn't, but before I could say so, headlights from the street swept the living room. A car stopped in our driveway.

In one lithe motion, Mark unfolded himself and moved across the room to pull back the drapes. "It's all right. It's . . ." He glanced back at me. "It's a friend."

Sometime during the night he had managed to put on socks and sneakers. With his dark clothes and bound hair, he looked like a prowler himself, and one hazardous to confront. Not the man I had lived with for six years.

"What kind of friend comes over at five in the morning?"

"Go to bed, Steve."

"You've not told me everything you know about this."

"Come on, now. Think about it. Do you really want to know everything?"

"You better believe I want to know everything," I snarled.

The creases around his eyes deepened. "Okay. So maybe you do. I'll get the door."

I heard him admit someone, heard his indistinguishable murmur answered by a woman's. A moment later, he ushered his early morning visitor past the foyer so that they stood in the opening to the living room.

Coral, with her back to me, shrugged out of a light jacket. "I don't know what you think we can do."

Mark touched her arm, and the intimate way he touched her, quickly, firmly, urgently, looked like a warning. "Later," he said. "Steve's in here." A brief jerk of his head indicated me.

Coral gave her jacket to Mark with a remark which I couldn't hear but which may have pertained to me, then turned and loosed a smirk.

"Hello, Steve. How nice to see you again." She had discarded the red dress, replaced it with amethyst colored leggings and tunic. Her hair was pinned back and face made up as it had been for the Dream Sugar reception. Mark stood behind her, looking over her shoulder with his customary noncommittal expression.

For one crazy second, the two of them seemed united together against me, the outsider.

No. This was my house, my home.

I managed a civil greeting. "Hello."

"Coral Varelli. I work with Mark at FIFA. I met you at your sister's wedding," she prompted, curiosity and something else behind her demure demeanor. Mischief, perhaps.

Mark, never indiscreet, had avoided talking to me about Coral.

Fee had been the one to reveal Mark had moved out on Coral.

"He didn't talk to Dan about it, but one of Coral's friends told him that Mark's way too possessive," Fee said over the phone, not aware Mark had already shown up in Atlanta, "and that if Coral wants him back, all she has to do is crook her little finger."

Fee's words twisted my heart. I had worried up until our wedding day that Coral would crook her little finger.

I no longer cared.

"You might not remember me," Coral persisted. "I came to Fiona and Dan's wedding. With Mark."

"I remember you." I said nothing about her being with Mark at the Dream Sugar unveiling, nor did either of them mention it.

Mark put his hand on Coral's shoulder to get her attention. A friendly gesture. No more. No reason for the rising suspicion of her presence in my house.

Besides, what if the casual caress did indicate something other than friendship still lay between them? I didn't care. Mark and I were through. He'd agreed to a divorce, hadn't he?

He ignored me to address Coral. "Coffee?"

Her face swung toward him, radiant. "It smells wonderful. You always did make the best coffee, Marco."

"Kitchen's this way." He directed her by nudging the small of her back in a gesture both practiced and personal, a touch signaling the familiarity of old friends. Or old lovers, in this case. "Check out the tabletop art in the hall. Druids are a favorite of mine at the moment."

Her scent, expensive and musky, drifted into the air as they passed.

Nonplussed by their unanimity, it took several minutes to realize that whatever had brought Coral here in the wee hours of the morning had nothing to do with Mark's art. They had excluded me, all right, but not because they were lovers.

Mark and Coral intended to talk about Hoo and the intruders, and he didn't want to do it in front of me.

How did Coral come into the picture?

By the time I reached the postage-stamp kitchen, she leaned against a counter near Mark, stiletto heels kicked off, hands behind her back, and one leg bent with its bare foot resting on the other knee in a charming crane-like pose. As Mark poured coffee, she listened with flattering absorption.

"Abner may not think it's my business but on the other hand, this has gotten kind of personal. Hoo's my friend. No matter what Abner says, I can't sit back and let—" He broke off his sentence at my entrance.

Abner. Always Abner.

Coral followed his glance. She slipped her feet back into her shoes. "What a night you've had," she said to me. Her voice throbbed with compassion, but her mouth betrayed her pleasure.

I could see her take in my old chenille robe and strained features before glancing down at her own outfit, sense her satisfaction as she compared her appearance to mine.

"Poor thing. You look washed-out and tired. And upset." Under cover of sympathy, she pointed out my shortcomings. "I'll bet you were scared out of your wits."

I had been, but she was the last person I'd admit it to. "It's certainly been an unusual night."

"A kind we're not accustomed to," Mark agreed.

"And Marco says you actually clobbered the creep." Coral cocked her head to one side in disbelief.

I could hardly believe what I'd done myself. For that matter, all the events of the past weekend seemed beyond belief.

Mark took two sugar substitute packets and opened them, pouring one and part of the other into a mug of coffee. He stirred the brew and handed it to Coral.

"Thanks, Marco." She used one hand to grip the mug and the other to stroke his knuckles. "I'm always amazed at your memory of what I like."

"And dislike." Without haste, Mark removed his fingers from beneath hers. "Such language you used tonight. I'd forgotten what a termagant you can be."

She made a crowing sound. "You know how I hate being woken up in the middle of the night, but since when did your knowing ever do me any good? When we were together, you never took any notice. I guess I shouldn't expect anything different now."

I could imagine why she would be woken up in the middle of the night when they'd been together and felt my cheeks flush at such private disclosures.

Mark took her remarks calmly. "You shouldn't. You know what an SOB I am. I didn't call and wake you up because I felt like reminiscing about old times."

Belatedly, I realized that Coral had been referring to his phone call instigating this meeting and not to previous sexual encounters. My face grew hotter.

Coral's impudent look said she could read my mind, and that my assumptions weren't so very far off. "I'm always available for you, Marco," she purred. "Any time. For whatever reason." And to me: "Your husband and I go back a long way. You don't mind, do you?"

"Why should I?" There may have been an edge to my voice, but not from jealousy. Coral was the type of woman other women instinctively mistrusted.

Mark turned his back to us as he poured himself coffee. "Steve, go up to bed. Coral's right. You've had a big night." He didn't ask if I wanted coffee.

"Don't tell me what to do." I had no intention of leaving, crowded though the tiny kitchen was with the three of us. "Why did you call Coral to come over here?"

Mug in hand, he leaned back on the counter beside Coral. The two of them were allied again against me.

But he spoke easily enough. "I wanted some company. Nothing against your conversation, love. Your conversation's fine, but I can tell you've about had it. Coral doesn't mind losing some sleep."

"I know whatever's going on has something to do with those men tonight and your friend. Why did you call Coral?"

He didn't answer.

The silence grew awkward. Coral leaned against the counter beside Mark and sipped her coffee with way too much satisfaction. Her observant eyes flicked to me and Mark and back.

Mark stood motionless so that the white kitchen fluorescent threw an eerie cast onto his skin and made him look like one of his own marble sculptures. He might put on a blank front but his mind must be churning.

"Why did you call her?" I repeated.

Mark either realized I wouldn't be sidetracked or else he decided it would do no harm to tell me. "Coral works with Hoo and me for FIFA. I knew she was in town and hoped she might be able to throw some light on what Hoo was doing. After our little problem tonight, I called and asked. Coral insisted on coming here." His gaze veered to Coral. "Instead of telling me what I wanted to know over the phone."

There may have been irony in his voice, or there may not have been. Mark was always hard to read.

"Do you?" I asked Coral. "Know anything about what's going on, I mean?"

She was as closemouthed as Mark, but her shrug said she knew a lot more than I did. "Probably not, but it's always nice to have an excuse to see Mark. I expect you know I lived with him before he married you."

"Coral." Mark didn't sound angry, but that same tone had captured Sweet Rowdy's instant attention.

Ignoring the reminder of Rowdy, I said to Coral, "I fail to see what your former relationship, or even your current relationship with Mark, has to do with this." There. My composure could match theirs.

Coral's eyebrows raised in frank surmise. "My current relationship with Mark? My, you do get to the heart of things, don't you? Aren't you the teensiest bit curious about our current relationship?"

"Coral, cut it out. Steve, Coral and I have a business relationship. Any other kind ended before our marriage." Mark looked at me with the same undisguised speculation as Coral. "Honest."

Great. Coral thought I was jealous of her connection with Mark, and now Mark did, too. I opened my mouth to deny it.

No. They counted on my denial. Counted on me being sidetracked on a wasted expedition so they wouldn't have to answer questions about Hoo.

"I'm not concerned with your relationship," I said instead.

Coral let out a trill of laughter, disbelief apparent. "What Mark said is quite true. You can go to your marital bed in peace. Your husband is perfectly safe. I promise. I'll send him up later, when we're through. Virtue intact. Or at least not irretrievably damaged."

She paused expectantly.

Coral might be able to manipulate a man however she wanted, but no way would she bait me into leaving. Maybe they wanted me out of the way for the same or different reasons, but I wasn't budging.

I spoke slowly and distinctly, the way I instructed a class of college freshmen who haven't quite realized they need to put forth their best efforts because they are about to have to compete in an adult world that is hard and biased and unforgiving. "If the two of you think I'm going to bed while you try to figure out what happened to Hoo and why he was looking for Mark, you can think again. In the past two days, I've lost my dog." My voice trembled and I had to swallow. "I've been broken in on at the lake house. I've been broken in on here. I've almost had my throat slit and nearly killed a man. Now what the hell is going on?"

"My, my. The puppy has teeth," Coral mocked.

"Leave it alone, Coral." A note seldom heard rang in Mark's voice.

I thought of his face after he first saw my neck with its cuts. I had been afraid of him then because his expression was so utterly alien to the picture of my husband held in my mind.

He didn't frighten Coral. "When Mark first met you, that's what he said you reminded him of. Did you know that? A little puppy needing somebody to take it home and look after it. I laughed. I had no idea he intended volunteering for the job."

Coral's disclosures left me unmoved. "I don't need anyone to look after me. All I need is the truth. And I'm still waiting to hear it."

She made a sound of disgust and threw up her hands. "I did try, Marco," she said to him. "I don't think your wife's going to be sidetracked."

"I could have told you that if you'd stopped talking long enough to let me." My husband aimed a half-smile at no one in particular. "Why don't you sit down and tell us what Hoo was doing down here, wild woman? The last I heard, he was working out of London."

Coral shunned the ladder-back chairs at the small table, choosing instead to vault up onto the counter beside Mark. Her long legs dangled in a homely fashion though she herself looked anything but. Against the background of plain oak cabinets and lemon wallpaper and off-white linoleum, she was an exotic orchid brought from a hothouse into a room of dandelions. "You always know how to work me, don't you? Well, I'm not going to lose my temper this time." She settled herself, using his shoulder to steady herself.

Her interactions with Mark disoriented me. Their tacit exchanges signaled she had a deeper understanding of him than I, although he'd been my husband for almost six years.

Perhaps she did. Perhaps in the past few months, they had resumed the relationship shared before our marriage. Perhaps their relationship had never been completely broken off. Perhaps all the times Mark had been gone, he had been working with her, sleeping with her. He might even have been with Coral when I was taken to the hospital, when my poor baby . . .

My knees started to fold. I pulled out a chair from the table for two that barely fitted into the cramped kitchen and dropped down like a blob of lead.

I was paranoid. The excitement of the past two days had caught up to me. Thursday night had been the last time I'd gotten a good night's sleep, and this was already Sunday. The nightmares of Hoo and Sweet Rowdy and the intruders were fresh. I couldn't think straight enough to put things into perspective.

The relationship between Coral and Mark, present or past, didn't matter. I wanted to find out what she knew, and how Mark's friend Hoo fit into the puzzle of Sweet Rowdy's death and the break-ins at this house and the lake cottage. If Coral had any knowledge at all, she would tell me before I finished with her.

Not that she understood my resolve. Her lip curled, scornful of my weak knees.

Mark, leaning against the counter where Coral sat, focused on her. "Well?" He sounded like he always sounded. Phlegmatic, patient. "Are you going to enlighten us, wild woman?"

"I'd love to enlighten you, Marco." Melting eyes turned his way.

A few drops of coffee sloshed out the side of her mug. "Except I don't have very much to enlighten you with. All I know is that Hoo was doing a special audit on site. An extremely confidential project. It's occupied all his time for the past five months. He couldn't even use his own laptop. He had one issued by Main Office especially."

"That's pretty unusual. What kind of project?" Mark handed her a napkin. "Who was he auditing?"

Coral wiped the mug with a languid, circular motion. "Some private business holding a government contract. No big deal, I'd think. Pretty ordinary. One of those we pick up all the time except more hush-hush. Hoo was going by the physical site one last time Friday morning. He emailed a draft report to Main Office, but he was supposed to bring the backup data he'd pulled to the field office in Atlanta."

I remembered the poor man in the boat. "He didn't make it."

Coral's expression blanked. "No."

"Why'd Hoo bring backup data to the field office?" Mark asked. "We normally send that up with the report."

Coral's answer was too glib. "Bob Colverton's our red tape expert in this part of the country. Since our contract came from Washington, all government requirements had to be met. You know, i's dotted, t's crossed. Bob would check the data against the final report before having it all couriered to Main Office. He'd make sure everything was there, in case the audit turned out not to be what the contractor wanted."

Mark poured himself more coffee before explaining for my benefit. "Bob Colverton's the field manager for FIFA in Atlanta." Then to Coral: "You said Hoo was going back to the site Friday morning. Why would he do that?"

Coral set her mug on the counter beside her hip. "I'm not sure." Scarlet tipped fingers played with a large square ruby ring. "From what I gathered, something in his notes bothered Hoo. He wanted to compare them to the actual records."

I spoke up. "How did he turn up at our dock?"

She hesitated, reluctant to acknowledge my presence. "We don't know. We'll be working on that tomorrow. Unless Marco here has any ideas."

"Actually, I do." Mark's index finger tested his coffee. "One of our housebreakers tonight was, um, cooperative." He sucked on the coffee-coated fingertip.

Coral avidly watched his mouth. "Knowing you, doll, I'm sure he was more than, um cooperative." A pink tongue touched her top lip. "Give."

"Hoo expected to meet Bob at Legacy Lodge, the lake resort, but these clowns had set him up. They wanted his data. Something must have made Hoo suspicious, though. When they grabbed him, he didn't have anything with him. They took him to a secluded houseboat to try to find out what he'd done with it, but he wouldn't tell them. Two left. Hoo knocked out the other one and stole a nearby boat. That's when he showed up at our dock. Unfortunately, they were right behind him."

I couldn't stop my sharp intake of breath at the meaning Mark didn't spell out. The men in the cruiser had carried off Hoo as I'd feared. Mark had known and never said a word. He wouldn't have told me now, had it not been for Coral's prodding.

Cold seeped upward to my throat, catching in a tight little ball. Hoo had been so close to safety.

I should have helped him. Instead, I had run away and handed him over to his kidnappers. Maybe Crooked Nose had lied. "If the men in the cruiser got him, what did they do with his boat?"

Mark's voice was gentle. "The small bass boat wasn't very heavy. They loaded it onto the cruiser and took it out into the lake and sank it."

My hands were clenched. I unclenched them and laid them in my lap under the table. Mark had known what happened to Hoo, what I had allowed to happen to Hoo, and he had said nothing.

Nausea rose, restrained only by force of will.

Coral had forgotten me. "Where's Hoo now?"

Mark shook his head, kept watching me. "Don't know. My informant stayed behind at the houseboat to clean up after a car picked up Hoo. Later, he got instructions to find out if Hoo gave anything to Steve."

So we still didn't know if Hoo was alive or dead. But if I hadn't left him, the men in the boat couldn't have gotten him. If I'd helped him up to the house, they couldn't have taken him away.

It was my fault he was missing.

If he was dead, I'd killed him as surely as I'd killed my baby.

No! I hadn't killed my baby. The doctor, everyone, had told me repeatedly my baby's death wasn't my fault.

My surroundings dimmed. I felt lightheaded.

CHAPTER EIGHT

THE DIZZINESS PASSED but my stomach churned, threatened to rebel with the roiling guilt over Hoo and my baby. I could barely concentrate on what the other two people in the kitchen were saying.

Coral had become the interrogator. "Who hired this asshole you caught?"

"A contact man. No names mentioned."

"Really?" Coral looked up from beneath her eyelashes. "Okay. What else?" She added with a dazzling grin: "Come on, Marco. Knowing you, I'm sure you persuaded your intruder to confide more than that. What else did you find out?"

"You're a hard woman, Coral."

"Marco," she coaxed prettily. A finger dawdled its way down his arm. "Tell me what else. I'm not going to leave you alone till you do."

And Mark told her. "He saw his contact man on TV, along with a lawyer who lobbies for the oil industry."

"Oh?"

I had the strangest notion this didn't surprise Coral.

"Really?" she murmured.

Mark noticed, too.

The blank face. The hollow tone. Did he wonder, as I did, how trustworthy Coral was?

She covered up well. "Come on, Marco. Give us your opinion. What do you think it all means?" Her adoring air would have distracted any red-blooded male, but she knew more about what Hoo Ogden had been involved in than she was saying.

No, I was being paranoid. Mark accepted Coral at face value. Why shouldn't I?

Mark's eyes watched Coral as closely as mine watched them both. "I don't know, Coral. Was Hoo by any chance doing an audit on one of the oil companies?"

Coral gave a huge shrug. She studied her nails, long and fire engine red, the color of the dress she'd worn to the reception. "You'd have to talk to Abner about that. He's the only one who'd know about Hoo's jobs."

Abner.

"Okay. The audit was for a government contract, you said. Which agency?"

Coral continued to study her nails. "Now, Marco, you know better than to ask things I can't answer."

"Can't or won't?"

"Marco."

"Coral." Their coffee separated them on the counter. He deliberately set both mugs to the side, so that he could slide over and drape his arm around her shoulders. It was his turn to coax. "You can trust me, wild woman."

"Oh, I know I can trust you." Coral took time from her manicure inspection to aim a meaningful glance at me.

He leaned his head close to hers. "Steve isn't going to say anything either. Are you, Steve?"

My lips were so dry I could hardly talk. "I don't know anything to say."

"So come on and give, Coral. You know I'll find out sooner or later. Tell me now and save us both the hassle."

Coral rolled her eyes. "Oh, Marco, you'll be the death of me."

"No way. Someone will surely kill you one day, but it won't be me. Not if you tell me who ordered Hoo's audit."

She sighed. "Well, as I understand it, the audit had to do with some kind of experiment a sub-agency is funding through a third party in north Georgia."

Mark's arm on her shoulder relaxed. "Sub-agency?"

"Yes, you crafty bastard. A sub-agency like DOE."

"Energy." Mark became abstracted. "Like oil."

"There isn't any oil in north Georgia." I might as well have kept my mouth shut.

"So, Marco," Coral said in her sultry way. "I've shared everything I know. Just as I always have with you. Now you know as much as I do."

Almost word for word what Mark had said to me earlier.

Except that Mark hadn't told everything. I didn't think Coral had either.

He let out his breath and picked up his mug and drank the rest of his coffee in one gulp. He still hadn't offered me any. I could have stayed upstairs for all the notice he took of me. He had zeroed in on Coral, something that for some reason left me forlorn.

I was the one who had been threatened and injured. I was the one who had lost my dog.

I had also been the one responsible for leaving a helpless man to be tortured, perhaps killed.

And if I hadn't been so obstinate about keeping our yard neat and tidy and trimmed, I might not have lost our baby.

I caught myself fingering the cuts on my neck and flushed. Not only paranoid, I was childish. And neurotic. There was no reason to blame myself for anything. Mark didn't, not for Hoo's disappearance or our baby's loss.

Mark hung onto every word Coral said because he needed her.

His hand cupped her arm. The same hand that had caressed my neck earlier.

"All right, Coral." His lazy tone said she had more to divulge. "You can dig deeper than that. What kind of vibes did you get when they sent you down here? Was there any indication that oil was involved? Like maybe deposits in north Georgia?"

He hadn't listened to what I'd said. "That's crazy. Any oil would have been found long before now if there were any to be found. I read somewhere that they've done all kinds of tests and turned up nothing."

The other two, engrossed in each other, ignored me.

Because they were trying to figure out what had happened to Hoo.

Coral aimed a secret, knowing smile at my husband. "That's all I have to tell you. You've drained everything, including the hot water heater, out of me."

My heart lurched. That was one of Mark's phrases. Or had been. After lovemaking, he had sometimes said that to me in pleasure and gratification, and occasionally awe.

Red might have tinted his cheek, but his gaze remained fixed on Coral. "So Bob called Abner when Hoo didn't show up, and Abner sent you down to find him."

"I didn't tell you that."

I broke in. "And nobody told you what Hoo was auditing that got him kidnapped?"

I resented her fashion plate appearance and the air of superiority she didn't mind shoving down my throat. I resented the rapport she shared with my husband, too. We might be splitting up, but for the time being, he was still my husband. The two of them had no right to shut me out.

"How did FIFA expect you to find him if you didn't know where to look?"

Coral threw out a tinkling laugh. "FIFA's never logical, hon. Mark can tell you that. God knows he's had enough experience with them. But what the heck. The pay is good and you meet the most interesting people."

She mocked me the same way Mark did. "Why did you come to the reception last night?

I had both their attentions now.

"I saw you there." I twisted the knife a little. "And I saw you go outside the lobby with Mark."

"Abner sent me down when Hoo didn't meet Bob on Friday." Coral spoke slowly, feeling her way. "When I got in yesterday, Bob told me about Mark's unveiling and I wanted to see it."

So Abner knew Friday Hoo was in trouble when he showed up at my boat dock.

"It was wonderful, Marco," Coral added, her voice dropping to a throaty intimacy. "I always said one day you'd make it big. Remember how I used to tell you that? I'd like to think you owe some little part of your success to me."

As Mark gave her a long ironic look, I noted for the first time the lines of fatigue around his eyes and mouth.

He had worked most of Friday night to set up Dreaming, his agent had said. And he had probably been up all Thursday night. And tonight. How long had it been since he'd slept?

Coral must have noted the lines, too, because she put out her hand to caress his cheek. "Poor Marco. That last probe in Africa had to be a bummer. But you shouldn't take these things so much to heart."

Stuff it, sister. Coral was laying the sympathy on with a trowel. Surely to goodness Mark couldn't fall for the old encouragement-sympathy-adoration ploy.

He could and would. Shaking off his fatigue, he reminded me of a lap dog, panting and ready to sit on command. "It could have been a lot worse. I could have been in Poughkeepsie."

Her chuckle was soft and seductive. "I've missed your terrible jokes. No one makes me laugh like you do."

Something stabbed my midriff. Not jealousy. I no longer had any right to feel jealous. Nor envy. I could have kept my place in Mark's affections had I tried. It had to be disgust, pure and simple, for her too-obvious machinations and his susceptibility.

There was no reason for me to sit here and watch them all but make out on the kitchen counter. I got up. The chair screeched on the kitchen floor and made Coral withdraw her hand from Mark's face and look toward me.

"What are you going to do now?" My voice sounded harsh.

She gave a drawn-out sigh as if she'd forgotten my existence and would have liked to continue to forget it. "Well, since Hoo went to this Legacy Lodge place, I guess our next step is to go there and look around, talk to the employees. About noon?" The dark curls bobbed toward Mark. "That'll give you a chance to get some sleep."

Picking up his coffee, Mark glanced in my direction and then into the mug.

Suddenly cold, I hugged myself tight to keep from trembling.

I didn't want him to go off with Coral. I'd be left alone in the house, and I couldn't stand it.

I couldn't.

"No," he said. "I can't go."

I breathed again.

Coral stiffened. "Why not? I thought you wanted to find Hoo."

"I do."

Coral pouted. "Doesn't look like it to me. If you don't go with me, what are you going to do?"

"Leave it to you and Bob, like Abner wants. This isn't my affair, remember?" His eyes crinkled at her. "Abner told me that on the telephone, and you told me that again at the reception. 'Stay out of it,' you said. 'Don't interfere.'"

So that explained why she had come to the unveiling. She knew Hoo had been at the lake house because Abner Crowley had told her and sent her to warn Mark to . . .

To what? Not to interfere? Why would Abner think Mark might interfere? Because he was Hoo's friend? And why shouldn't he interfere?

I disliked Abner more than ever.

Coral showed raw concern. "Not funny. That was before we knew about all this. We have to find Hoo. Come with me, Marco. Please."

He assumed the airy tone I hated. "Gosh, I would, Coral, but I've got big plans. I'm exhausted. After sleeping in, I'm going to sweep out my studio, then maybe wash the cars and read the Sunday papers. I don't think I'll have time."

Her eyes flashed like she wanted to say something rude. She contented herself with a mocking, "What a little homebody you've become. I'd never have suspected it of you." When she slid off the counter, she brushed her breast against his arm.

Intentionally.

Squeezing his shoulder to balance, she gave her brilliant smile. "Okay, Marco. I'm sorry I insisted on coming over."

"But Steve and I love visitors at five o'clock in the morning." He moved back so she didn't crowd him. "It's our favorite time to entertain. Of course, most of our friends are thoughtful enough to bring hors d'oeuvres."

Her hand dropped. "You shit," she said without heat. "Okay. Have it your way. Let me know if you change your mind."

Marco, she called him.

Had that been her pet name for him when they were lovers? I'd called him that once, and he'd said he didn't like it. Because Coral called him Marco? He didn't mind her using it tonight.

He yawned and stretched with sinuous grace, indifferent to my irritation with him and his old girlfriend. "Come on, wild woman," he said to Coral. "I'll see you out."

She took a long time to leave.

I rinsed the mugs and put them into the dishwasher without eavesdropping on what they were saying to each other in the privacy of the foyer. Maybe they spoke about Hoo or themselves. Maybe he told her about the breakup of our marriage.

No, they would have gone into that at the reception. What could they be doing?

As I removed the coffee filter, I heard her car back out of the driveway. Turning, I jumped.

Mark's rangy form propped against the kitchen doorway. There was no indication how long he had been standing there.

Bitterness tinged his laugh at my reaction. "Yeah, it's Jack the Ripper. Clear the way, folks, so I can pick a new victim."

"Don't make fun of me. I've had about all I can stand." One more smart remark and I would slap his face.

His sarcasm faded, his features gentled. "Go upstairs." He came over to take the filter from me. "I'll finish up here. You're so tired and edgy you don't know what you're doing."

Anger fled. I stood still, watching his deft, efficient movements.

In one elongated fluid arc of shoulder and arm, he flung the paper filter and its contents into the trash can. The plastic filter holder, washed in seconds, soon lay on the drain board to dry.

"Go on up to bed."

"Mark."

He didn't stop in the middle of scrubbing the pot. "Yeah?"

"I'm glad you're not going with Coral tomorrow. I don't like being left alone," I mumbled, ashamed of being afraid.

He nodded. "No problem. Go on up." He rinsed the pot, set it alongside the filter holder.

I couldn't look at him. "I'd rather wait for you."

There was no trace of laughter about him. "Sure. I've already checked the front door and turned off the lights. All we need do is set the alarm and close up."

Gratitude flooded that he didn't jeer or condemn my cowardice. I should have expected as much, knowing him as I did.

As I thought I did.

On the stairwell balcony, my steps lagged. I'd like to ask Mark to stay with me, but I didn't want him to misunderstand.

Nothing had changed between us, nor had I changed my mind.

Divorce was the only solution I could see, but while I didn't want to mislead him about our future, I was scared. I didn't want to be alone.

He went into our bedroom without my asking, folded back the sheet, and straightened the pillow. On noting the stained pillowcase, he got out a fresh one and put it on, competent as any maid. "Come on." He held out a hand. "I'll tuck you in."

I hung back. "There's no need."

He lowered his hand and stepped back. "I won't eat you. Go ahead and get in."

Awkwardly shedding my robe, I hurried to slip between the sheets. Maybe he wouldn't notice that the camisole top and tap pants were his favorite of my pajamas, the ones he'd picked out on our third anniversary before we decided we wanted to start our family. I saved them for special occasions, but they were the first ones to hand this chaotic night.

He tactfully pretended not to see them but busied himself pulling up the sheet under my chin and smoothing it around me. Careful not to touch me. "Okay?"

"Yes." I hesitated, and he started to leave. "No."

He turned.

"Mark."

He came back to the bed.

"I keep—" It killed me to confess my fears, but unlike him, I couldn't rein in my weaknesses or stash them away out of sight. "I keep remembering how I woke up and found that man beside me. I'm scared."

He didn't laugh, but Mark never indulged in ridicule or cruel mockery. "Sure you are. But it's all right. It really is, Steve." The springs creaked, the mattress shifted under his weight as he sat down by me. "Close your eyes."

I couldn't.

He smoothed back my hair from my face.

I didn't flinch.

"The alarm's set so no one can come in on us. There's no reason for anyone to bother us now. Everyone knows you don't have a thing to do with whatever Hoo was up to. I'll be in the next room. You can go to sleep in perfect safety."

His kindness persuaded me to close my eyes. He went on soothing me, telling me how tired he knew I must be, how much better I'd feel in the morning, how a good night's sleep would improve my outlook. All the ordinary things I wanted to hear.

At length, my body and mind relaxed. My eyes closed.

The mattress shivered as he slid off and stood up. "I'm turning off your light," he said quietly, "but I'll leave the bathroom light on and I'll be right across the hall. Okay?"

"Okay," I whispered drowsily.

No, not okay. It would never be okay again.

I thought I felt his lips brush my forehead but might have imagined it. As the house died into silence, I opened my eyes.

The door, partially open, allowed a pale glimmering inside the bedroom that sketched a penumbra around the dresser and chest of drawers. As promised, he had left the bathroom light burning.

My heart swelled. Mark was good to me in many ways. We'd never had a real argument, not about money or sex or friends from before our marriage that one of us couldn't stand. If we had never decided to have a child, if I had never gotten pregnant, we might still be the perfect couple.

If he hadn't left me to take care of the house by myself. If I hadn't tried to clean up the whole yard in one day. If I hadn't had to bear the pain without him.

If he hadn't made the marble baby, that hideous laughing statue of a dead baby.

Bands of misery suffocated me. I wanted my life back the way it used to be. I wanted my baby. I wanted Sweet Rowdy. I wanted my husband.

No, I wanted the husband I thought I'd married. A man who cared about me. The man who felt everything that touched me also touched us. The man Mark had turned into, a person unable to share anything but trivialities, was not the husband I wanted.

The ache in my heart passed. I could breathe again, but sleep still didn't come. My body, restless in spite of its fatigue, twisted and turned of its own accord.

I thought of Hoo and his pleading hand stretched out to me. I thought of Mark and how he had tucked the bedcovers around me. I thought of Coral and how she had looked at Mark with melting eyes. I thought of Mark and how he had held me in my terror.

Damn it, I was still terrified.

He oughtn't have left me alone. He knew I was timid. He knew about the horror I'd experienced during the past two days, knew I would be upset.

My subconscious might have grasped what was happening as I whipped up anger to quell the rising panic. My intellect did not.

Mark ought to know without my telling him that I shouldn't be left alone. This conclusion led to a logical decision, and I considered myself quite logical.

I flung off the covers and without stopping to locate house shoes, padded out of my bedroom and past the bathroom.

The door to the spare room gaped, but at its open invitation I hesitated. I wanted to be held and petted, to have someone to share the dark with. Nothing more. Would Mark understand that?

His shape lay beneath the covers, long and still. Asleep.

"Steve?"

The sheets rustled as he turned his head, but he remained an enigmatic form.

"What's wrong?" He sounded calm. Normal.

I shivered from the nighttime coolness and my inadequate pajamas. An unintentional sigh accompanied my footsteps taking my pounding heart over to the bed where he lay.

Every instinct screamed to turn around and go back to my room.

But at the same time, I couldn't bear awakening again to find a stranger at my throat.

Invisible wires drew me. I didn't want to go into the dark where Mark waited but wouldn't go back.

"I can't sleep," I said, meek as any child. "I'm afraid. I don't want to stay in there by myself."

His drawn-out sigh echoed mine. I wrung my hands and strained to see his face in the shadows.

"Please," I begged without shame. "Let me stay here with you."

"Love, you're asking too much." No flippancy, no jokes. "You know you are."

He couldn't refuse me. Panic rose, betrayed by frantic appeals. "Just for a while. I can't stay in that room by myself. I can't. Please don't make me."

"Steve—"

"Please." I bit my lip but couldn't stop the whimper. "Please, Mark."

He lifted the covers. "Get in."

My coming to him was a mistake.

I knew it the moment I settled in and he drew the covers over us, but I didn't care. The solid mass of his body reassured me. His warmth comforted me. I relaxed for the first time in a long while.

The full bed, smaller than the one we had shared, drew us together. I would have found it impossible to move away had I wanted to, but I didn't want to.

I finally felt safe.

When he didn't move, I turned on my side and backed up against him and soaked in his heat.

That was a mistake, too.

He put his arms about me, the front of his body cupping my rear. He wore nothing but the old boxers he preferred for sleeping. His chest touched my back, and his legs followed mine.

When I nestled against him, their coarse hairs tickled my bare calves and thighs. His arm went round my waist in the familiar gesture long disused, and his hand splayed on my stomach with a tentativeness unlike him.

He wanted me.

A burst of heat suffused my body, emerged through the entire surface of my skin, so that suddenly I was on fire all over. I stopped breathing, unwilling to give credence to this inexplicable hunger but wanting him as desperately as his body told me he wanted me.

It's wrong.

He can quench me, ease my body, I argued.

You can't do this.

I need him, my heart cried.

In the end, the physical demands overpowered conscience. I lay back, cradling his erection against my hips.

His hand gave a convulsive jerk on my stomach and then lay still. He didn't trust my reaction.

I pressed against him, my hand stroking his, holding it to my stomach, moving it in slow circles and downward.

"Steve?" His whisper at my ear was warm, husky with desire.

I groaned, half with longing, half with uncertainty.

Flesh and blood that had been numb as a block of stone for the past months came to life and made its own decision. My hand reached back past his arm to slide inside his boxers. My hips pushed against him of their own accord.

In another second, he had me on my back.

His face hung above mine, an indistinct oval in the dim illumination. I loosed his hair from its binding and tangled my hand in the thick waves and pulled his mouth to mine in a kiss long and deep and satisfying.

Sustaining the contact, he fumbled at my top and pushed the silk up. His fingers caught the back of my head and threaded themselves through my hair as my fingers had wound through his. The rough caress ended when he crushed me to him, so hard that our skin and bones seemed to coalesce. He drew back, quickly removing my top and throwing it aside before bending back.

My spine arched from pure pleasure as his tongue teased one

breast and teeth nipped the other. Pride and anger were forgotten, swept aside by a primitive emotion that filled me from head to toe. I wanted him desperately, wanted him inside me to fill the void, wanted him to begin the familiar strokes.

The usual preliminaries were superfluous tonight.

Pushing him back, I pulled at his shorts and reached for his length. By then he was nude and tearing off my tap bottoms.

His entry was swift and pleasurable, making me lose sight of everything else as he brought me one step closer to stanching my frenzied need. I moved against him, hearing him groan as he fought to delay.

"Don't," came his tortured whisper. "You'll make me come too soon."

I wouldn't stop. I couldn't stop. Not this close.

When I felt his shuddering release, my own came with dizzying suddenness.

In the end, we lay spent, Mark on top of me, his weight pushing me down into the bed. I didn't feel trapped as I had the last time he had lain atop me afterward, the one time we had attempted intercourse after I'd lost the baby.

I felt safe, protected, satiated.

Too soon, he rolled off and got up to bring me a towel. When he lay back down, still silent, I curled up against him. I was sated, mind and body. I could go to sleep now. The regular beat of his heart served as a security blanket.

Before I drifted off, I felt his fingers touch my ear, follow the curve.

"It won't work, Steve," he murmured. "You can't have it both ways. You'll either have to be my wife or not be my wife. Eventually, you'll have to decide which you want more."

I didn't want to hear what he said. I didn't want to think about his words and what they might mean.

I knew I couldn't stay with him this way forever. Yes, I'd have to choose one day. But I needed him tonight.

Later, when my strength returned, I would stand alone, and go back out into the world. Somewhere there would be someone else I could love. Someone who would share his emotions, make me feel this same overwhelming desire, give me the same feeling of security.

A different type of man. A man who would be at my side when I needed him. A man who wouldn't fling my grief in my face by carving a happy marble baby.

Strangely, there was only emptiness at the thought of the laughing cherub Mark had made.

The wild grief at his unfeeling gesture had passed, leaving me apathetic.

I shivered, but I didn't move away from the perimeter of my husband's warmth.

CHAPTER NINE

I DREAMED I was wandering through some sort of maze that contained a gurgling fountain.

A redheaded man led the way. A small dog led him in the wrong direction, but I couldn't catch them to stop them. "Em-i-leee." The mournful cry drifted back to me.

The Mark who was a stranger appeared from out of nowhere, grim and unsmiling.

The mists of my dreams evaporated as sleep left and sunlight streamed in. I woke in an uncomfortable bed, in an unfamiliar room. Delicate painted scenes on black lacquer Chinese furniture and bamboo wallpaper brought back reality.

I lay in the guest room of our Decatur house and Mark's side of the bed was empty.

He's gone! They got him!

Then the sound of running water came from the bathroom.

The shower. Mark was in the shower.

My pounding heart returned to normal.

I lay back, ashamed at the sickening fear that had overwhelmed me. I wasn't a child clinging to her parent's hand. No matter what had happened the past night.

Had a man really held a knife to my throat? I touched the base of my neck and found the clotted lacerations.

No, last night was no nightmare. Nor had I dreamed Coral's visit in the early morning hours to tell us about Hoo.

Depression returned.

We still didn't know where Mark's friend was, what had happened to him.

I shifted and tried not to think of my part in Hoo's disappearance.

Moving brought on unaccustomed aches.

I hadn't dreamed making love with Mark either. His scent lingered on the sheets and, when I put my arm over my face, on my skin.

I groaned and closed my eyes.

How could I have done it?

How could I have lost it so much that I'd practically raped him? And how could I apologize? What could I say this morning?

Sorry, our getting it on last night was a mistake. I can't live with you as your wife anymore, so don't think simply because the sex was good we can still work things out.

We hadn't used protection. What if I . . . ?

No, probably not. I'd finished my period at the lake house. We were probably safe for a few days. Maybe. If not, what would I do? What . . . ?

Worry about that later.

The shower stopped.

Mark's back, towel draped round slim hips, came out of the bathroom into the hall and disappeared into our bedroom. When he reappeared, he wore khaki pants and a short-sleeved madras shirt. One hand swung a belt, and the other held socks.

"Hi." He stopped inside the door. "I thought I'd let you sleep in. You had a pretty rough time last night."

He might mean the intruders or what happened afterward, but I wouldn't ask.

"Thanks," I muttered. "I was pretty tired."

No way could I meet his eyes, ashamed as I was of the cowardice that had led to my seducing him.

What if he and Coral were getting back together?

My behavior would put Mark in a touchy situation. Coral might not care if he'd slept with his wife, but then again, she might be insanely jealous.

I would have been.

"What time is it?"

"After one."

I grunted. "In the afternoon?"

"'Fraid so."

"I can't have slept so long." I propped up on my elbows, aching all over.

In contrast, Mark looked fresh, wide awake, and rested. His damp hair, brushed away from its widow's peak, dried in flowing waves that swung forward as he bent and picked up his deck shoes from the floor.

I had forgotten the satisfaction of lying in bed while Mark dressed, the pleasure of following his graceful, spare movements.

The unruly flutter in my stomach died when I took in his spotless pants and neat shirt.

When Mark worked in his studio, he wore old clothes, not good ones.

"Where are you going?"

"Thought I might ride up to the lake." His response was natural, unrehearsed. He set his shoes and socks down on the chest, and put money and cell in his pockets.

Fast learning to pick up nuances I wouldn't have noticed a week ago, my ear recognized the omission. "With Coral? To Legacy Lodge?"

He threaded the belt through his pants. "No," he drawled, as if analyzing my words and amused by them. "I'm going up to the lake house. By myself. From what you said, it's in a mess. If I'm going to have to live there, it'll need cleaning up."

My face reddened. He thought I was jealous of Coral.

I wanted to shout that I didn't care where he went or who he went with, but that wasn't true.

I did mind him leaving. I wasn't ready to be left alone. Not yet. "I won't stay here by myself."

"You should be perfectly safe." He finished fastening his belt.

"I will not stay in this house by myself." Forgetting my nudity, I threw the covers aside.

Cool air rushing over bare skin momentarily took me aback, and I looked to see Mark's reaction.

A few months ago my nakedness would have found him leering and making a lascivious comment on my helpless state. Today didn't bring even an indifferent glance.

"Suit yourself." He picked up his shoes and socks, and went down the hall.

I rushed to the door, modesty forgotten.

"Don't you dare leave me," I yelled at his retreating figure. "If you do, I'll just follow you."

"I'm going to put on my socks and shoes and then toast some bagels. If you want to go with me, be ready by the time I get through eating." He didn't bother to look back.

I showered in record time. After donning jeans and loafers and then twisting my wet hair up into a knot, I flew downstairs. Mark rinsed cream cheese off his knife before putting it and his plate into the dishwasher.

He always cleaned up after himself. He was neat and methodical in everything. Though he'd never said anything to me, sometimes I felt I didn't measure up to his standards.

Not that my inadequacies mattered. Not anymore.

The smell of coffee, fresh and tempting, floated over. He had toasted an extra bagel.

"I'm ready," I told him.

"So am I. That bagel's yours if you want it, but you don't have time to sit down and eat."

While he set the house alarm, I poured myself coffee, picked up the bagel, and beat him out the door.

He drove his car, a middle-class SUV, solid, comfortable, and dependable.

Neither of us had very much to say.

When we reached the four-lane, the halfway point between our home near Emory and the cottage at the lake, Sunday afternoon traffic thinned. I gathered up my courage.

"Mark, about last night."

Clichéd, hackneyed words.

I hated saying them.

Why hadn't I thought up something more original? "Look, Mark, the sex was great but let's not do it again." Or maybe, "Thanks for everything you did for me last night, Mark. I'm okay now and you won't have to be bothered anymore."

"What about last night?" His shuttered face was back in place. He wouldn't make my apology easier.

"I appreciate your, you know . . . I don't want you to think . . . I was scared, and you were there, close by . . ."

"Available," he supplied, with a hint of a drawl, looking straight ahead at the road.

A little twitch at the side of his mouth made me, watching his profile from the corner of my eye, suspicious. Either he was trying not to laugh, or else he was having a nervous spasm.

"Available," I echoed. "And I'm glad you were. I really appreciate your . . . being there." Couldn't I do better than this? Now he'd think I was coming on to him again. "Look, I haven't changed my mind. Just because I—you—we . . . I still want a divorce."

The smile playing round his mouth fled. He shrugged. "I assumed you did."

"I'm sorry." Aware of my part in last night's seduction, I felt guilty. I wished I'd never married him, never met him.

"So am I. Sorrier than you, I bet." He took pity on me. "Hey, stop heaping blame on yourself. Especially for last night. You didn't make it happen all alone. I could have stopped. I probably should have. But I never claimed to be a gentleman. If anyone's to blame it's me, love. I should have sent you back to your own bed and I chose not to. So don't worry about me. Believe it or not, I'll survive. And you will, too."

I sat back in my seat, ungrateful and inadequate and depressed. Despite his polite assumption of culpability, I knew where last night's blame lay.

We said nothing more on the ride to the lake house.

* * * *

THE INSIDE OF the cottage disheartened me. I had gone back to Decatur the day before, unable to tackle the jumbled evidence of the second break-in. Seeing the mess now hurt more than seeing it for the first time. Today I couldn't pretend it was a bad dream.

Mark wandered through, neither shocked nor dejected. True to form, he showed no sense of violation, no sense of the helplessness that had so distressed me.

"I guess Crooked Nose was telling the truth," he said, taking in the overturned flour and sugar containers, and the drawers turned inside out and the cushions ripped apart.

"What do you mean?"

He waved his hand. "They were searching for a bundle of papers so they didn't bother going through things like the tea canister. It's too small. The sugar canister might be big enough, if the papers were rolled up, so they dumped it. Are you sure Hoo didn't have anything that size with him?"

Analyzing again. Always analyzing. If it wasn't for worrying about the fate of Hoo, I would have been glad to forget the past two days. "Mark, surely to goodness I'd have known if he handed me a bunch of papers."

"Just checking, love."

"Don't—" I bit my lip.

"Don't what?" he asked absently.

"Nothing." Telling him not to call me *love* wouldn't do any good. This new Mark did as he pleased.

I started gathering up dishtowels strewn on the floor from cabinet drawers and took them into the utility room to be washed along with pulled-out towels. Mark picked his way through the disorder. The flour and sugar had to be scooped up and thrown away. The askew mattresses had been slashed so new ones would have to be purchased. Books had to be reshelved, pictures rehung.

There was too much to do in one day, though we worked for the rest of the afternoon. When the Rachinoffs came over to see how we were doing, they invited us to supper.

"Sounds good," Mark said in his laidback way. "Steve?"

"Sure, but . . ." I looked around at what we hadn't accomplished.

"We can't get it cleaned up tonight anyway. We can put quilts on the box springs to sleep on and finish up in the morning."

We stayed. Mark enjoyed the hammock on the cool porch. I slept on the box spring in the stuffy bedroom.

The small rug stained with Sweet Rowdy's blood had been

disposed of, but I tossed and turned, beating back embarrassing images from the past night and trying to convince myself that fears about the unknown intruders were groundless.

Twice I jerked upright at the outline of a jagged profile looking into the window before waking enough to discover it was a distorted tree limb next to the glass. Both times I kept from calling Mark and sank back into the pillows with thumping heart.

Mark must not have had trouble sleeping, for he arose early the next morning, clear-eyed and chipper. He made coffee and heated homemade cinnamon rolls Trina had pressed on us the night before, then set about finishing the clean-up.

Already the house looked better. There was nothing big that couldn't be put back in its place or mended except for the slit mattresses, upholstered chairs, and sofa.

Mark could buy new furniture.

My conscience would be clear after I helped him get the place habitable. Then he could move up here. Assuming he agreed to the compromise on the houses.

Loading up sheets and other items that had been dragged from the linen closet and dumped on the floor, I started the washing machine.

Mark stuck his head into the utility room. "It's nearly lunchtime, and I'm starved. Want me to run out and bring back some hamburgers?"

And leave me?

I cleared my throat, stared at the linoleum. I couldn't beg him to stay. I had to stop jumping at shadows. Or tree limbs. "Whatever. There's some canned stuff here that's okay if you don't want to go out."

"I don't want canned stuff. Want to go with me?" The creases around his eyes deepened. He was laughing at my weakness.

His scorn, however mild, stung. I might not want to stay by myself but he didn't have to mock me.

Stop being a wimp. No wonder he never wanted to tell me anything. "The machine sometimes gets off balance. I don't like to leave it running with no one around." I inhaled deeply, straightened my hands where they had involuntarily clenched. "I'll stay here."

The lines of laughter disappeared. "Sure?" he asked kindly. "I know you'll be fine, but if you're afraid—"

"I'll stay." I immediately spoiled my stoic act. "You won't be gone long, will you?"

"Thirty minutes or so. Just down to the shopping center and back." He waited to see if I would change my mind.

Time to show some spirit. Coral wouldn't think twice about being left, no matter what perils she'd endured. "I'll be okay," I said with fake confidence.

His teeth glinted white. "I'm sure you will be."

Mark's departure left an eerie silence. Surely, despite the washing machine's hum, the house had never been so quiet. No, the CD put on earlier had finished playing. Relief flooded me at the simple explanation. I put on another CD, and the music from *Cats* filled the cottage.

Mark and I were both fond of Andrew Lloyd Weber, one example of many matching tastes that should have spelled a long-lasting marriage. But our similar likes and dislikes hadn't helped.

I mopped the kitchen and thought of poor Sweet Rowdy and my failed marriage. Then I tried not to think of them. I also tried not to think of the rough intruders, or of the injured Hoo, or of my lost baby and Mark's marble one.

I especially tried not to think about what had happened in Mark's bed the night before last.

The cottage phone rang.

I jumped like it was a live snake.

No one knew we were up here today. It had to be a wrong number.

After tracking across my freshly mopped floor, I checked the caller ID.

Private. I didn't want to pick up the phone.

Stupid. If anyone wanted to break in, he wouldn't call first. Or if he did, it'd be to make sure no one's home.

My hand swooped out before I changed my mind. "Hello."

"Steve?" Coral's sultry voice asked.

I relaxed. "Hello, Coral." Suspicion followed the relief. She shouldn't have known I was up here.

"Mark isn't answering his cell. Is he around?"

A family joke from childhood popped into my head. *No, he's a square.*

That's what came from being married to Mark too long.

I resisted the juvenile impulse. "Not at the moment. He'll be back any time though. Shall I have him call you?"

"Yes. I'm across the lake at Legacy Lodge. He should have my cell number but just in case, I'll give it to you. Do you have something to write with?"

"Just a sec." I pulled a pen out of the pencil holder on the counter and scrambled through a drawer for a writing pad. Not finding one, I yanked off a paper towel. "Okay. Go ahead."

She recited the number, but the ballpoint pen balked. Its point refused to extend.

I cursed under my breath, heard Coral's long-suffering sigh and imagined her contempt at my ineptness.

"Wait a second, Coral. This pen doesn't work."

I threw it down.

A tackiness clung to my fingers. Like the plastic barrel was coated with wax or clay or some other sticky material. Before I pulled another pen from the holder, I wiped the stuff off on the white paper towel.

Ugh. Those nasty brown stains that felt so gummy must have come from the defective pen.

"Are you ready?" Coral's tone echoed her impatience.

"Uh, just a minute."

Coral would never have problems with defective pens. She would be efficient, organized, and totally in control of the situation at all times.

Like Mark.

I found another pen, tested it. "Okay." As I jotted down her number, memories clicked into place, one frame at a time.

The dock where I had laid down the unfinished list on the legal pad and the pen by my cellphone.

Hoo's bloody hand, catching at my tunic cover-up.

This phone where I begged for help as something poked me in the leg.

The pen pulled out of the pocket as I spoke to the dispatcher.

My hand putting the pen into the holder beside the other pens and pencils.

The deputy pointing out my tunic pocket soaked with Hoo's blood.

I squeaked. This was Hoo's pen.

"What is it?" Coral asked. "Is something wrong?"

"No. No, but I think—" Excitement built. "Coral, I think Hoo gave me a pen."

"What? Hoo?"

"Yes." I couldn't keep from blabbing. "I'm pretty sure Hoo gave me this ballpoint pen that won't write. I lost mine when everything fell in the lake, you see, so it couldn't have been the one I was writing with that day he showed up."

"A writing pen? Hoo gave you a writing pen?" Enlightenment crept in. "What kind?"

"Just a ballpoint. He must have put it in my pocket when . . . I thought he reached out for help, but he must have put it there because when I found it I thought it was mine only it wasn't. I'd lost mine. But this one was in the pencil holder so it's the one I stuck there when I came up to call for help. You see?"

Despite my garbled explanation, Coral picked up enough. "Are you looking at the pen now?"

"Yes."

"Listen, don't touch it, do you hear me? Put it down and don't touch it. I'm on my way."

I didn't like her autocratic tone, but I heard a car door slam and Mark's footsteps on the porch.

"Never mind, Coral." I could sidestep her commands. "Here's Mark. He can handle it."

Calm settled over me. I didn't want to see Coral. I certainly didn't want to turn Hoo's pen over to her.

I shouldn't have told her.

"Steve, don't hang up." Her words were sharp, demanding. "Let me talk to Mark."

Mark, coming in with a paper bag, raised quizzical brows as I handed him the phone. At my short explanation, he took the pen and put the receiver to his ear.

"Coral?" He listened, turning the pen round and round in his fingers. "No, there's no need."

I heard Coral's voice, quick and agitated, but couldn't make out what she said.

Whatever it was left Mark unaffected. Catching the receiver between shoulder and ear, he tried to unscrew the top from the bottom of the pen but couldn't.

I retrieved the pen and undid it. Inside the barrel, instead of the metal ink holder, was a piece of paper tightly rolled into a cylinder. When I couldn't get it out, Mark handed me a paper clip, still talking to Coral. "I do see your point, but I'm here now."

I straightened the paper clip and used it to fish out the paper. I tried to unfurl it, but my hand shook too much.

"That won't work either, Coral." Mark turned down what sounded like a demand at the same time he plucked the cylinder out of my fumbling hand. "Bob will never find this place. Have him come to Legacy Lodge. I'll drive over and meet you both there."

Again Coral talked, her voice rising with each quick word. She droned on and on as I watched the small roll spreading out.

Mark was immune. "Steve and I are about to eat. We'll come to Legacy Lodge as soon as we've finished . . . Yes, it looks like Hoo managed to leave a message . . . I don't know, but I'll see you in an hour or so . . . Yes, we'll bring the pen."

Coral was still yapping as Mark hung up.

"What is it? What does it say?" I couldn't pick out the faded words on the battered paper.

"It's a copy of a priority mail label. For Pickup Only. And it's addressed to M.L. Early. Buford, Georgia."

"What does that mean? That he's mailed you his data?"

"Guess so," Mark said. "We'll find out soon enough." He pulled his cell out and looked at it, not nearly as excited as me. "Battery's dead, wouldn't you know. That's why Coral couldn't get me. My charger's at the house."

"And the other's in my car. Guess you'll have to forego conversations with her for a while."

Too bad.

"Come on, let's eat before the fries get cold. I told Coral we'd meet her and Bob in two hours at the Legacy Lodge Resort. If we hurry, we can stop by the post office on the way."

How like Mark. I had been electrified and Coral had been beside herself, but Mark . . .

Mark wanted to eat.

* * * *

OTHER THAN MARK'S request to pour some canned colas left in the pantry over ice, he and I exchanged no words as we took out foil wrapped hamburgers and accompanying fries.

I brooded and Mark was quiet, thinking who knows what. He remained as enigmatic as ever as he washed his hands and emptied the bag on the counter.

I set drinks and glasses of ice at our places.

By that time, I'd come back down to earth. "So Hoo did give me something."

"Pass that mustard."

"If we hadn't come up here today, I would never have remembered. When I picked that pen up to take down Coral's number, and it wouldn't write, it jogged my memory. Hoo must have slipped the pen into my pocket, but I didn't realize it." I handed him the mustard, working my way up to the unwilling admission. "If I'd known, if I'd stayed there with him long enough to hear what—"

"Leave it alone. You found his pen and that's all that matters." Mark was curt. He didn't want to discuss Hoo's disappearance. "We'll soon see what Hoo sent and that'll be the end of it."

We sat down to eat, side by side at the counter separating the kitchen from the pine-paneled open-beamed great room. Beyond us, spread out through the front expanse of windows, lay the tranquil waters of the cove reflecting a clear blue sky. White drifts of blooming dogwoods scattered from house to lake hid the boathouse.

We had enjoyed the cottage during our marriage, but now I would never think of Lake Lanier with the same fondness.

Neither of us inclined toward speech. Mark appeared to have other things on his mind and I moped about what might have been.

We might never have known what Hoo had done with his papers. If I hadn't been on the dock, if I hadn't gone up to him, if I hadn't put the pen in the holder, if Coral hadn't telephoned . . .

"How did Coral know we were here?"

He answered too glibly. "I called her this morning and told her we'd spent the night here."

"Why would you call her?"

He opened his mouth to pop in a dill pickle that had fallen out of his sandwich. His eyes crinkled. "Jealous?"

Damn him. He had no right to take that tone with me, no right to laugh at me. "I couldn't care less what you and Coral have going on between you. Why did you call her? What are you keeping from me this time?"

He finished the pickle. "Not a thing, Steve. Not a thing."

"Then why did you call her?"

A corner of his mouth lifted. "To let her know about our wild and crazy night together."

He was lying and I knew it, but I didn't want to talk about that night, and he knew that.

Heat flooded my face and neck. I snatched up and attacked my hamburger.

He went back to his with studied satisfaction.

"Do you think Hoo's all right?" I asked when we were through eating and I gathered up food wrappers.

He put glasses in the dishwasher. "I hope so."

Mark didn't seem worried. Although with Mark, it was hard to tell. If he agonized over his friend's safety, he hid his concern well. But then he never revealed anything.

I brought the subject up again as we got ready to leave. "I don't see how he could be all right."

Mark understood who I referred to. "No?" He sounded unconcerned, almost bored. "We'll see."

He was evading me again. "What if he's dead?"

"Then he's dead." His voice frayed in the first instance since finding out about Hoo's disappearance. "And nothing we can do will change that. Hurry up, Steve. I told Coral we'd be there in . . ." He glanced at his watch. "Half an hour."

Inside his car, the silence once more formed a gulf. Someone knew what Hoo's reports showed that was so important he had been kidnapped and beaten, so important that I had been threatened and Sweet Rowdy had died.

If Mark didn't know, Coral must.

Absorbed, I almost failed to notice the change in Mark as we started over the road crossing Buford Dam.

When I did, it took the form of a vague uneasiness. Perhaps because my senses were newly honed from the weekend's events.

He shot a glance in the rearview mirror.

"What's wrong?" I looked back and saw nothing except a large brown pickup.

"You're the world's biggest worrier." His reassurance came quickly. Too quickly. Another glance in the mirror fueled suspicions. "Why do you keep thinking something's wrong?"

I sat back.

He hadn't told me everything. Mark was lying again.

No, not lying. Dodging the issue, as he always did, and leaving me in the dark.

The first crack in our marriage had appeared at the realization that Mark made a habit of keeping me in the dark about specific parts of his life.

Not that my overdue wisdom mattered. It was too late for analysis or understanding now.

Too late for anything. I gazed out the car window and tried not to think about my failed marriage and failed pregnancy.

The two-lane road followed the dam across the river in a narrow and crooked route that forced vehicles to slow to a crawl.

I hated this section, always had. One curve taken too fast would propel a car into the lake that lay on our left, deep and blue and serene except for a few motor boats plowing its waters.

One hardy soul skied in a wet suit to dull the water's wintry temperature. He cut back and forth across the wake, relishing the challenge of staying upright. A huge flock of geese floated sedately on the waves of a cove near the park.

On the right side of the road, the terrain plummeted.

Passing over the dam itself, I could look down and see the park beside the Chattahoochee River far below. Several tiny figures of fishermen perched on the boulders lining the banks. They cast their lines into waters that seemed thin and dark and insignificant after the large cerulean expanse of the lake.

I clutched at the armrest. I always clutched at it when riding across the dam.

Mark continued to monitor the rearview mirror. Then his shoulder muscles bunched. The tendons in his hand stood out as he gripped the wheel.

"Got your seat belt fastened?" He sounded almost lazy.

But the hidden tension came out.

"Yes." A glance out the back window revealed the brown pickup had edged closer. It was almost on our bumper. "Isn't he awfully close?"

About that time we reached the other side of the dam. When we came out of the final curve, Mark accelerated.

The pickup did the same. It pulled up alongside us.

I gasped. "He can't pass us here!"

Not on a solid yellow line.

Then it swerved into us.

CHAPTER TEN

THE SEAT BELT and harness contracted, held me fast during the collision.

Someone screamed.

The SUV swung to the side.

I was the screamer.

"Hold on, Steve." Mark's hands turned the wheel hard, brought us back into the road.

"What are they doing? They're hitting us!"

He held the wheel steady as the truck nudged our side again. "They want us to stop. They can't afford to hurt us, not till they get Hoo's papers."

A car coming in the opposite direction forced the pickup into line behind us.

We passed a park entrance veering sharply back to the right. Without warning, Mark made nearly a hundred and eighty degree turn.

The wheels lifted off the ground as our SUV slid sideways, righted itself, and went on.

The pickup, speeding straight ahead, missed the gate and left the road. By the time it had backed out of bushes and turned, we were halfway up the hill and nearing a fork. Mark elected the side leading up. I looked back at the looming truck before trees cut off my line of vision.

We came to the top of the hill and slowed.

Mark had unwittingly chosen a dead end. There was nowhere to go.

The road passed an empty pavilion before circling past deserted picnic tables and a large stone barbecue grill, then rejoining itself.

The pickup came up behind us, blocked the beginning of the loop, and waited.

Mark saw it and stopped beside the pavilion. He muttered something under his breath.

My teeth chattered in terror. "W-what are we going to do?"

He didn't answer directly. "I guess I'd better talk to these guys. Stay here and lock the doors." He looked down at the console. "Where's your cell?"

"In the lake. I lost it off the dock."

And his battery was dead.

He didn't waste time reproaching me for not telling him I had no cell. "Look, Steve, if worst comes to worst, see that ditch behind the pickup? Drive out through it. The SUV can make it if you cut diagonally across it. Go to the dam's operating office. You know where it is. The main road to the right, then over the hill and it's on the left. Go inside the office and wait for me."

"I don't—"

He opened his door, letting in a blaring siren.

The police.

No. Not the police. The siren came from the dam, not from any rescuers.

My stomach re-knotted.

The siren warned people to stay away from the river. It started five minutes before water was released for power generation and sounded every other minute down the river.

"Mark," I cried as he climbed out. "I don't think you ought to go over there."

The door slammed.

I was alone, speaking to empty air.

If worst came to worst?

"Mark!" I rolled the window down and called, to no avail. What did he expect to happen? If anything happened to him . . . "Mark!"

I relived the blade slicing at my throat.

The men in the brown pickup would be armed. Maybe with more than a knife.

They would be as merciless with Mark as they had been with Hoo and me.

As they had been with poor Sweet Rowdy.

I fingered the scabs on my neck and held back another scream.

A man, bald and short and powerfully built, got out of the truck.

A second figure followed. The man with the jutting nose.

The man Mark had tortured and then released. If anyone had cause to be looking for revenge, it was Crooked Nose.

My heart lodged in my throat. I shouldn't be sitting here while Mark walked into such danger.

But when the three met, Crooked Nose seemed to hold no animosity. He spoke while the bald man, built like a battering ram, stood back.

Maybe it would be all right. Perhaps there was a mistake. Perhaps Mark could settle with them.

My husband made an occasional gesture as he talked, but Crooked Nose seemed unreceptive. He shook his head negatively, speaking in turn. Mark listened then shook his head.

Crooked Nose shrugged and signed to his henchman, who clenched his fists and moved toward Mark.

Mark sprung forward, so quick that I couldn't follow. He hit the other man first in the face because the impact flung the bald head up and back.

And his next blow must have caught the groin, because the bald man clutched at that part of his body and sank to his knees.

But Mark moved so fast that, as the one man went down, he'd already swung round to face Crooked Nose.

Crooked Nose, standing slightly back, reached inside his coat. When he brought out his hand, metal gleamed.

A gun. He had a gun.

Mark was at him before the gun swung up. He caught the man's hand and held on in a struggle that made the two look as though they were engaged in a macabre dance.

One of them stumbled, dragging both combatants down onto the pavement. The gun jarred loose, went spinning into the ditch as they wrestled in the road.

The baldheaded man got to his knees. He stayed on them, bent over at the waist, too dazed to stand.

Mark needed help.

I remembered the crunch when I hit the man in my bedroom.

If a little statue could do such damage, a wrench or tire tool could surely do as much or more.

Getting out, I ignored the siren still wailing down at the river and opened the hatch. Shifting aside a blanket and a bag of magazines ready to be transported to the recycling station, I found nothing I could use.

Damn, damn, and double damn.

Mark owned a thousand tools. Where were they?

The siren stopped abruptly, making me look up.

Mark still grappled with Crooked Nose. The other man, the one with the bald head and chest like a barrel, had disappeared.

Searching for the gun?

I fumbled beneath some old canvas drop cloths, hoping for anything suitable for a weapon.

Then, at the front of our car, I found the missing man.

Baldy had crept up to the hood. His lip and nose were bleeding and starting to swell. He saw me over the gaping car door at the same time I saw him.

We both froze. Then, as before when I'd awakened to find an unknown man inside the lake house, my mind dissolved.

I fled.

Past the pavilion. Away from peril.

Baldy lumbered after me.

I veered onto the beginning of a hiking trail. My feet flew over the packed pine needles.

Fading azaleas and dogwoods blurred. At one point, the scent of magnolias washed the air.

Because the path led downhill, toward the river, my progress was rapid.

When the trail divided, I went left. Down.

All the time, I imagined I heard heavy footsteps behind me. Imagined because the siren had begun its screaming again, leaving no room in my ears for important sounds such as a pursuer's footfalls or heavy breathing.

I must be gaining distance on the man chasing me. I'd covered so much ground . . .

Oh no! The trail doubled back on itself.

My pursuer had stopped on the path directly above me.

Why was he standing there? What was he waiting for? What had I overlooked?

Then I saw what the man above had already seen. The trail I followed led back up in a circle. If I continued on, I'd run right into that massive figure.

I slid to a halt on the pine needles. Panting and out of breath, I tried frantically to plan as he and I stared at each other through the lacy tips of a redbud sapling.

He began to retrace his steps in a route that would bring him directly in line with me on the upper path.

I realized too late what his vantage point had already shown him. He could cut through the thin underbrush separating us and get down to the lower trail in seconds.

Get down to me.

How to escape? I could crash through the undergrowth myself, but the thickness off this side of the trail discouraged me. A step forward revealed an obscure path leading off to the left.

Without a thought as to where it might go, I plunged toward it and into a drenching sweetness of honeysuckle. I glanced back once to see the man pushing through the bushes above the spot where I had stood a moment before.

The siren had stopped again.

The next time it sounded would mark the third time.

Then waters held back by the dam would be loosed, to ripple and tumble and fill the Chattahoochee riverbed to its brim as it would have done a hundred years ago before the dam was constructed.

I knew this, somewhere in the back of my mind, but there was no time to dwell on it. I had to escape Baldy. I had to get help for Mark.

A dead end halted my flight.

When I got to the bottom, the trail led to a deck overlooking the river some distance away.

Trapped.

Here in this lovely glade smelling of jasmine and fresh woodland growth, I would be hurt, maybe killed while Mark might already be . . .

I touched the scabs at my throat again.

Then I saw the stairs on the other side of the deck, to the side and almost concealed by verdant spring foliation.

Hewn from granite, dark and narrow and steep, they sprang up through the vegetation like fairy steps, and led down toward the river below.

Without hesitation I took them.

Later, I couldn't recall my feet hitting a single tread. I seemed to float down their mossy slopes and maybe I did, I went so fast.

The granite slabs turned into a wooden landing with wooden steps.

At their bottom curved a paved road that led round to the parking area beside the dam.

Beyond the road flowed the Chattahoochee, with a few fishermen standing up at the top and heading toward the bridge spanning the river where they could watch as the dam gates opened. They carried stools and reeled-in rods gathered up before they left the lower banks of the river that the water would soon cover.

I started toward the road that led to the parking lot.

With so many witnesses, my pursuer would have to turn back.

And I could get help for Mark.

Mark. What was happening to Mark?

I tired but no footsteps echoed behind me. Had Baldy given up and turned back? Reaching the road, I started toward the bridge with renewed hope.

Then my heart sank.

My pursuer had gained. He had zigzagged, maneuvering through a deep ditch to reach a section of the road between me and the bridge ahead.

I couldn't go forward. If I turned back, he had a clear path to cut through to me. All he had to do was keep coming at me.

The river.

I left the pavement and stumbled down to the riverbank. Amid odors of damp leaves and shaded earth and sun warmed stones, a path through the spring foliage led to a small sandbar.

The sands were deserted, as was the small bordering footbridge, but across the river an elderly couple carrying folding chairs and rods climbed up the high bank opposite.

Escaping before the Chattahoochee was set loose.

They knew about the oncoming flood and didn't want to be caught.

A glance over my shoulder revealed Baldy sliding down the grassy bank toward me, puffing but obstinate.

Somehow I found myself across the sandbar and at the edge of the river. Placid water blocked my way in a gentle curve through sand and rocks.

I looked at it and then back at the man approaching the sand. I could stand here and let the river hold me captive, or I could brave the water and try to make it to safety before the dam gates opened.

Mark.

No choice.

I stepped into the water.

The edge dropped off. Numbing cold embraced me. I sank.

This is how people drown. Caught by the cold water, unable to breathe.

I surfaced sputtering, and began to swim for the other side.

Just a few yards. I can stand the cold that far.

Halfway across, the siren went off again.

The water release had begun. The lazy Chattahoochee was about to become the turbulent, churning power nature intended.

People had died from being swept downstream by that power.

Panic gave me a fresh burst of adrenaline.

I can make it. I will make it.

I did make it.

Scrabbling up onto the harsh stones on hands and knees, I sobbed thankfully.

The elderly man came halfway down the steep rocky bank to pull me up by the hand when I emerged. He looked frightened, red-faced.

It took a moment to make out his words. "—you trying to do, lady? Kill yo'self? We gonna get caught up in them flood waters if you don't hurry."

Despite my feet being at the mercy of the sharp rocks—I'd lost both shoes to the river—I hurried after him, icy cold, dripping wet.

Thousands of gallons of water flooded the river as the dam began generating electricity.

But I was safe.

The man led me past the dank line of rocks that marked the height to where the river would rise. There, my foolhardiness hit and my knees trembled, partly from the cold but mostly from fear.

I could have been caught in the deadly currents. I could have been swept away and drowned.

At the top of the rocks, I looked back.

The stocky baldheaded man stood on the sandbar across the way, hands on hips and furious. He spotted the footbridge spanning the river further up and hesitated. He didn't know whether to follow me into the river or go back up to the road and cross at the bridge.

The elderly man, from the safety of the bank, yelled at him, but Baldy ignored the cries.

He didn't understand what the fisherman was trying to tell him. The flood gates were open and the waters, seeming to quietly roil, would within minutes become turgid and deadly.

Since he didn't know what was happening, he took his time in deciding what to do. By the time he started to retrace his steps, he trudged through waters beginning to swell.

The other fisherman, a white-haired woman who wore a bright cap sporting a rainbow-colored assortment of fly hooks, came up. "Land, gal. What in the world were you thinking of?"

Horrified, I stayed riveted on the unsuspecting man across the river.

The woman beside me watched him, too. "Your friend over there better run."

"He isn't my friend." I was shaking uncontrollably.

"Well, whoever he is, don't he know he's about to be trapped?"

He didn't.

He stumbled as the stealthy river covered the sandbar.

When he got up, the water raked at his knees. Belatedly understanding the danger, he tried to run, but the sands mired him down. The water clung to his legs and made him clumsy.

He stumbled a second time.

The Chattahoochee kept rising.

He got up, again had his feet washed from beneath him.

This time he did not get up.

The water, whirling merrily round the rocks in the middle of the river, caught him up in its great billowy grasp and took him with it in its downstream surge toward freedom.

The elderly woman gasped beside me. "Oh, land! Gully!"

"I been watching that idjit, Verna. I reckon I better call for help. Here." The man who had pulled me up the rocks handed the woman a blanket and pulled a cellphone out. In his nervousness, he dropped it. "Hell and damnation! 'Scuse me, ma'am," he added.

Embarrassed, he walked away to make the call.

The siren stopped its mournful wail.

The sound of the waters flooding the riverbed replaced the hush, until finally the gentle innocuous murmuring filled and reverberated throughout the basin, and drove out all memories of the strident siren.

Peace returned, though the Chattahoochee remained flowing full, dancing and foaming and spewing with its potency of deliberate release.

Below me, their faces pointed downstream where the stocky man had disappeared, shocked people gathered.

"Didn't y'all hear the siren?" the elderly lady asked as I shivered beneath the blanket she draped round my shoulders. "I can't believe you jumped in that water. Ain't you lucky? You could'a been washed away like that other poor soul."

She didn't seem to need an answer as she chattered.

Just as well. The cold of the river had seeped through to the very bone, and my shoeless feet ached. The climb over jagged rocks to safety had left cuts and abrasions.

Worse than that was remembering the way my pursuer had looked caught up in the current, how his arms had flopped like a rag doll as the water bore him away.

I couldn't stop shivering.

If he died, it was my fault. My fault.

A car horn blew. My mind jumped from the man in the river to Mark.

I had forgotten Mark.

What happened after I ran away? Across the river and up the steep hillside beyond, the top of the pavilion jutted over the wall of trees.

What were Mark and Crooked Nose doing up there?

Nerveless fingers let the blanket slide off my shoulders.

I had to get to Mark.

Again, the insistent car horn blew and kept blowing.

The woman beside me grumbled as she caught and readjusted the blanket round me. "Listen to that crazy fool. Don't he know he ain't helping matters none?"

She nodded toward the lot across the river beside the bridge, to an SUV pulling up with a screech of brakes.

Mark's SUV.

I cried out with joy before caution prevailed.

What if it was Crooked Nose in Mark's car? What if Mark lay up at the pavilion, dead or dying, looking as Hoo had looked?

No! I didn't believe it. I couldn't bear it. If anything happened to Mark . . .

The driver got out to stand beside the hood, and despite the distance, the khakis and madras shirt made the long-limbed figure easily recognizable. My entire body sagged with relief.

Mark.

My cut feet, the cold, my wet clothes. None of that mattered.

Mark was all right. He was safe.

"He's all right. He's all right." I heard a broken voice repeating the words over and over. It was mine.

"Now, now, child." The woman with the fishhooks in her cap mistook my words, thinking I meant the man swept downstream. "Sure, he's all right. Why, if he's smart, he'll catch hold of a rock or a tree branch till they fish him out. Gully's already called for help. They'll get him out in no time. No need to break down now."

"Y-yes," I stuttered, still watching Mark's figure. He beckoned. He wanted me to cross over the bridge to the dam.

I slipped out of the blanket as the SUV took off up the hill. "I have to go."

The elderly woman's mouth gaped. "You can't run off."

"I must. Thank you. Thank your . . . Thank Gully, too. I can't tell you how grateful I am."

"You're like to take pneumonia. And you gotta talk to the cops."

"I'll be fine," I flung over my shoulder.

I left her, a small figure in baggy jeans and colorful hat, glaring after me.

Hurrying toward the dam, I reached the wide plank footbridge that led across the Chattahoochee to the parking area on the other side. My bare feet, slashed and bruised, throbbed.

No matter. Despite them and the stitch in my side, I sprinted across the boards and up the asphalt walk. A few minutes after I got to the parking lot, Mark pulled up close to the walk entrance. All I had to do was hop into the open car door.

"Oh, Mark, that man got washed away, and I was so scared," I babbled across the console. "I wanted to help you, but he came and I ran, and I didn't know if you were all right or not, I was so scared."

I would have thrown my arms around him, but he gave me no chance.

"Buckle your seat belt." The past half hour might never have happened. My husband started the car before my door closed. "The county police'll be here in a minute and the last thing we need is a lot of questions we can't answer."

I subsided, giving in to cold and shock and fatigue.

The old Mark sat beside me, obviously in control, obviously needing to concentrate on his driving. He spared no time for explanations, no time for apologies, no time for exchanging fears and hopes and emotions. There would never be time, and that was one of the reasons we were divorcing.

He accelerated up the hill leading back to the road, breaking every speed limit sign we passed.

For once, I didn't remonstrate. Who cared how recklessly he took hairpin curves and ran stop signs? I said nothing when, on reaching the main road, he swerved onto it without decelerating.

I couldn't tell when he reverted to a more sedate pace. I was too intent on holding back tears and gathering up shreds of dignity to match Mark's steely composure.

We slowed, but not until we came to a complete stop did I realize he had pulled off the road where a little abandoned store sat. By that time, he'd undone his seatbelt and was unfastening mine, preparatory to taking me in his arms over the console.

I let him.

I buried my face in the curve of his neck and breathed in the scent of him and felt the solid warmth seep through me. I allowed him to comfort me as he must have known I would.

"I'm sorry, love," he murmured again and again into my hair. "I'm so sorry. It's all my fault."

The tears gathered up inside my throat in big clumps, making my voice tremble from the effort of restraining them. "I was so s-scared." I held onto him for all I was worth. "That man—I didn't know—I looked in the trunk for something to hit him—I wanted to help you. Where are your t-tire tools and things?" I asked plaintively, idiotically.

A smothered note of laughter overrode the concern. "Under the liner." The next minute, his laughter vanished, and he stroked my hair and held as tightly to me as I held on to him. "It was my fault. All my fault. I thought my warning the other night would take care of everything. I didn't know Hoo had left the pen with you. I'm just so sorry."

When the numbness and fear abated, I recovered enough of my shattered esteem to draw back. "I ran away. I left you there." The loss of his warmth hurt worse than I had imagined. I folded my arms to keep from falling on him again.

"What else should you have done?" He scanned my face as he leaned over the console. "If one of them had got you, I'd have had no choice but to give up whatever it is they want."

"They want what Hoo sent you, don't they?"

"Apparently."

"Do you think it's his audit paperwork?"

Caution settled over his features, punctuating his weariness. He had a nasty cut over his left eye that seeped blood and several abrasions on both cheeks and chin. The left side of his mouth had begun to swell.

"Probably. But whatever it is, Hoo risked his life to keep it out of these people's hands. That's enough to let me know they mustn't have it."

I wanted to reach out and wipe away the blood from over his eye, kiss the side of his swollen mouth.

But that would be too intimate a gesture for the present state of our relationship. Instead, I asked, "How did you get away from that man?"

He must have seen something in my face, pity or empathy, for he whipped the rearview mirror around and examined himself. "This is a fine thing to happen to a rising young sculptor who's probably going to be interviewed and photographed in the next few days. I'm going to look like hell, aren't I? For your information, I left Crooked Nose flat on the ground. If he's wise, he'll be long gone by now. And I'll bet he looks worse than me."

Smugness in the last remark grated.

Until yesterday, I would never have put Mark in the macho category. But it seems all men possess differing amounts of testosterone that must occasionally find an outlet.

"You're lucky that's all he did to you. He had a gun." I recalled the silver gleam bouncing into the ditch. Fear returned. "He would have killed you."

"No, he wouldn't."

"How do you know?"

"I'm bigger than he is."

I closed my eyes, wishing he'd take what had happened seriously, wishing he didn't feel the need to shrug away everything important with a cute remark. All right, I could be as nonchalant. "What are we going to do?"

"Excuse me, love."

He reached over to open the dash of the car and take out a small container of tissues. Daubing at the blood over his eye, he proved effectively that he didn't need my ministrations.

He was self-sufficient, my husband. He didn't need anyone. Not me, not Coral, not anyone.

"What will we do?" I prodded. "Once we find out what Hoo sent you?"

He finished his clean-up and dropped the tissues into the litter bag. "Let's see what Hoo left first, before we go making decisions about what to do with it." He leaned over me again.

I didn't shrink away as he reached across toward the window.

His left arm paused against my right shoulder and breast, imprisoning me. His eyes met mine.

I saw past the dark spots into the greenish depths and thought he was going to kiss me. A hard kiss that would demand a response.

What should I do? I didn't want him to kiss me. I didn't.

I held my breath.

But the old fires arose deep within, stoked by the gray-green intensity and the sweet widow's peak and the bruised line of his jaw disappearing into the thick hair.

I dropped my gaze away from the challenge in his, found the curve of his lips that brought back the memories of how they had played upon my body two nights past.

We sat there a full twenty seconds, his face barely two inches from mine.

Then he smiled, a rather crooked smile that narrowed the fringe of lashes and deepened the familiar laugh lines. That in turn left a fiery trail of nostalgic desire racing through my stomach. He pulled my seat harness down across my breasts to my thigh, hooking it with slow deliberation.

I let out a long sigh.

Of relief? Or regret?

I didn't know. My head was spinning, my feet were hurting, and my stomach churned from the ordeal. I was scared and wet and cold, not thinking straight.

Mark ought not to confuse me like this, knowing what I'd been through.

At that moment the obvious question occurred. "Mark."

He was in the middle of fastening his own belt. "Um?"

"Those men. Were they after Hoo's package?"

"I imagine so."

The men might have been following us all day, but we would surely have noticed long before we reached the dam.

And they had tried to run us off the road to get the pen.

"Mark, how did they know we found Hoo's pen?"

Dark eyes that were really green flickered my way. The silence dragged into a vacuum with us caught in the middle. He didn't reply and I doubted I could make him reply no matter how I pleaded.

He cranked the car and we resumed our trip, but he did not drive to Legacy Lodge.

Coral waited in vain for us that day.

Coral, the only one besides Mark and me who knew what Hoo had left.

CHAPTER ELEVEN

HOO HAD CHOSEN a post office in Buford, one of Atlanta's northern suburbs. The area was far busier than expected on a Monday afternoon.

As I sat in the car nursing my feet, Mark stood in a straggling queue to pick up Hoo's letter. Forty minutes passed before he came out. He held a large bulky manila envelope.

I had assumed that once we obtained whatever Hoo had sent, Mark would examine it and deliver it to the field manager at Legacy Lodge with Coral.

But Mark stowed the package under his seat, unopened, before we left Buford. And, though we were on the same side of the lake as Legacy Lodge, we did not head in that direction.

As he drove, and my clothes dried and the pain in my feet subsided, I wondered why not.

But there were larger worries.

If those men were after Hoo's papers, someone had to have told them about the pen. And the only person besides Mark and me who had known we were bringing it to Legacy Lodge was Coral.

Was Coral the reason Mark was so quiet? Did he suspect his old lover of setting Crooked Nose on us?

Or Mark might be allied with Coral in some way. She might have invited the interception at the dam as he had done the invasion of our house.

That wasn't so farfetched. After all, Mark had got out at the park, said he wanted to talk to the men. Had talked to them. If he and Coral were . . .

No, that was crazy.

I trusted Mark. I might be divorcing him, but I trusted him. Mark wouldn't do anything to harm me. Not Mark.

Apprehension reseeded itself as we got on the Perimeter.

Where were we going?

We exited the Perimeter not far from Cumberland Mall and pulled into a nearby discount mart. The crowded area, where we had no reason to be, lay far off our usual route to and from the lake and farther away from our house near Emory on the other side of Atlanta.

"What are we doing here?"

"Shoes. What size do you wear?"

"Oh." I looked down at my feet, seeing the tiny cuts and dried flakes of mud. "Eight."

"I'll be right back."

"I have shoes at home!"

Too late. He slammed the door.

From the car, I could see the store entrance. He stopped in the foyer almost out of sight. I could make out a phone at his ear. He stood there long enough to carry on a short conversation.

With Coral? Was he reporting what had happened?

Fifteen minutes later, he came out with a store bag which he handed to me. "We'll have to make another stop later. My cell battery died, but they don't carry any chargers that will work."

Inside, I found cheap tennis shoes, sanitizer, and a roll of moisturized towelettes.

"Go ahead and clean up your feet and put on the shoes. You need to come in, too."

"Like this?" My jeans and shirt were drying but uncomfortable and stiff from the river. "Thank you just the same, but I'd rather not be seen in public until I go home and change clothes."

"Go home?" His mouth dropped open in horror. "And waste this beautiful afternoon? I thought we might eat out, take in a movie. Here, give me one of those wet thingies."

I stopped in the middle of cleaning my feet, unable to figure out what he planned, and who he had called. The workings of his mind had never seemed more removed from mine.

"I want to go home."

He took a towelette, became engrossed in wiping his face in front of the mirror. "We'll go. Ouch." The cut over his eye started to bleed again. "Ugh, that smarts." He used a tissue to apply pressure. "We'll go home, Steve. Only not right away."

I put on the new sneakers. "Why not?"

"I don't feel like cooking." He got the bleeding stopped and readjusted the mirror and opened his door. "Hurry up, love. Time's a'wastin'."

"Mark." I tied haphazard bows and jumped out as he left. "Will you please stop with the jokes? I hate it when you do this. Are you saying it isn't safe to go home?"

He didn't stop walking. His dispassionate voice floated back. "Look, you're not stupid. You know as well as I do that you and I and Coral were the only people who knew about that pen. If Coral told Bob, he might have told someone else, but who knows? Until we do find out what's going on, I think we'll stay out of sight. Besides, I want a chance to look over Hoo's papers before they go to Main Office."

So it wasn't safe for us to go back to the house near Emory.

I'd suspected as much, deep in the back of my mind, but I hadn't wanted to believe it. A chill, as disturbing but completely different from that caused by the cold water, enveloped me.

He'd strode on ahead.

I scurried past rows of parked cars to keep pace.

"Pick up some toothbrushes and toothpaste, would you?" he asked as we went inside. "And some disposable razors. And while you're at it, why don't you get a pair of jeans and a blouse?"

Too many unanswered questions were running around loose in my head to argue with him.

"Okay."

"And I think we'll be staying at a motel tonight. You might want to pick up some pajamas. Unless you prefer sleeping in the raw." He leered at me, though I could tell his heart wasn't in it.

Perhaps thoughts of Coral distracted him, made him wonder whether his one-time lover had betrayed us.

I didn't rise to his bait. "What will you be doing?"

"Oh, I'll be in men's underwear," he said airily, taking out a shopping cart. He pushed it into my unwilling hands. "You can come with me if you like. I could probably use some help choosing some boxers." His voice dropped suggestively. "And afterward I could help in picking you out a nightie, one of those sheer things kind of like a bathing suit with a little matching jacket to—"

"Shut up." I pulled the cart to me and wheeled it away, not knowing whether to laugh or cry.

He was impossible. And I was afraid.

"Try to make it snappy, okay?" he called after me. "I've got things to do."

It seemed I didn't. Slipping behind a tall display of purses set out in the wide middle aisle, I peered around a fake alligator shoulder bag in time to see Mark heading back out the door.

I'd noted the two pay phones in the foyer when we came in. He went straight toward them.

All right. "Keeping Steve In The Dark" seemed to be the name of the game. As had been true throughout our marriage. If that's how he wanted to play it, fine.

Seething, I snatched up jeans, blouse, socks, panties, bra, and a chaste cotton gown that happened to be on sale. My shopping took twenty minutes flat. Mark, minus any articles of underwear or anything else, met me in the pharmacy as I threw a pack of disposable razors into the cart. I couldn't hold back a tart comment on his empty hands. "What's wrong, didn't they have your size?"

"Huh?" He remembered the boxers and grinned. "Oh. Actually, they didn't have my color. I couldn't see myself in chartreuse. I guess I'll wait."

After choosing toothbrushes and toothpaste, we went toward the checkout line. A prominent array of white cotton briefs, stacked alongside gray and maroon and navy boxers, blocked the first three registers.

I pointed them out with some malice. "However did you miss those nice muted colors?"

What have you been up to? I wanted to ask. Who did you call? Who've you been talking to for the past twenty minutes?

But I knew he would offer that absent grin and not answer. Or if he did answer, he would manage to evade saying anything of importance.

He plucked a folded pack of boxers off the top of the stack of underwear and put them into my cart. "Come along, Elvira," he said, taking my arm masterfully.

I hoped the boxers would be two sizes too small.

He put me in line. "You know we don't have time to chat. We've got to get home and slop the hogs."

A bleached blonde matron ahead of us overheard Mark's words and turned. Dressed in expensive running shoes and a silk jogging suit, and trundling a cart full of toiletries and a top-of-the-line toaster oven, she shrank away as if we smelled.

Which might very well have been true.

Her expression made me glad to get to a fast food place where I could change clothes in the ladies room.

With Hoo's sealed package stashed between us in the booth, Mark picked at fried fish and hushpuppies. I let him know how annoyed he made me with his selfish, irresponsible, maddening refusal to confide what was going on.

In fact, I let him know at length how annoyed I was with him in general.

He listened courteously until I ran out of steam. "Well, love, it's like this," he drawled, spearing a fried potato with his fork and dragging it through a little pile of mustard he had squirted onto his plate. "Somebody put those men on us today. How do I know it wasn't you?"

"What?"

My voice carried. Five people sitting across the room—two in one booth, the others in enviable solitude—turned to look at us. I sank as low as I could into the booth, trying to be inconspicuous.

"Listen, Mark Early," I said, furious, but trying to speak quietly, "after all I've been through, now you have the nerve to tell me you think I . . . Oh, you . . . Don't you laugh at me."

He munched on his nauseating mustard-drenched potato. "Okay," he said, doing an about- face. "Let's attack your concerns from another angle. So far, you're perfectly innocent of any involvement in this thing except accidental. I'd like to keep it that way."

"It's too late for that."

"No, it isn't. Unless you know something to make you interesting, love, no one should bother you. Besides, how can I tell you something I don't know myself?"

His reasoning was flawed, but I couldn't think how. "I hate you."

He was unperturbed. "No, you don't. You may dislike me intensely at this point, but you don't hate me." He forked another potato and waved it in the air. "I know you inside and out, Stephanie Early, and you've never hated anyone in your entire life."

He plunged the fry into mustard and popped it into his mouth, looking smug.

He was wrong, but it wasn't worth arguing over.

* * * *

AFTER WE ATE, we drove around until Mark chose a motel out of the many encircling the Perimeter. Safely checked in and locked away, we tackled the package picked up from the post office. He, in his deliberate way, slit the end.

Its contents turned out to be a large stack of accounting papers for some firm called GENSYN Oil.

I picked up a few sheets and studied them, but they seemed straightforward.

There were last year's balance sheets and cash flow statements and income statements pulled off a computer, along with photocopies of journal sheets and accounts payable listings and checks. Mixed haphazardly among the stack were letters from vendors confirming expenses and handwritten worksheets where Hoo had compiled his audit information.

Everything was jumbled together, with no notes of explanation, no draft of a final report.

Just the normal statements and worksheets any accountant might deal with. None important enough to get the auditor kidnapped and beaten.

Disappointed, I said, "There's nothing here."

Mark had more patience. "We'll see. Why don't you bathe and

put on some clean clothes while I look through these? You'll feel better."

What he meant was that my help was unnecessary and unwanted. When he made this plain by turning his back and spreading the sheets out on one of the double beds, I retreated to the bathroom and the luxury of a hot shower.

As I shampooed my hair, I thought about Mark and Coral.

They might still be lovers. Not that it mattered, except that for the time being, to help my peace of mind, I would rather they weren't. *If they aren't, I can trust Mark.* That was why I hoped he and Coral weren't lovers. I didn't want them plotting behind my back.

Scrubbing the stretch marks on my stomach brought back memories of my pregnancy and its unhappy conclusion.

The glorious autumn day spent raking leaves and clipping grass and trimming shrubs, the effort to ignore the spasms, the bleeding, the rush to the hospital, Fiona's tears afterward.

I'd thought myself inured to FIFA's demands until that afternoon.

Mark had been away on one of FIFA's episodic assignments when I had the miscarriage. My first call had been for an ambulance and the next to FIFA's emergency 800 number, the only way to contact Mark.

Later, I had lain on the gurney taking me through the hospital doors. I remembered rolling down the corridors into the bowels of the OB section beneath the dazzling lights, wishing for Mark, gritting my teeth again the worsening pain.

I told the nurse putting a stethoscope to my stomach, "He isn't due for another ten weeks."

My obstetrician appeared to give me an injection. "To see if we can't stop the cramps and bleeding."

There is a certain point when the agony of rending body muscles and tissues and nerves gives way to a numbing of the mind. A trance where one is aware of what is happening but is equally aware that nothing can be done to stop it. At that point, the pain becomes a monstrous entity of itself which must be borne one way or another.

I had reached such a point in my labor when, mental faculties separate from the physical ones, I listened to the doctor's low voice giving instructions. ". . . an IV . . . just in case . . . I can't . . . monitor doesn't . . ."

The numbness blocked my understanding. Something was wrong, yet I felt curiously removed. "My baby's all right, isn't he?" The disembodied voice belonged to someone other than me. "He isn't coming now, is he?"

More people in hospital scrubs had materialized.

Certain things came back with vivid clarity.

The doctor's set mouth before her mask covered it. The coldness of the stirrups as they placed me supine with knees in the air. The cheerful voice of the nurse as she moved around putting instruments on a tray. My wrists being strapped down. The stick of a needle.

I quietly watched the forehead and downcast eyes of the doctor between the intervals of cramping, until my pain-induced stupor failed, and I could no longer hold back a cry.

And finally the truth when my baby was extracted.

"Ohhh," the nurse said before clamping her lips together as though forbidden to speak.

"What is it?" I whispered, sweat cold on my face. "What's wrong?"

The doctor, working frantically to revive the tiny pale morsel of humanity that was my son, snapped at the nurse, "Did you put in that call for Dr. Calandaris?"

"What's wrong?" Dread fortified my voice.

"No heartbeat," a man I didn't remember seeing, said from the side. He operated some sort of machine.

"Is he dead?" I asked him because he was the only one who looked at me, spoke to me. "Is my baby dead?"

He didn't answer.

I knew.

After the hard labor, I shouldn't have found the strength, but the scream rolled up from somewhere deep inside me and frightened everyone including me with its raw howl of denial.

"She's hemorrhaging." The doctor looked up. "Put her under." Her voice was calm as Mark's as she gave up on reviving my baby and turned away.

I fought the needle but lost that battle, too.

Only that scene with the doctor working over the tiny motionless form that was my child, my son, remained seared into my heart.

As did the days afterward, spent in the hospital with Fiona, who'd flown in from Virginia.

And the entire time we waited and wondered where he was, no word came from Mark.

Not when I came out from the anesthesia to find that my baby was dead and that I had nearly died myself. Not those first awful hours spent alone in the hospital before Fee got there, nor the other nights when she sat beside my bed.

During those days, Fee called FIFA's emergency number to leave countless messages, but still no word from Mark.

When it became obvious there would be none, Fee came up with excuses. "They may not be able to reach him."

"In this day and time?" I didn't believe her excuses, had known she didn't believe them herself.

That marked the beginning of the end.

No matter that, on the same day I came home from the hospital, five days after my first call to FIFA, Mark showed up bearded and unkempt, carrying his flight bag along with an armload of blood-red roses. As Fee withdrew to find a vase, he bent down to kiss me where I lay on the sofa. "Hey, pretty lady, are you okay?"

I nodded, numb, aching, unable to answer.

He seemed concerned and quieter than usual, but he didn't speak of our loss. "I've brought you just the thing for couch potatoing." Unzipping his bag, he brought out an elaborate Japanese silk kimono. "It looked like you. All delicate and elegant and beautiful."

A silk kimono to replace a dead baby.

He saw my face and his fell. "I'm sorry, love, I'm so very sorry for everything. I did try to get here." When he took my hand and put it to his lips, his fingers felt cold.

Fee came back with his roses in a vase. Though he continued to hold my hand, her presence stemmed any apologies for his absence, any outpouring of grief to mitigate mine that he might have extended.

Not then nor later, after Fee's departure, did he offer more than the conventional comforting phrases.

At the time I'd told myself he kept his pain to himself as he always did.

It had taken the carved marble baby to make me see Mark couldn't share, couldn't understand my grief.

The kimono had been packed away, never worn.

Here in the conventional motel bathroom, I took out all the old memories and looked at them one by one.

The ache in my heart was unexpectedly diminished. Maybe I was at last starting to heal.

Streams of water drenched me, hot and cleansing and, strangely, considering my churning uncertainties, soothing inside and out.

Putting on the inexpensive gown from the mart, I came out of the bathroom to find Mark bent over the bed. He shuffled and reshuffled little stacks of paper.

"Need some help?"

He straightened, looking troubled. "These pages aren't in any kind of order. They're all mixed up. And Hoo's the neatest accountant I know. If I hadn't recognized his writing, I would have said he didn't do this."

"Maybe he didn't have time to put them in any kind of order." I picked up a paper at random. "If he knew someone wanted to steal them, he may have loaded them up in the envelope any old way so he could get them in the mail."

He looked at the piles. "You're probably right. I guess he knew those damned goons were after him."

With the cut over his eye and one entire jaw turning black, Mark looked like a goon himself.

The old suspicions came back. I only had his and Coral's word that nothing illegal was going on, but Coral's word was questionable. If she and Mark were lovers, his veracity was as suspect as hers.

Who had he called as I was buying clothes? Coral?

Wanting to ask but afraid of being rebuffed, I watched him thumb through the stacks. "Is there anything I can do?"

The audit sheets absorbed him so he didn't hear me. I had to repeat my question.

He looked up, eyes glazed and unseeing. "What? Oh, no. Thanks." The glaze disappeared and a twinkle I hadn't seen in months appeared. "Or maybe I ought to find out what it is you have in mind before I turn your offer down."

He surveyed me hopefully.

Heat flooded my neck and rose to my face. "I meant," I said plainly, "is there anything I can do to help you with those accounting sheets."

"Hmm, I was afraid that's what you meant." He lost interest and went back to the papers. "No, two people doing this would be too many. It'll take one person working alone to put this mess into any kind of order."

Still unneeded, or at least unwanted, I doctored my feet, then climbed into the unused double bed and clicked the television's remote control.

The late news had a story about a man being swept downstream by dam release waters.

I turned up the volume. The body had not been recovered, the perky African-American anchorwoman told us with a pretty frown. People were warned again not to ignore the sirens that signaled the imminent release of reservoir waters.

No one mentioned my swim across the river. Nothing about a woman's presence at the dam at all.

"Did you hear? They didn't say anything about me," I said to Mark, who had moved some of the papers over to a table.

Absorbed in his work, he said, "You're pretty, love, but lots of pretty women are running around for the reporters to photograph."

"Can't you be serious?"

"What's there to tie you to a man caught up in the dam release waters?" he asked sensibly, laying some papers to the side. "Nothing." "He was chasing me." I shivered at the memory. "Everyone there saw him chasing me."

"So? They probably figured drowning served him right. Anyway, just because a woman was on the scene isn't enough to start a manhunt for her. Don't worry about it."

"I think we should go to the authorities."

"We will, as soon as we know what Hoo was mixed up in. If they can't find you," he continued, as though assuming concern for my own well-being lay behind my fretting, "it'll soon blow over. The authorities have too many real criminals to worry about to spend time chasing a phantom woman. Okay?"

He seemed callous about our escape that afternoon.

I had never understood him. Now I saw how very far apart we were. "Don't you care that a man died today?"

His unfathomable gaze flicked from the papers spread on the table to me. "Sure. But I'd have cared a lot more had it been you." He went back to poring over Hoo's worksheets.

I despaired of digging any real emotion out of him. What would his reaction be if his friend Hoo turned out to be dead?

No, no, he couldn't be.

Surely, Hoo was alive somewhere. Surely, someone had tended those bloody wounds, found him a doctor.

But he had been so pale and weak. Would his captors have cared about his injuries? If he died because of them, it would be my fault.

I pulled the pristine sheets up under my neck and tried not to think of the mangled face. Remembering Mark's telephone calls, I got up enough nerve to ask, "Who did you call when we were at the discount store?"

He took his time answering. "The field office."

I waited.

And waited.

Damn him, I deserved to know. "Well? What about?"

He straightened, feigning surprise. "I let them know we'll be in tomorrow. That they shouldn't bother calling us, that we'll call them." He went back to his papers.

"You called them twice?"

He didn't bother to look up this time. "I called the house to check for messages, too."

"Were there any?"

"A couple. One from Fee, nothing important she said, but call her when you get a chance. And somebody from the DeKalb Police. We have to go Thursday at two to sign statements."

Still dissatisfied, I sank back against the pillows to channel surf.

Mark moved more piles of papers to his work table and, with a pen, checked off figures on the audit sheets.

If he would let me, I could help him, I thought resentfully, but he obviously didn't want my help. He didn't need my help.

He didn't need me.

CHAPTER TWELVE

AFTER SWITCHING OFF the television, I turned my back to Mark and tried to sleep.

Instead of a deep revitalizing slumber, I fell into an intermittent doze, rousing often from fitful dreams to find his lanky form stooped over the table. The lamp behind him cast a faint halo around his hair as he worked.

I woke this way several times, until in the midst of a nightmare where I raced before a flood of water with a man on my heels holding a gun, I opened my eyes and saw nothing.

The room was pitch-black, and the dream so real that I shot bolt upright in bed, whimpering.

Run. Get away.

I scrambled out over the bottom of the mattress.

"Steve."

My name hit me out of the dark. My feet hit the floor.

Get away, get away!

Disoriented, I rushed toward where the door would have been at home but in the motel room I struck a wall headlong. I bumped the side of my nose and a cheekbone, stunning myself amid increasing confusion.

Where was I?

Mark's arms came about me from the back.

"Steve." His voice was sleepy. "Wake up."

"I am awake!" Reality returned with his familiar presence. His arms tightened around me, and my head sank back against his shoulder for support. "I am awake," I repeated in a whisper.

For a moment we stood there, my heart thumping so loudly that I could hear nothing else, my body shaking. Aching nose and cheek were forgotten. I turned to face him, felt the hard warmth of his chest as I caught the sides of his ribs. Of their own volition, my arms slid around him until they hugged him as hard as he held me.

He was strength and stability and safety in an unknown dimension. I clung to him because I was afraid, not only for myself but for us.

"It was just a dream," he murmured, still groggy with sleep.

"I know. I'm sorry I woke you." But I didn't move, nor did he. We stood there, clasped together.

My shaking stopped. I felt his desire, awakening and rushing through him. My body converged into his. I could feel his blood heating and coursing, so that it seemed we shared the same veins, the same heart.

I put my lips against his neck, felt it pulse beneath my mouth, felt his lips caress my neck.

I moved my mouth upward, and he did the same. The lobe of his ear thickened and throbbed under my bite. Mine did the same as his teeth clung to it.

My face turned and so did his, so that our lips touched gently, once, twice, before joining and melding together.

My hand skimmed down his back to his waist, slowly, softly, reveling in the feel of his bare skin.

His hand did the same, sliding beneath my gown to caress me lightly, tantalizingly, before it moved to my waist and massaged the small of my back.

I drew my fingers across his waist to the side, delving into his shorts to trace his navel and the hairy trail leading to his sex, hovering just short of touching there.

He followed my lead, using his thumb to roll back and forth on my belly before pausing at the pubic area.

Mirroring my movements.

He spoke, his words muffled by my hair confirming my intuition. "I don't want to have to apologize tomorrow morning." His tongue brushed my earlobe as mine had done his. "And I don't want to have to listen to your apologies either. I want it understood, Steve. Anything we do tonight is because you want it." His whisper warmed my face.

I didn't want to hear what he said. I wanted to go on feeling what I was feeling. "Mark—"

He went on, his breath hot at my ear. "I mean it. Whatever happens won't be because you're frightened from your nightmare, nor because you're grateful, nor because it's easy for you to give in to your desires. You have to want me as much as I want you, love. I'll go as far as you say. It's up to you."

I understood him but didn't like it.

His aggressiveness would be guided by mine. He would make me lead before he reciprocated. He would force me to admit that my own will drove us and not his.

I didn't know if I could meet his demands, whether it would be honest to try. I wanted him badly, so badly that I burned all over, but somewhere in the back of my mind, I knew I had to hold myself aloof or I would be lost.

Agreeing to his conditions would begin the process of rebinding me to him, and I couldn't have that.

No, not that.

"Yes," I got out, trying to twist my ear away from his mouth. "Yes, I want you, but it won't change anything between us. I'm half out of my mind right now."

"You're only just coming to your senses." His lips fell on the top of my ear. His tongue slowly, deliciously made its way inside its curl. "You've been out of them for months, Steve. You've been another person, lost and bitter and not my Steve, not my love. Bring her back, Steve. Let her come back to me."

What he said was untrue, but the passion eclipsed his words.

What did it matter whether I agreed or not? I could stay silent, let things take their course.

He wouldn't refuse me.

Massaging his chest, I found his nipples, bent to nip at them and bring them erect. Straightening, I looped my hand in his hair before leaning back in his arms and letting him imitate my motions on me.

"This won't change anything." I wasn't so far gone that I didn't warn him.

Even as his tongue made ever-widening circles over my heart, I tried to be fair.

He stood upright, threaded his fingers through my hair and left them entwined so that we held each other by the hair, faces all but touching. "I'm playing by your rules, love. Remember? You're calling the shots. I'll go as far as you do."

Sex always roughened his voice, thickening it, making it breathy.

Its ragged edges sent familiar signals to my body. Had I been afire before, I was now engulfed in a volcanic eruption.

"You're confusing me," I got out before I relocated his mouth and words no longer seemed necessary.

My hands slid down, felt his butt tense. His hand, slipping beneath my gown, cupped my hips. The bulge in the front of his shorts bit through the silk and cotton. I pushed the boxers down until he could kick them off. He lifted the gown above my head and threw it away in one swift motion.

We fell on the bed, rolling back and forth with hands roving and lips caught together in a long kiss. I wanted him desperately, knew he wanted me as much. I also knew that I couldn't accept him passively, that I'd have to be the aggressor.

No question as to whether or not I would comply with his conditions.

My body was too far gone to brake.

When after a period of increasing fervor he made no move to end the prolonged kiss, no move to advance to the final stage, I rolled on top of him, pinning him down, drawing up my legs.

Before he allowed himself to be encompassed, he held me away. The near pitch-black room hid his face, but his hand splayed on my chest, keeping me from pressing my breasts to his chest.

I knew what he did, would have been angry except for the other dark sensations commandeering and binding all sanity.

"I told you before, you're going to have to make up your mind." No hint of laughter about him.

"Not now," I murmured, pushing his hand away and impaling myself on him.

He gasped. "No." His voice trembled. He gasped again as I moved slowly on top of him. "Not now."

I had won this match. Despite Mark's insistence on a decision, I had succeeded in putting off the inevitable in the heat of the present.

I put my hands on either side of his face, offered a breast for his amusement, sighed at its acceptance, leaned back, and reached down where he was joined to me.

In a short, unexpected movement, he tumbled me off and was astride me, so that he chose the rhythm to control our coupling.

I couldn't resent his actions. The things he did were what I wanted. He knew how to caress and touch and reveal all the secret places ready for plundering. I fondled and held and met him strike for strike.

When I came to the top and plummeted, I felt him going with me, and my cry mingled with his as we collapsed among the tangled linens.

* * * *

I SLEPT RESTLESSLY for what was left of that night. Each time I came awake, Mark's even breathing as he lay beside me soothed me.

I felt guilty but couldn't understand why. I hadn't committed a crime. Making love with my husband wasn't illegal.

Except that I didn't want to enjoy anything with my husband anymore. I didn't want Mark for my husband anymore. I wanted us to go our separate ways.

Or did I? Did I hope the spontaneous sex would lead to . . . ?

I moved out of his reach, away from the feel of his skin that made my carefully constructed rationale crumble.

For the first time since our baby's death, I took a long honest look at myself.

I had blamed Mark for our baby's loss, but underneath, hadn't I been afraid that it was my own fault for Mark's and my growing estrangement?

Hadn't the final unbearable fear, that the responsibility for our baby's death rested squarely on me, been what led me to the point of divorce?

Maybe if I had taken better care of myself, or if I'd given up my classes that last semester, or if I hadn't insisted on working outside in the yard . . . Maybe things would have been okay. Maybe if I'd been wiser, smarter, more careful, our baby would be alive. Maybe our baby's death was my fault.

But Mark had never once uttered a word of blame, no matter how I had pushed him.

Such as in our exchange on the day I'd found the marble baby. Unable to challenge him about his work, I had instead criticized him for being absent when I'd lost my child.

He'd overlooked my spleen. "I know how my absence hurt you. I'd have given anything to have been with you."

"You didn't have to go away."

The lines of his face took on the set detachment that I'd come to recognize as his shield against revealing too much of himself. "I go whenever FIFA sends me. It's in my contract. You know that."

I seized the opportunity. "Is your contract more important than your marriage?"

"Of course not. You can't compare the two." He'd tied his hair back in the ponytail he customarily wore when working and blobs of clay stained his clothes. He lifted one hand. "Love, I'm sorry I wasn't here when you needed me. Yes, I should have been here. Maybe I could have done something if I'd been here. But I wasn't, and you . . . You had to bear it alone. Steve, we have to live with what's done. We can't change it."

"Your being here wouldn't have made any difference."

"No?" He had disputed me for the first time, coming close to giving me the fight I spoiled for. "That's not what you've been thinking."

"You don't know what I've been thinking." Nor had I known what he had been thinking. I never had known. Not for the entire length of our marriage.

He'd drawn back from a full-fledged quarrel. "I'd like to promise you that I'll be here next time you need me, but I can't. Not so long as I work for FIFA."

"Quit." I was irrational, but I didn't care.

With great patience, he spoke as if I were a child. "My contract runs through November. Besides, FIFA's the reason I can afford to sculpt."

"Then quit sculpting. Quit FIFA. Now."

My demand shocked him. I remembered how distinct the sound of our breaths, mine quick and panting and his long and soft, had been in the silence. "I know you've had a tough time, but try to be reasonable."

With that, he had left to hide out in his studio.

"Be reasonable," he had said. Was it unreasonable to want your husband beside you when you were giving birth? Was it unreasonable to expect him to rush to your side when you nearly died?

Was it unreasonable to be nauseated by the sight of a laughing, healthy baby sculpted in marble when your own baby lay unmoving in the ground?

In the dark, against Mark's soft breathing, I tried to whip up the old defiant anger.

So what if Mark had never condemned me for losing the baby? It could be that he blamed me without voicing his feelings. After all, I'd never told him how the sight of that marble laughing baby had affected me, had stabbed me in the heart.

Because it wouldn't matter. I grasped the top of the sheet and smoothed it away from my chin.

He cares more about his work than he does about me. He cares more about his sculpting than he does about anything. How can I possibly love a man who cares for nothing but lumps of clay and stone?

I had no answer by morning.

* * * *

I GOT UP and fled into the shower before Mark awoke. When I came out fully dressed with a towel wrapped around wet hair, I found him sleepy-eyed and yawning, sitting at the table in his boxers, going over Hoo's papers.

"Did you figure anything out last night?" I asked, toweling my hair.

Knowing crinkles rimmed his eyes. "Concerning what?"

I couldn't handle sexual repartee at this hour of the morning and said as much.

The smug expression didn't go away. "Want to see if they have room service?" At my exasperated look, he hastily added, "For coffee. It might make you feel more human."

"Did you or did you not find anything in those papers that told what your friend was doing?"

At mention of Hoo, the carefree air fled. "Maybe."

"What?" I threw the towel down. "What did you find out?"

He lounged back in the chair and stretched out his bare legs. Clad only in his shorts and with a full day's growth of whiskers concealing part of his bruised face, he looked ready to commit mayhem or murder. And he still evoked a physical response from me I distrusted.

"What did you find?"

"I'm not sure. I need to talk to Bob first, see if—" He stopped.

"You spoke to Bob yesterday."

His head checked, gave a slight negative shake. "Actually, Bob had taken a personal day."

"But you said . . ." The truth dawned on me. "Oh?" Anger made me imprudent. "You lied."

"I didn't lie." His quick response was the expected evasion. "I left a message on the answering machine at Bob's office." He turned his back to me, avoiding my glare.

"You didn't tell me that before."

"I'm telling you now."

I knew with absolute certainty he had spoken to someone besides answering machines yesterday, and with as much certainty, I knew who that someone was.

"You talked to Coral, didn't you?"

A muscle on his back twitched. He decided to play it lightheartedly. "You caught me, love, but there's no need to be jealous. I let Coral know we weren't coming to Legacy Lodge. No sense having her worry about us."

"Oh." I felt deflated at his easy admission, annoyed that he had called Coral, but more annoyed that he hadn't admitted the call to start with. "Did you tell her we'd be here?"

"No. I didn't know where we'd be." Mark threw down some papers. "I have a pretty good idea of what this audit showed, but it doesn't hang together unless Bob can fill in the blanks with the right data. Do you understand me?"

Of course I didn't. How could anyone understand a person so flip and oblique as this man? I did understand he wanted to distract me from the previous topic. "What else did you and Coral talk about?"

He swung around to grin at me. "Still jealous?"

"Don't count on it."

The eyes narrowed with his sigh. He ran a hand through his wavy mane. "Look, love, it's like this. I don't know, but I suspect, this audit was for energy planning purposes."

I picked up the damp towel off the floor and hung it on a rod. "I can follow that much. I'm not a complete idiot."

"You're not an idiot at all."

His compliment brought me no pleasure. After six years, I recognized a stalling tactic when I saw one. "Go on. The audit was for energy planning purposes."

"All right, say this company, GENSYN Oil, isn't trying to find oil reserves in north Georgia." He leaned back in his chair, put one foot up on the table, and crossed it with the other. His bare legs were muscled and fit, his stomach flat and hard. "Studies have been done on the soil in that area. You're right about oil there being unlikely."

I stopped staring at his body, squashed the tingle building inside my own. "All right. Then what is this company doing?"

"Aha." The feet swung down to the floor as he sat up straight and turned back to the desk. "That's my question." He fumbled through some sheets, came up with a payable worksheet he handed to me. "Look at this. Thousands of dollars spent on chemicals, thousands more spent on plants. Green plants. In particular, kudzu—"

"Kudzu?" That was the last thing I was expecting. "Kudzu?" He must be mistaken. "Let me see that."

Sure enough, black and white entries on the accounts payable sheets confirmed it. There were also letters Hoo had received from several sellers confirming the amounts collected for GENSYN.

Mark spoke from behind my ear. "For months, they've been buying kudzu, gradually increasing the volume. Also a lot of other chemicals."

I blinked. "Why?"

Kudzu, a vine imported from Asia to control erosion, had turned out to be more of a curse than a benefit. It was tenacious and rampant, and grew as much as a foot a day to cover and eventually wipe out entire forests if not kept down. People crafted baskets from the vine and cooked up novelty recipes using its leaves and roots, but the only practical utilizations were for animal forage and stemming erosion.

Certainly no use would involve such enormous amounts of the pesky weed as these listed on Hoo's sheets. No one in his right mind would pay for kudzu when they could start a patch and grow it with minimal effort.

My mouth gaped as I realized exactly the amounts involved. "What are they doing with this much kudzu?"

"Another good question." He took the paper back from me. "I don't know, but I've got some wild guesses. What if GENSYN is using kudzu to manufacture a synthetic fuel?"

"A synthetic fuel?" He must have lost his mind. "From kudzu? Come on. Get real. We would have heard something."

"Not necessarily. Not if it was kept secret."

He couldn't be serious. But he wasn't laughing. "No, no, that's not possible."

"Of course it is. Don't you remember Senator what's-his-name's speech at the Dream Sugar reception Saturday night? Look, Steve," he said patiently, putting the paper back in its stack. "You have this company experimenting with producing an artificial fuel. You have the Energy Department asking for an audit—"

"We don't know for sure that it was the Energy Department. Coral said it was a sub-agency. If you can believe Coral. All you know is—"

"That's one of the blanks Bob should be able to fill in," he said easily. "Now, if some branch of Energy does turn out to be involved, and if this branch is studying the feasibility of producing artificial fuel by looking at the books of a company actually making it—"

"It's been studied before," I objected again. "Lots of times. The process to make artificial fuel, ethanol or anything else, is too expensive for anyone to be able to produce any kind of volume large enough to sell in the open market. Not enough to replace gasoline. That's why they're turning to electric—"

"Ah, using the old methods to produce it. But what if this—" With his excitement, Mark strode across the room and back in his boxers. "What if this new microorganism the Senator referred to at the Dream Sugar reception really can break down any kind of green plant and convert their energy to sugars used for ethanol?"

I tried to remember the speech and failed. "Is that what he said?"

"Yes." Mark pushed his thick mane of hair back. "And what if using this process brings us nearer the point where the costs of making a synthetic fuel and the costs of producing gasoline coincide?"

That I understood. "Then we'd be better off using a renewable energy source to make a synthetic oil."

"Instead of buying or importing regular crude at high prices," Mark finished. He stopped pacing.

"What's that got to do with Hoo?"

We frowned at each other.

"I mean, if that's the case, the news will leak out sooner or later," I said. "Whoever's after Hoo's worksheets . . . What can they hope to accomplish by stealing them?"

"Hm." Mark breathed deeply. "Another good question."

He resumed pacing back and forth, running his hand through his hair, wincing as he unintentionally rubbed the cut on his temple.

"It has to be the oil interests," he said to himself. "The guy I beat up—"

"Crooked Nose," I intervened. "And he did a pretty good job on you, too."

"Crooked Nose." He looked at me but he didn't really see me. "He told me he saw his contact man alongside an oil lobbyist on TV once. He may be a lobbyist for oil interests in the Middle East or Mexico."

"Or here."

"Or here." Throwing his head back, he stretched and yawned and rubbed his eyes. "What would an oil producing country, or a conglomerate of oil companies, want with Hoo's notes?"

"Maybe they're trying to get the formula. Or make sure it stays a secret?"

"What do Hoo's notes have to do with the formula?"

"True." Hoo had mailed Mark audit papers. Obviously they were important.

"They might," I said, trying to reason it out, "need to know the breakeven point on the synthetic fuel so that they can price their oil accordingly. Low enough to keep the synthetic stuff from being developed, but high enough to take all the profit they can."

Mark's pacing stopped for the second time. He bounded over to where I stood by the dressing area and seized my upper arms. "Damn, you're smart, Steve. I believe I'll keep you."

For some reason, I picked that moment to burst into tears.

As with most men, Mark was helpless when dealing with a female on a crying jag. "Oh, God, love, don't do that." His high spirits fell away as he pulled me to him. "Please don't."

"I c-can't help it," I sobbed. "I keep thinking of Hoo and Sweet Rowdy, and those m-men at the dam. Is that what this whole thing's about? People are hurt and little d-dogs are killed, for, for . . ."

"Money," he finished quietly, still holding me close. "Money's nearly always involved in anything like this."

I disengaged myself but not without reluctance. He was substantial and comforting. After getting a tissue, I wiped my eyes and blew my nose. "Is this the kind of work you do for FIFA, Mark? Chasing down figures and adding them up to find out who's doing what? Adding up while people are being beaten, maybe dying—" My voice broke.

He looked sick.

We stood in silence for a long moment, me thinking of my baby and Mark's friend Hoo and Sweet Rowdy, and Mark thinking of God knows what.

Later, much later when it no longer mattered, I wondered if, in that particular moment, both of us weren't on the brink of opening up to one another for the first time in our marriage.

But as always, Mark drew back. "Let me get my shower. Then I'll call Bob."

While he bathed, I realized his diversionary tactics had succeeded. He still hadn't told me what additional interesting things he and Coral had discussed in his phone call the previous day.

CHAPTER THIRTEEN

WE WENT OVER to Cumberland Mall and found a Waffle House for breakfast. Afterward, I waited in the SUV, and Mark went inside the mall to get a cellphone charger.

Could I trust him?

An involvement with Coral made him susceptible to her influence. And if he wasn't involved with Coral, why had he called her yesterday?

It was obvious that she had something to do with leaking our discovery of the pen. Did he really plan to call his field office? Could he and Coral be working together toward some end I couldn't comprehend?

Either Mark had been expecting the men to intercept us at the dam or Coral had double-crossed him and sent the men without his knowing.

I couldn't believe Mark had known.

He'd admitted expecting the men at our house, but not at the dam. He had been as surprised as me despite his composure.

No, whatever Mark's feelings for Coral, the two were not in league against me. The idea was ridiculous, a remnant of the paranoia that had gripped me earlier. Mark might be impossible to understand, but he would never deliberately plot with anyone against me.

He would never do anything to hurt me.

Mark slid back into his seat, the old mask not quite hiding the fatigue about his eyes.

"Well?" I asked. "Are you going to call Bob?"

"I called from the mall." He attached his cell to the new charger and plugged it into the car outlet.

Naturally he wouldn't want me to hear his conversation. "Did he know what department contracted the audit?"

"I didn't talk to Bob." He spoke carefully, deciding how much to reveal. "I talked to Coral."

"What's the matter? Is Bob taking the whole week off and leaving Coral to manage?" The jibe slipped out.

He ignored it. "Bob's late getting in today. Coral was already there." When he leaned over to crank the car, a hank of hair, unbound because sometime during the night he'd lost his rubber band, dropped to curtain his profile.

I tried to hide my animosity. "And what did Coral have to say?"

He slung back his hair with a toss of his head and raised his brows. "Ow." He winced, having forgotten about the cut over his eye. "I think I've started bleeding again."

"No, you haven't, and don't change the subject. You didn't talk to Coral about the weather."

His mouth opened and I read his mind.

"And don't try to fob me off by accusing me of being jealous, or by telling me what intimate details of our sex life you were whispering to Coral."

"Ouch. You don't leave a man much leeway, do you?" A vestige of the old humor appeared as he pulled out of the mall and headed toward the Perimeter. "All right, ma'am, I surrender. I'll talk. Coral still says she doesn't know what Hoo was into, or exactly which government office ordered the audit. All she knows is that it's a sub-agency of the Energy Department."

I sniffed. "That's the same thing she said the other night. Do you believe her?"

"Give me some slack, will you, love? I need to watch out for these damned drivers."

Traffic around Cumberland Mall stayed busy, even on weekday mornings. Still, Mark had always been able to drive and talk simultaneously before. Dread swept me as he checked the rearview mirror. I twisted to look behind us but saw just the usual jumble of cars.

No brown pickup or any other dubious vehicle.

I sank back into my seat.

His mouth twitched. "Looking for somebody special?"

"You know what I was doing."

"Yeah, I know." He sobered as his eyes returned to the road ahead. He got into the lane for the Perimeter ramp. "Relax. I've been watching. Not one suspicious character in sight. You're as safe as in your own—" He cut himself off abruptly before finishing. "As safe as can be."

He had started to say as safe as in my own bed. The memory of waking up with the knife to my throat would stay with me always. The knowledge of my own vulnerability would never allow me to feel safe again.

And was I?

I had a hard time reading Mark's moods because he always displayed the same balanced temper, but didn't he seem grimmer than usual today? Grimmer because of something I didn't know about?

Perhaps he was simply tired.

I felt rested and relaxed after sleeping much of the past night—I refused to think about the totally, uninhibitedly awake part—but Mark had sat up late going through Hoo's notes. The night before, at the lake, he'd slept in the hammock. And Saturday night, we'd had the intruders. For two nights before that, he'd been preparing for the Dream Sugar unveiling.

He had to be exhausted.

Engrossed, I didn't realize where we headed until we got off the Perimeter onto State Road 400 going north.

"I thought your field office was inside the Perimeter."

"Gosh, I think you're right." He gasped, surprise blatantly feigned. "I guess we're headed up to the mountains."

The grim undertone from earlier must be pure fancy on my part. Mark was his usual enigmatic, incorrigible self.

"I thought we were going to take Hoo's notes to your field office."

"Did you? What gave you that idea?" Pressing the cruise control, he settled back.

Mark looked more at ease driving than anyone I'd ever seen. He lounged in his seat, paying no attention to anything, yet managing to find openings in traffic and avoid wild drivers with perfect complacency.

I had forgotten how good he drove, indeed how good he was at everything he did. From the time we'd met, he was always on top of things. Unlike me, who could barely muddle my way through. That had been part of his attraction.

Now I felt isolated, bereft, and adrift in circumstances out of my control. "Don't tease me. Where are we going?"

His glance gauged how much I could stand to hear. "Hoo's notes had the directions to the place he audited. I thought we might ride up that way."

No, I was right about his strange mood. His lips held their perennial curve, but his eyes were opaque and his jaw set deliberately, both at odds with his cheerful appearance. It didn't stem from the bruises. My sense of abandonment was real, and its origin emanated from Mark.

Mark was keeping something from me.

All the times during the past six years when I had felt this way, I'd had a valid reason. Mark had kept things from me then, too. He'd treated me like a little girl to be cosseted and protected.

Now he'd used traffic as an excuse to end our conversation about his phone call to Coral, and I had allowed it to keep from hearing what he might say.

No longer. "What else did Coral tell you?"

"That she doesn't know how those men found out about the pen."

"And that's all?"

He tried his normal evasive tactic. "What else would she tell me?"

"Don't shut me out." I didn't intend to sound so sharp. "I'm tired of being shut out. I've been shut out all our married life, and I'm sick of it. Don't think you're doing the right thing by keeping me in the dark. All you're doing is making me more certain than ever that a divorce is necessary."

"And you've never shut me out?"

The quick retort caught me by surprise. I paused, regrouped. "Not intentionally."

"Huh." With the ugly scabbing wound over his left eye combined with the vivid purple welts across the jaw, he looked menacing. "Sure of that?"

"Never intentionally," I repeated.

Despite the feelings of security he engendered when I lay beside him, I wondered again how well I knew my husband. Women had been married to murderers and rapists before and suspected nothing. I knew . . . No, I felt Mark couldn't do anything evil, but I didn't know.

I didn't know Mark at all.

I moistened my lips. "Tell me, Mark. Please. Whatever it is you're involved in, nothing could be worse than my conjectures."

"I'm not involved in anything." He concentrated on his driving, giving me his profile. Most of his bruises and cuts were hidden, bringing back the image of the obliging man I'd married. "Maybe you're right. Maybe we should stop tiptoeing around trying not to step on each other's feelings. Coral told me . . . She had some bad news."

He paused, not wanting to say the words. When he did, they came out in a rush. "They found Hoo's body last night."

My heart stopped. "His body?"

"Yes."

Hoo. Dead.

Mark didn't try to sugarcoat it, and I was grateful for that, but the truth let in empty despair. "I left him," I said to no one in particular. "I left him there alone. If I'd stayed—"

The car swerved, whipped back into its lane. "If you'd stayed, you could be dead, too," Mark snapped. He ground his teeth before continuing, his sentences coming out in rapid-fire bursts. "Don't start heaping guilt on yourself again. I'm sick and tired of you playing the martyr. Everyone's to blame for something at one time or other in their lives, and you're no better than anyone else. Everybody else picks themselves up and goes on living. You can do it, too, if you'll make the effort."

The viciousness of his attack sent me mentally reeling. This was worse than the confrontation in the Dream Sugar parking deck because this time, he had singled me and my actions out.

There was no reasonable reply. I sat in my corner of the car and tried to gather my shattered pride and keep my waffle from coming back up as we sped toward the small county in north Georgia and the location of the company a dead man had audited.

* * * *

"THERE'S NOTHING HERE but woods."

Having recovered, at great effort, my composure after Mark's unmerciful and personal assault, I surveyed the thick trees and unkempt undergrowth of the wilderness around us as we jounced over a dirt road in need of grading and gravel. "Why would anyone put a business out in the middle of nowhere? Are you sure the directions are right?"

Mark cut the wheel to avoid a deep rut. "Oh, yes. This is the place all right."

"But there's nothing here," I repeated, holding on to the strap over the door for dear life.

"Sure there is." The SUV stopped without warning. "And right here it is."

We had come to a solid metal gate chained shut on which the words KEEP OUT were painted in bold letters. Attached to the gate, a daunting fence ran out of sight on both sides. It was at least nine feet high and made of sheets of plywood put together without breaks to conceal what lay behind. When we got out for a closer inspection, we saw a smaller notice to the side.

A warning that the enclosed premises were United States government property and that trespassers would be vigorously prosecuted, substantial fines levied, and stringent jail terms handed down. No exceptions.

Mark perused the sign. "Sounds like a threat to me."

"Is this GENSYN Oil?"

The area around us was deserted. A forlorn air hung over the trees and road and rocks in a way peculiar to sites once bustling with traffic before being abandoned due to economic recessions or company relocations.

"Has to be." A breeze ruffled Mark's hair, lifted the ends, and playfully draped one strand around his chin. He shook the chain in case the padlock opened, but it held securely.

"There's no sign saying it's GENSYN. And why would they put up a fence like this without having a guard on duty at the gate?"

The absolute hush, with no raucous birds or chattering squirrels to soften the surrounding woods, got on my nerves.

"I'd think there would be workers needing to get in and out. Unless they're closed on Tuesdays."

Mark paced alongside the fence.

I noted his purposeful steps with alarm. He was searching for an opening. "Where are you going?"

"I'm going to walk this fence a little way. You can sit in the car."

And be left alone in this desolate place? "No, thank you. I'll walk with you."

"Better stay here. It may be rough and I'm not going to wait." True to his words, he had already taken long strides away from the gate.

Naturally, I followed.

He hadn't lied. Keeping up with him made my tender feet throb. I'd also let myself go during the last months. Complaining muscles and tendons reminded me how out of shape I was, but I trudged after him until the area around the road gave way to wild untended woods.

At the edge of a knotted, twisted undergrowth of straggling laurel and brambles, a spreading plant resembling poison oak blocked the way. Mark had no compunction in wading through its midst.

Not me. "Mark."

He didn't answer. Another second, and he disappeared beyond the scrub trees.

"Mark!"

"Stay put a few minutes." His voice floated back. "I'll be right back."

I set off after him, pushing through the briars and avoiding the poison oak.

I hoped.

Seeing a bit of madras dropping down from a tree branch onto the other side of the fence, I stopped, scandalized.

"Mark!" Thoughts of the sign and its threats sharpened my voice. "Don't go in there. Don't you remember the signs?"

"What signs?" floated back over the high fence. "Stay there. I won't be a moment."

He knew quite well what signs I meant.

The tree he'd used to cross the fence was about eighteen inches in diameter and without any discernible footholds. How had he managed to scramble up it? I couldn't. I didn't want to climb it badly enough to try.

Fuming, I made my way through the underbrush beside the fence. There had to be an easier way to cross.

There wasn't. Whoever had erected the fence had made it tall and impossible to scale.

After some time spent pushing aside fragrant honeysuckle and dodging pine cones and getting caught in wild blackberry bushes, I stumbled over a root and fell, rolling head over heels down a low embankment.

I sat up, groaning. No real damage, though. What were a few more scratches added to my growing collection? Besides, the layer of dirt and leaves would probably hide them.

Discouraged, I floundered to the top of the bank and brushed myself off before limping back to the spot where Mark had disappeared. At the tree, I searched up and down it for footholds I might have missed seeing.

I ought to at least make an attempt to cross the fence, but one of us in trouble was enough. If Mark got caught, I'd have to bail him out.

If the feds allowed prisoners bail.

All right. I was a coward. So what? Lots of people were cowards.

If I hadn't been one, I would have helped Hoo up to the cottage. He would have been safe with me while I called for help.

And I'd have been taken away by his murderers. Maybe killed like him.

Mark was right. Guilty of abandoning Hoo I might be, but what was done, was done.

I tramped back toward the gate simply to be doing something, to help contain annoyance with the delinquent Mark and discontent with my own character.

At the locked entrance, the signs stared at me ominously.

"I hope you have to pay a fine and serve time," I muttered balefully to my absent husband. "It would teach you a lesson for ignoring rules."

No one appeared to catch him in his disreputable activities. Unless a watchman waited inside the grounds or someone else came along, Mark seemed to be in no danger of imminent arrest.

Too bad. The thought of Mark behind bars appealed to me.

For about five seconds.

If he got caught, I'd be caught, too.

To the left, I spied another small sign on a post nearly covered by some kind of vegetation. The vine didn't look like poison ivy but to be on the safe side, I found a stick to push back the clinging tendrils.

The metal of the sign was bent and rusted. I could barely make out the letters spelling out Helton Industries.

Helton Industries. A well-known engineering firm, it employed hundreds of people in plants through the United States. It also worked closely with the government, often leasing its facilities for special contracts.

So Helton owned this property that the government had placed a warning sign on.

Wasn't there something about Helton owning a north Georgia tract of land that I ought to recall? A few minutes of hard thinking brought back bits and pieces of nearly forgotten information.

Yes, Helton Industries had owned acreage up here at one time. A newspaper article years ago had reported on their holdings in this county. But what had it said?

I chewed on my lip. Something about how the old Helton Industries property had been condemned and boarded up. How vandals were sneaking inside despite the fence and warning sign. The article had pointed out how dangerous it was because . . . because . . .

Damn, damn, double-damn. Why couldn't I remember?

Frustrated, I started back to where Mark had disappeared. His faculty for collecting all kinds of weird and unusual trivia amazed everyone. Perhaps if I told him what I recalled, he could add more. At the end of the open area, I stared at the tree he had climbed and shivered. I wished he would hurry and come back so we could get out of this spooky, melancholy place.

Spooky place. Helton Industries in north Georgia.

They were doing some kind of experiments for the government, weren't they? Fuel experiments, maybe? But not synthetic fuel. No, synthetic fuel didn't sound right.

Something touched my back.

I screamed and hit out.

"Hey." Mark grabbed my wrists for self-protection. "Hold on, love, it's just me."

"You imbecile!" Fright turned to anger. I shook all over. "Why did you sneak up on me like that? Don't you know I've been scared to death, worrying whether or not someone was going to catch you and put you in jail?"

Amusement wrinkled his nose. "I'm fine." His fingers kneaded my wrists and then slid up. Their warmth pervaded my entire body and eased my shivering. "And gratified to know you were worried about me."

"You?" I disabused him of the notion that his safety was my main concern. "I was worried about having to pay a fine to get you out of jail. And you have the car keys. I wouldn't have had a way home." I looked over his shoulder. "Where did you come from?"

"Couldn't find a place to climb out. Had to loop back about a hundred yards," he replied cheerfully. Trespassing might have been an everyday event.

Even trespassing on a dangerous piece of ground like this.

Dangerous ground.

Another snippet of the newspaper item came back.

Remonstrances were forgotten.

"Now I remember! This is where Helton Industries did all those experiments for the government." His hands continued to hold my upper arms as I seized his shoulders and shook them. "This property is supposed to be radioactive."

He took my news calmly. "Yes, that's right."

"You knew it and you went in there anyway?" My voice rose. "How could you be so stupid?"

The Mark I thought I knew would never have done such a thing. Not without a good reason.

He didn't defend himself, but his hands dropped away from my arms, leaving mine with no choice except to draw away from his shoulders. He isolated me again, kept me wrapped in cotton wool, left questions unanswered and fears disregarded.

All right. I could be non-communicative, too. I wouldn't beg.

"Ready to go?" He headed back toward the gate.

Struggling with my pride, I followed.

Pride lost. "Mark, why did you go in that place?"

"To see what was there." The rhythm of his step never broke.

"Did you find what you were looking for?"

"I didn't find anything."

I hurried to catch up. "What about a factory? The one using the kudzu?"

"There was a building that looked like a factory."

A fantastic idea struck me. I grabbed his arm. "Do you suppose the government put out those warnings about radioactive property to keep people away? So they could secretly work on a synthetic fuel?"

The lines around his eyes deepened, but I could see he was preoccupied. He used my hand on his arm to pull me close, so that he could reach around and bite at the lobe of my ear. "You know as much as I do. Let's go."

My ear lobe tingled from his mouth. It was unfair, the methods he used to sidetrack me from my train of thought. "You've got no right to do that to my ear."

"I had to do it to your ear." He plucked a leaf from my hair.

"You've got dirt and leaves everywhere else. You ought to brush yourself off. Who've you been rolling around on the ground with?"

I would never understand him. Never.

* * * *

BEFORE WE NEARED the Perimeter, Mark chose an exit and pulled into a fast food place with a sign advertising chicken.

At the sign, my heart sank. My stomach threatened mutiny. "We ate hamburgers yesterday for lunch and fried fish last night and waffles this morning. I'm sick and tired of junk food."

So what if I sounded like a sulky five-year-old? I refused to continue suffering in silence.

Mark undid his seat belt and opened his door to get out.

"Did you hear me?" I wouldn't budge. "I don't want greasy fried chicken for lunch. I want a salad. I want veggies."

"Hm?" Mark looked at me with faraway eyes. He closed his door, carefully so that its latch barely clicked, and reached for my hand. "Okay. Sure. Look, Steve," he began.

He'd already forgotten my rebellion against junk food.

I steeled myself for what was to come.

He played with my hand, tracing the outline where my wedding ring should have been, making a circle of his fingers and putting them around mine. "I don't like holding on to this package Hoo left me."

"I'm not happy about it either, but what else can we do?" I snatched my hand away. "Besides, we know what's in it now. And they have to know that we know. So won't they give up?"

"I don't think it matters." He chose his words with care. "I don't think that our knowing what's in the envelope will make a difference to these people. I don't think it's safe for us to keep it."

Not safe. "You think they'll still be after Hoo's papers? Won't our knowing what they want cut down on the audit's value to them?"

"Hoo died to keep his work from these people," he said dryly. "I don't think they're going to quit trying to get it simply because you and I happen to have seen his papers."

I hadn't thought that far ahead. I had assumed that once we recovered the package, things would go back to normal.

No wonder Mark thought me naïve. "Should we make a copy then? In case we lose the originals?" To those people.

He grinned in the familiar upbeat way. "Costs too much."

"Will you please stop—?"

He cut out the teasing. "No, I don't think we need go that far, Steve."

"Why not? If they're after—"

Mark took a patient breath. "The people wanting this package can't have access to the records Hoo used or they wouldn't be trying so desperately to get these reports. FIFA has access. Hoo's computer should have backed up to theirs daily. Or, if something went wrong, they can always do another audit."

"Oh." I finally understood. "FIFA will be able to re-create the reports."

"Right. And copying the papers would double the odds these people might get hold of one of the sets. Now, any suggestions on what we do?"

"Destroy them?"

"I don't want to do that. Not until I'm sure FIFA does have all of Hoo's data."

"Put them back in the envelope and mail it to FIFA."

He remained unnaturally serious. "No. I don't want to chance them getting lost. I think what we'll do is put the envelope in one of the public lockers at Perimeter Mall. Then we can give Bob the key and let him worry about it."

From the way he spoke, I knew he had reasoned everything out before talking to me and made a decision. I sighed. At least, he had consulted me. Even if it was after the fact.

* * * *

ONCE WE LEFT the package safely stowed away, we stopped at a cafeteria in the mall. Starving for real food, I filled my tray till it overflowed. When we got to a booth, Mark unloaded his and made a beeline to the restrooms.

Another call to the field office, I bet.

My appetite shrank markedly, but I set a fluffy piece of pie to the side and started on the rest. Spinach salad, blackened grouper, broccoli rice casserole, scalloped potatoes, grilled veggies, and homemade rolls.

If he caught Coral, he'd tell her the location of Hoo's package. Naturally.

He sauntered back in a few minutes. "We're to meet Bob in an hour," he said, sliding into his chair and beginning to eat.

"Just Bob? Or Bob and Coral?" I couldn't help the tiny ironic twist I gave her name.

The fork stopped halfway to his mouth, before finishing its trip with its load of green beans.

"Just Bob," he said after chewing and swallowing. At the same time, he gave me a speculative look that bordered on amusement and made me flush.

"I'm not jealous of Coral."

"I like the way your eyes shoot little blue sparks when you're mad."

"And I'm not mad. I'm worried."

"You needn't be." He made a sweeping gesture with his empty fork. "Coral's a good friend, but that's all."

"I don't care what Coral is to you!" I gritted my teeth, remembered the people around us, and lowered my voice. "I'm worried because—"

I stopped short of blaming Coral for setting the men on us at the dam. I told myself my reticence stemmed from knowing Mark would laugh at me. But deep inside, a part of me acknowledged the truth. He might be angry rather than amused at my accusations. Angry because he cared too much for Coral.

Maybe I was wrong. Maybe Mark wasn't keeping Coral informed of our every movement. Maybe she wasn't the one responsible for Mark's bruises and my injuries.

For whatever reason, I closed my mouth. Let him misconstrue my concern however he liked.

He pushed his plate aside, complacency written all over him. "Better not eat all that dessert. Bob's meeting us at an ice cream place."

"You should have told me earlier," I snapped over the remains of my coconut cream pie.

"Didn't know," he said cheerfully.

"Why can't we take the package to Bob's office?"

Mark put his napkin to the side and his elbows on the table to consider me. "Whoever wants Hoo's papers is certain to know where the field office is and is probably watching it. We don't want to have any more unpleasant incidents."

I pushed away the unfinished pie, my appetite gone.

CHAPTER FOURTEEN

INSIDE THE COZY ice cream parlor with its red-checked curtains blocking the afternoon sun, glass-topped tables and white wrought-iron chairs stood ready to accommodate customers. Customers who, in this modern age of bustle and scurry, preferred to dash in, purchase their cups or cones, and dash out to eat on the run.

Though a constant flow of people came to stand at the counter and contemplate the list of flavors before making a decision, ours was the sole occupied table. I was full from lunch but couldn't help eyeing Mark's banana split.

Bob Colverton, Mark's field manager, had been waiting for us when we arrived.

A plump man in his forties, with thinning hair and round face, he peered through thick spectacles while popping the last bite of a waffle cone into his mouth. He carefully ignored an untouched locker key that lay on the table in front of him.

"Sorry, dude," he said to Mark, "I can't help you. Main Office says they don't want me handling Ogden's stuff."

I thought he looked relieved, not sorry at all.

When Mark said nothing, he went on, "They're sending a special courier for them." He raised hopeful brows. "Unless you want to deliver them yourself?"

"Coral's down here." Beneath a sign boasting two hundred twenty flavors of ice cream and yogurt, Mark lounged back in the chair much as he did when he drove. He looked lazy and comfortable and not dangerous at all if you discounted the marks of combat. Nor did he seem dismayed at Bob's revelation. "What's to keep her from taking the papers back with her?"

Bob took off his glasses and polished them in obvious discomfort. "Well, er, actually, there's a little problem."

"With Coral? I would think she'd be the logical person to take charge of them." Mark toyed with the half-eaten banana split. Occasionally, he made a desultory attempt to fish out the cherry.

He might be determined to ignore the signals, but instinct told me what Bob didn't want to say. "You think Coral might be how those men found out about the pen, don't you, Bob?"

I thought so, too, but until now, hadn't been brave enough to voice my suspicions to Mark.

"Well." Bob put on his glasses and brushed at crumbs on the table. "It's certainly a possibility."

Mark, on my right, threw down his spoon. He made no move to pick up the key.

A family came into the shop, the father holding the hand of a little boy about three feet high. A young baby with a pink ribbon circling her fuzzy head clung to her mother's neck.

My eyes lingered on the baby as the man behind the counter waited on them. The father said something to the small boy and grinned at his response. The mother joined in with a jolly laugh.

The baby, mouth open in a toothless grin, reached up and pulled at the mother's hair.

The mother laughed harder.

I looked down at my hands.

Bob, aware of Mark's resentment, amended his words, "That is to say, I don't think Coral intentionally did anything wrong. But Main Office is wondering how these people knew you were on your way to Legacy Lodge with Ogden's pen, Mark."

Mark sounded deceptively gentle. "I've wondered about that myself."

I voiced my secret belief. "They think Coral was the one who passed along the information, Bob. Is that right?"

Bob gave Mark an apologetic look as he used a napkin to dab at a spot of yogurt on his tie. "It does seem strange. I know you and Coral go back a long way, Mark, but you must admit it's strange. And she might not have realized the importance of it."

"I've certainly considered Coral." Across the glass-topped table, Mark's affable expression didn't change. "On the other hand, there were people besides Coral who knew we would be crossing the dam, Bob. You, for instance."

"Me? No, I did not." Bob sat upright, words tumbling out to repudiate Mark's accusation. "My family and I went up Friday afternoon to Chattanooga. We took a cruise on the riverboat Saturday and spent all day Sunday at the Aquarium and drove home Monday. I'd promised my wife a getaway weekend, strictly family. I turned off my company phone and left it at the office. That's why I didn't know a thing about all this till late yesterday."

Mark didn't say anything.

"You can check with Flo if you don't believe me." Bob leaned over the table. "She knows my phone was here because she stuck it in her desk drawer when she left work Friday. I had to ask her where it was this morning because I thought I'd misplaced it."

The young family got their ice creams, cones for the father and son, a cup for the mother, and sat down at a table on the far end of the shop.

Mark's eyes had followed mine, and Bob his, so that we watched, all three of us, as the small family arranged themselves. The father placed the small boy into a booster seat and the mother settled the baby on her lap.

"How convenient," Mark said at last in a neutral tone.

Bob spluttered. "Now look. I'm not involved in this. I tell you I didn't know anything about you being involved till I heard the message Coral left me."

Mark shifted in his seat. "I'm not accusing you of anything. Don't get excited."

"I'm not excited." Bob, willing to be mollified, bounced the wrought-iron chair backward and took off his glasses to fidget with them.

"I guess Coral didn't know you'd be gone this weekend." Mark picked up his spoon. "When she found out Hoo had left his pen with Steve, she planned for you to meet us at Legacy Lodge."

"Coral might not have known." Bob replaced his glasses on his nose. "Flo said she didn't talk to her. But I can't see that it matters. Coral's the only person who knew you'd found that pen. And she knew you'd have to cross the dam to get to Legacy Lodge." A trace of yogurt on one side of his mouth marred the effect of Bob's sanctimonious nod. "No, if Coral isn't your leak, it's someone else she talked to. Not me."

"If you didn't know we were on the way to Legacy Lodge, it has to be Coral." I avoided Mark's face by watching the mother feed ice cream from her cup to the baby.

The locker key reflected a ray of sunlight as it lay on the checkered tablecloth.

Mark fiddled with his cherry, pushing it around and around. "It doesn't matter at this point."

I'd been holding my breath and released it in a rush.

Mark didn't blame Coral for what had happened at the dam, but I couldn't understand his reluctance to see the truth. He was usually so reasonable, so logical.

Unless he and Coral had resumed their relationship.

That might explain his reaction, but it didn't explain the weight that settled on my heart.

"The main problem is those reports. I want to get rid of them." Mark looked up from his cherry to address Bob, abandoning the debate of who had known our plans. "Steve's been assaulted and nearly died because someone thought she had access to them. I want them as far away from her as possible. I want you to keep them till FIFA gets someone down to pick them up."

Bob shook his head. "Sorry, can't help you. Abner says they stay with you till the courier comes. It ain't my hot potato, pal. It's yours."

Mark, spoon paused over the cherry, considered him. "Are the papers really that important?"

"Guess so. Don't know. First time I heard anything about them was when Abner called last week, told me to meet Ogden and help him draft his final report. He didn't give me a clue as to what Hoo was working on. Whatever it was must have been too valuable to be trusted to me." He thought a second before adding, "Must still be." He didn't look sorry.

Customers, a chattering trio of one man and two women, came in, were served amid much noisy dialogue with the counterman, and left.

Mark waited until the door closed. "So you don't know what the project was about, or who contracted the audit?"

"Nope," Bob said. "I don't know a thing about any of it because I never got a chance to go over Ogden's work. I went to meet him, but he never showed."

Putting down his spoon, Mark used his fingers to go after the cherry in the midst of the melted ice cream. At the same time, he eyed the key on the table with hostility. "All right, who's picking up the papers and when?"

Bob eyed him uneasily. "Brown. Joel Brown. Flying in this afternoon. You know him."

"Yeah." Capable fingers lifted the cherry. "What do you suggest Steve and I do in the meantime? Do you want this, Steve?"

"Want what?" So he still refused to admit Coral might have revealed our whereabouts.

"This cherry."

I did—my lunch seemed long ago—but shook my head. "No."

Mark popped the cherry into his own mouth and licked the sticky residue off his fingertips. His grin at Bob bared his teeth.

"And your suggestion is?"

Bob didn't budge. "Up to you, guy. There's a MARTA train going downtown or there's the mall up on the hill. Good places to get lost in, either one."

I was confused. "Shouldn't we stay at your office? Wait there for whoever's picking up the reports?"

Both men looked at me with indulgence.

It was my husband who explained, eyes narrowed and lips curved into something resembling a smile. "Bob doesn't want us there, Steve.

We're a little too, um, popular, for Bobby to have around the office just now. Right, Bob?"

"'Fraid so, guys." The bottle lenses couldn't conceal Bob's harassed expression. "Look," he explained to me, "The office is just that. A field office. It consists of me and Flo. We don't have any security because we've never needed any. You and Mark would be sitting ducks if the folks looking for Ogden's papers discovered you were there. Chances are they're watching now, waiting for you to show up. I made sure I wasn't followed, but you don't want to go near the office."

"No," Mark agreed in a toneless voice. "Guess not."

"And, uh, Coral's in and out, too." Bob ducked his head awkwardly. "Main Office thinks you ought to stay away from her. Till they make sure, you know?"

"Yeah." My husband retrieved the locker key. "We can't count on your help. And Coral's under suspicion. So you think we should go downtown or to the mall?"

"Yep." Bob inhaled, relief obvious. "Either place. Lose yourselves for an hour or so. Call me about four. I should know then where you'll be meeting the courier."

"About four," Mark repeated.

With a brief farewell, Bob pushed back his chair. Mark and I sat at the glass-topped table and watched him go.

The little boy at the other end dropped his ice cream cone on the floor and howled. Father and mother, after the first unanimous exclamations of shock, scurried around to clean up the mess and utter soothing noises. They bought him another cone.

Mark bought me one, too, but the ice cream didn't cause the coldness in my stomach.

* * * *

MARK TRIED TO leave me.

After our talk with Bob Colverton, we checked into another motel near the Perimeter where we showered and shampooed, getting rid of the north Georgia dirt and any stray ticks or other insects picked up tramping around the woods.

At this rate of bathing, my hair would start falling out from dryness.

Afterward, as Mark shook out his rumpled clothes and put them back on, he said, in his nonchalant way that revealed so little and meant so much, "I've got to go out. I'll be back as soon as I can."

I rocketed from the bed where I'd collapsed in my nightgown, the only clean thing I had to wear despite it being three-thirty in the afternoon, and rushed over to block the door before proceeding to tell him in no uncertain terms that he wasn't about to abandon me and leave me stranded in a strange motel room by myself.

"Well, all right," he said, putting on a long-suffering look that wouldn't have fooled a child. "I thought I'd go out and buy some more underwear. I could use some feminine advice if you want to join me."

I didn't budge from my post in front of the door. "I let you use that excuse to keep me from overhearing your phone calls. I'm through playing the game your way."

"Oh. Okay. I'll stay here and we'll make mad passionate love. Like we did last night," he said heartlessly. His tone lowered, became intimate. He put both hands against the door, trapping me between his arms as he leaned forward. "This time, I'll start out on top and you can end up there. How about it?"

"Stop making a joke of everything." I snatched at one of his arms with both hands and slung it aside. A beginning hysteria launched into a black upward spiral. "You're not leaving me, I tell you."

"Steve." He uttered my name quietly, dispassionately, and aimed a pointed stare at the red mark on his arm where I had pinched him. "You'll be all right. You're quite safe here, and I have things to do."

The mind-bending spiral reached the top.

I fell on him, shrieking and hitting.

All my anger so carefully controlled, all my fears, all my frustration, all my grief, everything came pouring out in an incoherent rambling statement that Mark couldn't possibly have understood because I didn't understand it myself.

I remember hearing Sweet Rowdy's name and Hoo's name, and bewailing my isolation and Mark's detachment, and blaming myself for losing the baby and Mark for his hard heart that capitalized on my loss by turning it into art.

I beat on his chest and bawled.

"Steve, Steve." Mark was shaken out of his indifference as he tried to catch hold and calm me. "Love, please. Don't do this to yourself."

I knocked away his hands and sobbed about his insensibility and generally behaved like a demented woman who ought to be locked away. "Don't you see? I don't know you. I've never known you, I thought I did but I don't. You won't let me get close to you, you're so damned independent and you don't want me to do anything for you and I'm always afraid of saying the wrong thing, doing the wrong thing, I can't stand it anymore."

The phrases poured out of me by rote. No time for stammering or stuttering while I groped for words. I knew too well what I had been feeling for too long. "You won't let me share what you feel. I never know what you're thinking, what you aren't telling me, whether you're leaving things out I ought to know."

"Steve—"

"And you laugh everything off, like everything's funny, even your friend's murder and Sweet Rowdy's death and our baby, our own baby. You just shrug and crack a joke and I'm so tired of you making fun of everything when I'm hurting."

"Don't." He caught my flailing wrists, pulled me to him. "Steve, love, please stop tearing yourself up like this."

"No!" I twisted in his embrace, fought a useless battle against his hold. "I can't stand it when you laugh and you should be crying, when I'm crying because it hurts so much inside. You're wrong, Mark. I am capable of hating. I hate you, oh, I do hate you."

By that time, despite my struggles, he had me encompassed tightly in his arms, cocooned so I couldn't move. "Love, love," he crooned, "don't you know I laugh to keep from crying? Don't you know I die inside whenever you hurt? Don't, Steve, don't. I can't bear to see you like this. Steve, love. Please."

Depleted, mentally and physically, I laid my head on his shoulder and let the beating of my heart subside. I could see the back of his neck, a tiny vein pulsating beneath the hair as he held me and murmured my name over and over.

Empty. Nothing inside me but emptiness.

All the emotions kept bottled inside for the past six years had gushed out in a torrent as relentless as the release of the waters from the dam. And like the flood waters, they had washed my soul downstream against its will, carrying it to a point from which my old self might never emerge.

My heart, that part comprising the core of my soul and spirit, was numb.

We stood unmoving, me locked in Mark's clasp, for what seemed like hours.

Eventually, his warmth reached me, comforted me, gave me back the familiar security.

A great sadness fell over me, but I didn't know why.

"That wasn't true." My words broke into the steady rhythm of his heartbeat. "What I said. I don't hate you. I didn't mean that. I'm tired and very afraid. Don't leave me alone."

"No." His voice, muffled against my hair, sounded as sad as I felt. "No, I won't leave you."

* * * *

AN HOUR LATER, we behaved like two strangers, polite but ill-at-ease in each other's company, when Mark pulled his SUV into the lot of a large hotel off the Perimeter. I didn't know why we were here, but my outburst had convinced him he couldn't leave me behind.

With as little to say getting out of the car as during the ride, we entered a side door of the hotel, then shunned lobby and elevators to walk up three flights to a room halfway down the hall.

Mark knocked.

After a rustle at the peephole, the door opened to reveal Coral with bare feet. "Marco."

I took a step back. Bob had clearly warned Mark to stay away from Coral.

"Do you have Hoo's package?" was her first question to him after she gave me a dismissive glance. She drew back and motioned us in.

I hung back, but Mark pulled me inside. "No, but it's in a safe place."

The hotel room, done in Dresden blue and white with burgundy accents, showed no hint of wear. Two blue upholstered Queen Anne chairs sat on sculpted carpet beside a round table and a straight wooden chair at a desk.

An ordinary hotel room except for signs of Coral's occupancy everywhere. An open suitcase on the dresser. A laptop on the desk. A briefcase on the floor. A book and nail file on a night table. A purse on the round table between the two armchairs. Satin house slippers beside the bed.

Mark stepped between a pair of red heels kicked off by impatient feet, lying haphazardly in the middle of the floor. Crossing the room, he pulled back the drapery and looked outside. Satisfied, he fell uninvited into one of the wing chairs.

I stood, uncertain as to what we were doing here.

Coral, instead of taking the other arm chair, chose to perch on a section of bed across from Mark. Her knees almost brushed his.

Taking the desk chair let me see them both, inspect Coral's neat navy dress and meticulous makeup. I brushed at a dirt stain on the knee of my jeans.

"Where have you been since yesterday, Marco?" Coral scanned his bruises. "What's up?"

Mark told her forthrightly what Bob had implied.

Her jaw dropped. "Bob thinks I put those people on you?" One outstretched hand, its nails matching the scarlet trim of her short navy dress, beat at her chest to exhibit her disbelief. "You know better than that."

"Sure." Mark threw off a chair cushion and settled back, giving her knees plenty of space. "So who'd you tell?"

Coral's smooth forehead wrinkled. "I left a message, several of them, on Bob's office phone and cell after Steve found the pen. When he never got back to me, I thought it important enough to call Abner at home. He said to wait for you at Legacy Lodge and take charge of whatever Hoo had left."

Mark slid further back in the chair and put his elbows on its arms. He planted his feet apart, flat on the floor, ready to hop up at a moment's notice. "You didn't talk to anybody else?"

"To the state investigators when I identified Hoo's body. But I didn't say anything about him leaving anything. I didn't think that was any of their business."

"No, it wasn't," my husband agreed at once, as if accustomed to employing his evasive techniques on the authorities as well as me. "Anybody else?"

"No. Except you."

Mark believed her. I didn't understand why, but I tried to give her the benefit of the doubt. "Could someone have heard the message you left for Bob on his office phone, someone who told those men we were coming to Legacy Lodge?" My back stayed prim and erect in the straight chair. "Like his secretary?"

They looked at me in amusement, the two of them merging into that solidarity that excluded me, the solidarity that I detested.

Coral spoke first. "Flo?"

"It's possible." Mark could be a lenient parent humoring a child's imaginings.

Coral wasn't as tactful. "Flo's been at that office longer than Bob. Besides, she wouldn't have known what to make of the little I said."

"Okay." Dislike swelled. *Keep an open mind about Coral.* "What about somebody else. Could someone have broken into the office and listened to your message and understood it?"

The lines about Mark's eyes deepened. "I'm sure Bob would have mentioned his office being broken into."

He was laughing at me.

"If Bob's telling us the truth." Coral crossed her legs and tapped one long red nail against a dimpled knee.

She and Mark looked at one another, sharing an unwelcome conjecture.

Bob Colverton had accused Coral. Coral shifted the suspicion right back to Bob.

"Bob was gone." I broke into their tacit exchange. "In Chattanooga the whole weekend. Till Monday morning."

Mark and Coral both shrugged in a way that dismissed my objection as immaterial. My hackles rose at their collusive, patronizing manner.

Damn them both, I was not a spoiled child. Why did they make me feel that way? Why couldn't I be on the same wave length with them?

"Hey, people." I laid my cards on the table. "I'm not used to anything like this, but obviously, the two of you are." My voice grew brittle. "You'll have to spell things out for me, make them a little clearer before I can follow you. My ideas may seem stupid to you, but I may be able to help."

Mark was quick to reassure me. Too quick, perhaps. "Your ideas aren't stupid. And you have a good point. Bob may have been in Chattanooga as he claims. Or not. So far as I know, no one's checked."

Coral nodded as if willing to go along with Mark, as if humoring the poor little wife. "Or Bob's family may have gone to Chattanooga without him. We have no way of knowing whether or not he heard my messages and passed them on to someone."

"We have no way of knowing whether you're telling the truth either." I carefully kept my face impassive.

"I'll vouch for Coral," Mark said quietly.

Coral saw my involuntary flinch and laughed outright. "Oooh. You didn't have to put it so unequivocally, Marco. Now your puppy thinks the worst of us." She stood up and sat back down on the bed with one leg curled beneath her. Toenails at the end of sleek feet were painted the same red as her fingernails.

I swallowed. "I only wonder whether anyone can vouch for another person's honesty."

Would Mark have taken my word as quickly as he had accepted Coral's?

"Mark's known me for, hmmm." Coral calculated in her head. "Fourteen, fifteen years? Has it been that long?"

"Fifteen this fall," he said promptly. "You and Hoo and I started college together at the Institute. I was fresh out of the army, and you and Hoo were babies, still wet behind the ears."

Coral put up a hand but not before I saw her stricken face. "Hoo was such a happy person. Slow sometimes, but so sweet no one cared."

"That's something I've wondered about." Mention of their friend did not affect Mark as it had Coral, but then I knew firsthand how impervious to sorrow he was. His attention stayed focused on the problem at hand. He could postpone grief indefinitely. "Hoo was, like you say, a nice guy but not always quick on the uptake. Why did Abner assign him to something like this?"

Coral dropped a hand, turned its palm up in query. "Why not? It was a simple audit."

"It's turned out to be fatal."

Coral twisted the huge ruby round and round her finger. "No one knew what would happen."

Mark yawned, stretching his arms over his head and his feet out before him. A patch of bare ankle showed between the khakis and his deck shoes. His right leg came within inches of Coral's left knee. "Hoo's specialty was small departments of government. Why did they pick him for this audit?"

"The contract came through the government." Coral got up and moved past him to draw back the heavy burgundy drape from her window. "I'd guess they asked for him." She peered out at the view of parking lot and surrounding buildings as Mark had done. "They know Hoo . . . Knew him from his dealings with the different departments. They must have asked for him."

"That makes sense."

Dropping the heavy curtain, Coral stepped over to frown down at him. "But you don't believe it."

The moment Coral voiced the words, I knew she was right. She could read my husband better than I. Of course, she'd known him for fifteen years. She'd had more time to learn him.

I wondered how long they'd lived together, whether they slept together when they worked together.

Nausea started in my stomach, had to be forcibly kept down.

I shouldn't have insisted on coming with Mark.

CHAPTER FIFTEEN

I DON'T CARE.

It didn't matter to me what Coral was to Mark.

When I found each of my hands squeezing the other, I forced them to relax. I parted them and made them rest on my thighs in a casual manner that would cause no comment, reveal none of my discord.

Coral dropped back onto the bed under Mark's considering stare.

"Which government agency ordered the audit, Coral?"

Coral's eyelashes flew up to her brows. "Marco." She put a finger to her lips. "That's confidential. Even if they'd told me. You know better than to ask something like that."

"You know which one it was, wild woman, and I know you know."

Coral might be his friend or more, but Mark was as implacable with her as with anyone. I was glad Coral was the object of his unswerving tenacity.

"Come on, I won't tell Abner that you blabbed. Which agency?"

Coral crossed her legs and swung her foot back and forth. "I've already told you. A sub-agency of the Energy Department."

"I have a connection at the Energy Department who checked for me. They have no record of FIFA being hired."

Coral's foot stopped swinging. "If it was one of their sub-agencies, they wouldn't, would they? You'd have to go directly to the sub-agency involved."

"Tell me, Coral." Mark didn't relent. "You know."

"I can't." Her voice murmured. Her lashes drooped. Her mouth pouted. "Don't ask."

The thing that resembled a smile curved Mark's lips. His eyes were hard. "Then call Abner and tell him I can't produce Hoo's papers."

"Marco, you're going to get me and you both in trouble." A red-tipped toe reached across and played with his calf. "Big trouble."

His leg didn't respond. "Call him right now."

She drew her toe back and stuck both hands up in the air, fingers spread in concession. "The Office of Renewable Energy Alternatives." The tone was wry, the implication unmistakable.

"Okay." Mark nodded as though he had known she would give

in. As though he knew what she would say. "That fits Steve's theory. We're to call Bob in a half hour or so." He yawned again.

He must be exhausted.

Mark went on, "He's going to tell us where to meet the courier. What do you think about that?"

"Bob?" Coral's raised brows exhibited doubts.

Mark pulled in his legs and uncoiled his lanky frame from the chair. "That's what I think, too. I believe I'll set up other arrangements with Abner myself."

She looked away. "That might be best."

I didn't like Mark telling Coral his plans. His affection for her might blind him to her faults, but I didn't trust her.

Assuming Bob told the truth, and he seemed more credible than Coral, there was no getting around the fact that Coral had known that Mark and I would be traveling over the dam yesterday to get to Legacy Lodge.

What's more, the time between my finding the pen and our reaching the dam had been slightly over half an hour. To get to the dam in thirty minutes, the men must have been no farther away than the Perimeter.

Say, for instance, this hotel.

On the other hand, the length of time to the dam from Legacy Lodge, where Coral purportedly waited at the time I discovered the pen, was also about thirty minutes.

No, I did not trust Coral at all.

Mark came past the round table to pull me up by the hand. Turning his back to Coral in an attempt at privacy, he drew me slightly aside and into the spacious dressing area of the room. "I'm going to leave you here with Coral while I run down to the lobby," he said *sotto voce.*

My face must have reflected my outrage. I opened my mouth but before anything had time to come out, he shuffled me into the bathroom and, without closing the door, spoke into my ear. "Hush, don't hurt her feelings. I know you don't trust her, love, but I do. I've worked with her too long not to. I'm asking you to have faith in my judgment."

"When it comes to Coral?" Her name stung my tongue as, like him, I whispered. Except mine came out as a hiss. "You don't think the way you feel about Coral might be clouding your judgment?"

He looked mystified. "The way I feel about Coral?"

"It's pretty obvious. You drool every time you get near her."

"Drool?" The old lines of laughter succeeded a dawning awareness. "Maybe Coral was right all along. Maybe you're jealous."

My shoulders sagged. "I am not jealous."

I was tired and empty and I wanted . . .

What? I didn't know what I wanted any more. "If you and Coral have a thing going, I don't care. Just don't let it blind you to the truth."

Mark kissed me.

He seized me by the back of the neck and the back of the waist and pulled me up against him and took my unwilling mouth and made it willing. His tongue stifled my objections, his touch reduced me to mush.

"The truth," he said, coming up for air, "is that I've known Coral for fifteen years and worked with her for eleven. And, yes, I lived with her for a year, too. Lord knows Coral has her faults, but dishonesty is not one of them. If she says she didn't tell anyone else, she didn't."

I was breathless, weak in the knees, unable to stand except by clinging to him. "Mark . . ."

"And no, I never loved her like I love you, Steve." He looked smug, even cocky. "I've never loved anybody the way I love you. Any more questions you want answered?"

This was unfair. Dazed, I shook my head.

"Okay." He got back to business, his hard body still holding me up against the bathroom wall as he spoke into my hair. "This is the deal. I'm going out to call Abner, see if I can't talk him into letting me hand this locker key over to Coral. He knows her as well as I do, and I might be able to persuade him."

"Call him from here."

"I don't want Coral to overhear in case Abner says no."

"Then let me go with you."

"No. It won't take long. I'll be right back."

I tried to push him away. "I won't stay here with her."

He held me tight. His whisper was urgent. "Hush. This is for your benefit, Steve, since you're so suspicious of her. With you here, she can't call anybody to tell them what we're doing or where we are. Understand?"

I did but didn't want to. "I guess so."

"I won't be gone long, and you'll be fine till I get back. I promise you."

"You promised me those men wouldn't bother me again." I still wanted to rebel. "But they did."

He crushed me to him again, as if he could pull me inside the heart of him. I felt his heat, my own answering need.

"I know," he whispered with a sincerity that distorted his voice. "I'm sorry, love. You don't know how sorry. I can't let it happen to you again. That's why it's so important for you to do what I ask now. Please." His hands massaged my back, holding me to him.

I tried not to soften, tried to avoid the huge yawning pit I foresaw swallowing me whole if I let myself give way to his unfair physical persuasion. If I let myself believe him. "I don't want to stay with Coral."

"Somebody needs to babysit her." His tongue found the place on my neck that reduced my stomach to mush.

"Don't." I gasped. "Don't do that. I can't think. All right."

He raised his face, put his nose against mine to look me directly in the eyes.

I fell into gray-green space and gulped painfully, trying to draw back from the waiting abyss. "You'd better not be gone long."

"Ten minutes, twenty at most," he promised, looking at me and smiling. "Oh, hell. Why is once never enough?" He kissed me again.

My legs were so rubbery that, when he let me go, I sank down on the edge of the tub to keep from falling.

At the door, he turned back. "Oh, another thing you may have been wondering about," he said, an impish glint making the black specks dance, "I haven't slept with Coral since before you and I got together. To be specific, the night before Fee and Dan's wedding, at approximately twelve thirty-three in the morning if I remember correctly."

"I don't care!" I picked up a stack of Coral's clean towels off their low shelf and threw them at him. "I don't care! I don't care!"

The door pulled to before the towels hit. As they slid to the floor, I heard his muted laughter from the other side.

I got up from the edge of the tub and began to laugh, too.

* * * *

CORAL SAT ON the bed, going through the strewn out contents of her purse. She glanced at me when I emerged in time to see Mark's back disappear outside, but she didn't comment on my dishevelment.

"I want a cigarette," she said. "Do you have one?"

"I don't smoke."

"Hunh." She made it sound like a jeer. "I'm sure that pleases Marco. He keeps harping on me to quit, but it's frigging hard. Especially at times like these."

I sat down. "I'm sure it must be."

Coral was stunning with her olive skin and dark hair and liquid eyes. How could Mark have brought himself to leave such a sensual, fascinating creature? Whatever had caused their split, it hadn't been her smoking habit, I'd bet. Something must have happened. A quarrel, perhaps, when she'd demanded he reveal himself to her.

I'd also bet she hadn't pitched a fit like me. Memories of my near hysteria earlier made me blush. What a wonder Mark was still speaking to me.

Coral plucked a battered pack of gum out of the clutter on the bedspread. "Nice guy, our Marco."

"Yes." . . . *our* Marco. "He is."

She uncurled herself from the bed and stood up. She straightened the short dress by wriggling shoulders and hips in a lazy manner suggesting provocation and seduction and unadulterated sex. With the same unconscious movements, she offered me a stick of gum.

I declined it.

Taking a piece herself, she sailed the pack back toward her opened purse. "So what's wrong with him?"

"Mark? I don't know of anything wrong with him."

At least nothing I'd discuss with her.

She took the paper off her stick, folded and popped it into the voluptuous mouth in a way that must have been practiced, since nothing else could explain the tantalizing way her lips engulfed the gum. Her small nose wrinkled in distaste at the inadequate substitute for nicotine.

My nose caught a whiff of peppermint. I could see firsthand how fascinating Coral was.

"I can read Mark like a book, hon, and I can see something's wrong." She used the same conversational tone as Mark. "He had a tough time on his last job, I know, and I'm sure your baby's death—"

"I don't want to talk about the baby." Shock waves hit me, exposing every nerve in my body, at her of all people bringing up that subject. "I don't want to talk about Mark either."

Her jaws stopped. "I see." Her calm reminded me so much of Mark I wanted to scream. "Let me guess. The two of you are having problems."

"I don't want to talk about it."

Resuming chewing the gum, she dropped into the chair opposite mine and studied me the way a cat studies a bird. "Fine. Good. Very good."

My outrage must have shown because she laughed. "Let's be honest. You don't like me and I don't like you. You have Mark and I don't. But he's wanting loose now, is he?"

"No, he isn't. I'm the one—" I stopped too late.

"Better and better." The black lashes—they must have been fake; they were too long and thick to be real—lowered in satisfaction. "So trouble in paradise is what's eating away at poor Marco. And all the time I assumed it was the shit he went through in Africa."

Trouble in paradise.

Her words mocked at me.

I got up and went to the window as she and Mark had done earlier. The open curtains allowed visual access to the cars and tops of trees in the parking lot as well as the buildings beyond.

The view didn't matter. I wanted to get away from her.

She said to my back, "I'm sorry for Mark because I hate him to be unhappy, but I told him all along you two weren't suited."

"I'm sure you did." Why wouldn't she? Everyone else had said the same thing.

"I'm glad to see you can stick up for yourself. He's pretty overwhelming. Of course, there are lots of women who don't mind being overwhelmed."

I pivoted. "You, for instance?"

"I don't overwhelm easily. In fact, I think Marco and I are very well matched. I wouldn't mind having another whirl with him." She inspected her nails. "Men like him aren't easy to find. Are you leaving him?"

I would have bit my tongue out rather than admit to this woman that I was divorcing Mark. "I suppose you're right. Men like Mark aren't easy to find."

"Hunh. In other words, mind my own business, eh?" She took her purse and raked the items on the bed back into it and laid it on the dresser.

Her silence galled me as much as her speech.

I spread my hands. "Look, what do you want me to say? Go ahead and take him and welcome? Mark would have to be the one to decide that."

"I guess you're right. But it's a nice fantasy. You throwing him out. Me getting him back."

She walked around the bed, if you could call the leisurely, swaying way she moved across the room walking. Plumping up pillows against the headboard, she sank down among them. Polished toenails glistened as bare feet swung up onto the Dresden and white spread. "What happened?"

"Nothing happened."

"Sure it did." She burrowed back among her bolsters and crossed her ankles. Except for the snapping gum and the short dress and the modern surroundings, she looked like Cleopatra on her couch.

Exotic. Seductive. Compelling.

She brushed back her hair. "A year ago, Mark was busy with the

Dream Sugar commission. You were expecting his first child, life was good, and our Marco was happy as a little clam."

I looked away.

"Now, after his big unveiling, despite all the media hype and critical acclaim, he's not happy at all. Oh, did you see the papers?"

"No."

"Well, believe me, the coverage of Dream Sugar's opening was nothing short of sensational. Our Marco and his statue were the main topic. A whole section in the Atlanta rag."

She folded her hands over a nonexistent stomach. The skirt, rucked up to the top of her thighs, displayed legs as unblemished as the rest of her. She didn't so much as tug at the hem. "But now, when he's got it made, right when he ought to be on the biggest high in his life, it's like someone died."

"Someone has died," I said coldly. Hoo and some other unknown man and Sweet Rowdy.

And my baby.

Her face clouded. "This is a different kind of death, hon. We're talking about Mark." Picking up a cushion, she cradled it in front of her. "Was it the baby?"

"I told you I don't want to talk about my baby."

Her upper lip curled. I guessed she couldn't understand what Mark saw in me. "*Your* baby? Nothing to do with Mark?"

The tiny sign of contempt brought me back to myself. "Look, this is a very personal subject, okay?"

Languid jaws worked the gum. "Wow. I'll bet coming back to you after barely getting out of Africa alive must have been a real thrill. Some festive homecoming for poor Marco."

"Not festive for either of us." I could heap ashes on myself by the truckload if I wanted, but I'd be damned if I let some ex-lover of Mark make me feel guilty. I was the one who'd suffered, who'd lost a baby, who'd nearly died.

Coral's nostrils flared, scenting a kill. "What happened? Did Mark come home whimpering, expecting the little woman to nurse his wounds, and instead find he'd been relegated to second place behind a dead baby?"

"If you know Mark so well, you'd know he doesn't whimper."

She smirked because she had goaded me into a response, and chewed her gum.

It took a few minutes for her remarks about Africa and Mark barely getting out to soak in. It took another few minutes to decide whether or not to ask about them.

If I were any kind of wife, I should have known what Coral was talking about. I didn't, but I wanted to find out. Enough to swallow my pride.

Mark had vouched for her honesty.

"What do you mean about Africa and Mark's wounds?"

"You know. From his last job."

"His last job was in Africa?"

The jaws stopped working. Her expression bordered on incredulity. "He didn't tell you, did he?"

I started to explain, excuse my ignorance. "Things were not . . ." What was the use? This creature had probed into my consciousness and subconscious, and brought out every indecent characteristic I possessed. She knew Mark better than I, his wife.

I said humbly, "No. He didn't tell me."

Her surprise faded. "He wouldn't. Keeps hard stuff like that to himself, our Marco does. I asked him once why he didn't talk about it, get it out in the open."

My tongue felt parched. "What did he say?"

She gave me a sidelong glance. "That it doesn't do any good to dwell on the past, that what's done is done and all you can do is learn from your mistakes. Or words to that effect."

That sounded like Mark. Ignore anything unpleasant on the theory that tomorrow was another day and bound to be better.

So he was in Africa while I had lain in a hospital bed alone. "My sister put in a call for him. We wondered why we didn't hear anything."

I didn't realize I had spoken aloud until Coral answered, "The phone lines and electricity went out when the massacres started. You didn't know about them either, right?"

She sat waiting for me to reveal the extent of Mark's and my estrangement. No point in lying. "He never talks about what he does for FIFA."

"No?" Coral chewed and pondered. I didn't like the way she looked at me. She'd taken my measure and found me wanting. "I guess he wouldn't. With Marco, you have to ask, pin him down. Otherwise, he'll change the subject or refuse to answer. The only way I get anything out of our rugged, stolid, silent male is to ask and keep asking."

Mark was the strong silent type. The type who never showed hurt, never shared his problems, never shared his suffering with anyone. Not even a wife. But underneath that stoic exterior, occasional frustrating glimpses of the real man peeked through. Frustrating because as soon as he realized his walls were sagging, he fortified them again.

"What happened to him in Africa?"

"If he didn't want you to know, it isn't my place to tell," Coral said virtuously. Her complexion had taken on a subtle glow, as if she'd discovered something to her liking.

"You mean you won't." I didn't like her, but I was beginning to understand her. And maybe Mark a little. Perhaps if I asked him like Coral did, and kept asking and pinning him down, perhaps I could come to understand enough about him to unravel the puzzle of the man I had married.

Coral chewed her gum in silence for several long minutes. "Look, hon," she said finally. "I'm going to be straight with you. It was my own stupid fault I lost Mark. He's not a man to take for granted. If I had it to do over again, I'd be a little more, um, circumspect about my personal life. And I'd be a damned sight more careful about how I treated him." She took out the abused gum and put it, a little gray wad, into an ash tray. "I don't want to see him unhappy, but if you're determined to sabotage your marriage, I'm the last person in the world to try to counsel you on how to make it work. Get it?"

Yes. Coral wanted my husband back and wouldn't mind how she went about taking him.

I couldn't condemn her. Hadn't I myself once felt the same way?

I went back to staring out the window.

* * * *

WHEN HE RETURNED, Mark came directly to me, oblivious to the chill hanging over the room. "Okay. I'm back. Time to go."

"Did you get Abner?" Coral asked. She looked provocatively tousled, with her dark curly hair falling down over her shoulders and no shoes on her pedicured feet.

I still didn't see how a man could leave a woman like Coral. She must have done something terrible to drive Mark away.

But he'd come to me afterward.

"Yes," he replied to Coral. "I got Abner."

I picked up my purse. "What did he say?"

He spoke to Coral, not me. "Abner's not happy with the situation. He's flying in himself to take the papers."

Coral's eyes and mouth widened. "Abner?" She looked appalled. "Abner? He never leaves Main Office. Never."

"Scary, huh? Murphy's law applied and in action." Mark grinned at her but took my hand. "See you, Coral."

She grabbed his arm. "Where are you going?"

The crinkles deepened. "Shopping."

She sighed then stood up on tiptoe to cup his face with her hands and kiss his mouth. "Don't do anything stupid. One of us is already gone."

His countenance darkened at the oblique mention of Hoo, but he chuckled. "I won't do anything you wouldn't do, wild woman." He moved his hands.

"That's exactly what I'm afraid of." She stood back, reluctantly, worry on her face she tried to conceal.

I wondered if she and Mark would get back together after the divorce.

How could he resist her?

* * * *

"I DON'T FEEL like shopping," I said when we got into the Explorer. "We could go back to the motel."

He managed to raise both brows, close his car door, and leer at me simultaneously. "Really? We can if you want to." His mouth curved in a manner that brought back remembrances of the past night.

Goose bumps riddled my body as I recalled the way his lips had felt against my skin, the way his hands had cupped my breasts, the way his leg had nudged mine aside.

I quashed that train of thought immediately. "Not for that. We could keep out of sight there."

"We could."

His agreeable answer was suspect, especially since he put the key in the ignition and leaned back in his seat without making the slightest effort to start the car.

"How'd you and Coral get along?" he asked.

"Fine." Like two dogs marking their territory.

"No phone calls?"

"She didn't make any or get any."

"Good." He didn't turn the key.

It was left to me to ask, "Are we going to sit here all day?"

"No." His eyes focused on a point past my shoulder.

I turned. Through the SUV's window, he could see both entrances to the parking lot along with the hotel portal. We were parked between a small mimosa growing inside a break deliberately left in the asphalt on our right and a dumpster shielding us on the left. Cars and people coming and going could be monitored in relative obscurity.

"Mark, are we looking for someone?"

"I don't know."

"What's wrong?"

"Maybe nothing."

Discouraged, I sat back and closed my eyes.

Within ten minutes, he stiffened.

I opened my eyes to see a brown pickup entering the parking lot and gasped. "Is that the same truck that tried to run us off the road at the dam?"

"Yes, love. It's that very same one." The direct but careless answer might be pointing out a particularly interesting acquaintance.

By this time, I was too battered to feel anything but bewilderment. "What are we going to do?"

"Sit right here and see what happens."

From behind the sheltering mimosa leaves, we watched the pickup stop and a man emerge. He had a prominent nose and it, along with other parts of his face, was as puffy and bruised as Mark's eye and lip. He walked slowly, with a curious gait as though both legs pained him.

"He looks worse than me, don't you think?" Mark murmured with a certain amount of satisfaction. "I got in several pretty good licks."

Like a little boy who'd beat up a rival. How in heaven's name could he sound so pleased with himself with that man hot on our trail?

When Crooked Nose disappeared into the building, Mark started the car.

"How did he know to come here?" I blurted. "Coral?"

"Good question." He no longer defended her. "If Coral phoned the moment we left, they must have been right around the corner."

"So you think she might have been in touch with them all along?" I tried not to sound triumphant.

He took the back exit away from the parked brown truck. "I work with Coral regularly, Steve, and have for a long time. I'd stake my life on her honesty. She's registered under her own name. All someone would have to do would be call around and find out where she was staying."

"But the timing seems odd."

He didn't answer.

So he worked with Coral regularly.

I had suspected that, hadn't I?

And he continued to defend her. There was no winning when it came to convincing Mark that Coral was untrustworthy so I changed tactics. "Is that why you don't want to go back to our motel? Because they could be calling motels to find us?"

"Aren't you the clever one? No, I don't think we'll go back there.

What did we leave? Jammies? Toothbrushes? Underwear? We need to go shopping, okay?"

I was tired and miserable, for more reasons than one. "No, it isn't. I'm tired of shopping and how you can talk about it with all this happening is beyond me."

"Easy for you to say. You've had a change of clothes," he pointed out in righteous indignation. "I've had on this shirt and pants since Sunday morning. They're getting pretty ripe after all my sweating and rolling around the pavement, not to mention the tree-climbing. Besides, your clothes look pretty bad, too, after your digging in the dirt this morning."

Naturally, he had his way.

As we left the area, Mark pulled into a convenience store where his sharp eyes had spotted a rare pay phone.

"Got some change?"

"No." I wondered why he didn't use his cell.

He went through his pockets, found some coins, and got out.

"Abner again?" I asked on his return.

He grinned disarmingly. "No. The police. I think they ought to know a brown pickup connected to a man's death in the Chattahoochee below the dam is parked in the hotel lot back there with its driver inside."

His motivations mystified me.

I sighed.

"I didn't give my name," he said as if I had protested.

I shook my head despairingly.

CHAPTER SIXTEEN

WE DIDN'T VISIT Perimeter Mall where he'd left Hoo's papers, nor did we take the train to Underground Atlanta. We drove to Lenox Square and took our time going through the shops.

I bought another set of underwear, a loose cotton dress, and some canvas slippers. Mark got a pair of khaki shorts and a polo shirt along with three pairs of silk boxers and a ponytail holder.

"On sale," he told me, waving the boxers in my face.

"Whee. Can't pass up a deal like that."

We used the restrooms to change into our new clothes before heading for the food court. While I paid for iced tea and coffee, Mark put in a call to Abner.

Naturally.

He did not talk long.

"All set." He sat down in a chair across the small table from mine. "Abner's already left Virginia. He should get into Atlanta around six." He glanced at his watch. "We've got plenty of time to pick up the package and drive over to Hartsfield."

"Are we meeting him at the airport?" With its crowds of people, it would be an ideal place.

He reached over the table to push a strand of my hair off my cheek. "On the edge of the south runway."

I opened my mouth to object.

Mark forestalled me. "You're so easy," he said, grinning. "No, love. We're going to find one of those lots where you park your car and they shuttle you to the airport. Then we'll call and leave a message at the terminal for Abner, telling him which shuttle to get on. Does that meet with your security arrangement satisfaction, Mrs. Early?"

He left unspoken what we were both thinking. No one except us would know where we could be found.

"Ready to pick up the package?" he asked as I dawdled.

I finished my tea and got up.

* * * *

WE SAT IN the car, the package containing Hoo's paperwork in the seat between us.

Mark had parked about a hundred yards away from the one

entrance to the shuttle lot, positioning the Ford so that the gate beside the office was in plain view.

"Does it seem to you that all we do is hurry up and wait?" he asked, trying to be inconspicuous about looking at his watch.

"Yes." I thought about Coral's words, what she'd said about his assignment in Africa. "Does your work usually involve something like this? Is this normally the kind of thing you do?"

"Gosh, no. I'd hunt another job if it was." He leaned his back against the window, stretching out as much as he could. He avoided my eye.

I remembered how he had darkened our house and left off the alarm and waited for the intruders to break in. I remembered the confident way he had walked from the car to meet the men who'd forced us off the road. I remembered how quickly he'd picked up on Bob's fear, the studied calm with which he'd met it.

"I don't believe you. Things like this have happened to you before."

"No. Not like this."

I stared at him.

He reiterated firmly, "Nothing like this."

"You're lying."

"No, I'm not. Most of my work's so boring I can hardly stand to talk about it. Honest."

"So that's why you don't." My mouth dried. My voice sounded harsh.

Mark's eyes shuttered.

"What happened on your last job for FIFA?"

He gave no visible sign of tensing, but I felt his muscles coil, his nerves gear up.

Something flickered behind the eyes that weren't really dark, was quickly replaced by the usual amiability as he caused his muscles and nerves to relax.

"You know what happened," he said easily. "I went out to do an audit and when I got back, you'd lost our baby and nearly died. And our life started falling apart."

His words about the baby skimmed by, the memories hurtful but fleeting.

Coral had advised me, unwittingly, before she knew the entire situation between Mark and me.

With Marco, you have to ask, pin him down.

"What happened on your audit in Africa?"

His expression didn't change. "It was just an audit."

"That isn't what Coral says."

His features shifted, settling into the expression that, I'd learned during the past six years, meant he was hiding disclosures too private.

"Coral doesn't know," he said coolly. "She wasn't there."

"Neither was I."

Pin him down.

Coral's words egged me on. "Mark, I tell you everything that happens to me. I tell you about the good students and the crummy students and the ignorant students and the pompous administrators. I tell you about the lady down the street who had a heart attack, and about the ice cream truck running into the car at the end of the block. I tell you about the man who cuts my hair who's fighting with his boyfriend and the couple from India opening the new boutique. I share everything with you. Everything. Why won't you share something with me?"

He turned his head away. His profile could have been chiseled in stone. "Not everything. You don't share everything, Steve."

He meant the baby.

"I would have," I said with as much sincerity as I could muster. "You weren't there to share it with."

His eyes remained downcast. "I wanted to be."

"Then why weren't you?" burst out before I could stop it.

He lifted his left hand, ran his index finger over the curve of the steering wheel. "We've been over that. You know why." His words were so low I could barely hear them.

"No, I don't know why. Tell me."

"I had a job to do."

"I know you had a job." I swept aside his half-hearted excuse. "But why did it take you so long to get back? You should have been there the day after it happened, after I . . . Instead, there was no word. No phone calls, no Mark, no nothing."

He glanced at me, quickly looked away. Had I imagined the guilt?

"Don't close yourself up again." I wouldn't let him equivocate any more. "Tell me."

"God, Steve." His left hand gripped the wheel so tightly I could see the knuckles turn white. "You don't make it easy."

I had the strangest sensation of walking across a fragile glass floor. One false step on my part would cause a fissure that would spread and allow the entire structure to shatter, and whatever future Mark and I might hope to build together would be lost forever in the shards.

"It kills me that Coral knows more about you than I do," I said carefully. "It makes me feel like Coral's closer to you, that she means more to you—"

"That isn't true." He leaned forward over the console to take me in his arms, but I used both hands to stop him.

His caress would be another diversion.

Mark knew too well how to divert me.

"What is true?" If I lost track of my train of thought, Mark and I would be back where we had started, and I would have no other chance to mend us. "I had to learn from Coral, and not until today, that you were in Africa when I lost the baby. You didn't even tell me that much. What happened there?"

He hesitated, stretching his hand out to stroke my face.

I moved my head to the side, away from his fingers.

He deliberately closed them over empty air and let them drop. "It isn't something you need to hear."

"Let me decide that."

"What if I don't want to talk about it?"

I couldn't deal with this. "All right. Don't. I guess I was right all along. You're incapable of opening yourself up to anybody, and I'm tired of living with a man who won't."

I suppose he saw by my face that I was serious.

Or he might have weighed his options and wanted as desperately as I to salvage something from the past six years.

He finally began to talk. Reluctantly, haltingly, sometimes ambiguously.

But he did talk.

"FIFA sent an auditor over to a little African nation you've never heard of. It'd been fairly stable for several years." He stopped, forgot his hair was tied back and tried to run his fingers through it. "Its government contracted with FIFA as a preliminary to getting a loan through the World Bank."

Taking off the band holding his ponytail, he fanned the strands in an absent gesture.

"Turned out the legitimate government didn't know about some sidelines. Like its treasury running on drug money. Our auditor couldn't quite pin down how, so they sent me. Money laundering's my specialty," he added almost apologetically. A sideways glance gauged my reaction.

"Money laundering. I see." That was another of the things I hadn't learned about my husband during our six years of marriage. How much else was there to discover? "Go on."

He looked down at his hands as if afraid I wouldn't like what I heard. "It took some time to figure out how they were doing it and trace the other countries involved. FIFA, with the prime minister's permission, consulted an international law enforcement agency. Then, for legal purposes, FIFA agreed to take control of the actual records. I had to bring them out of the country."

He fidgeted, shifting to face the steering wheel. Both hands gripped it hard. When he resumed, he enunciated his words with precision. "The morning Abner got word to me you'd gone to the hospital was the same morning I left. I picked up the records at the palace. But on my way to the airport, we ran into . . . There was a coup going on, backed by the drug runners. Attempted coup. Everything went haywire. There was such a mess—" He took a deep breath, went on. "The turmoil, the chaos . . . Unbelievable. To make it short, I couldn't get out for several days."

The creases around his eyes looked like lines of worry instead of laughter. "So that's what happened. That's why I couldn't get to you. Satisfied?"

I remembered Coral's surprise. *He didn't tell you about it, did he?*

"I don't think that's all."

A hand that had relaxed on the wheel, tightened. The eyes were open, but they held a haunted weariness. "It's enough. There's nothing else I want to talk about."

"Was it enough for Coral? She was surprised that you hadn't told me what had happened. You must have confided in her. Why can't you tell me?"

"I didn't tell Coral anything." He folded his arms across the steering wheel and rested his face on them so his words were muffled. "And you don't need to hear about the crying children or the flies moving in clouds over the piled-up corpses."

My heart sank. I swallowed. "You're wrong. I do need to hear."

"No!" His fist hit the wheel. "No normal person should have to know what happened there. I've never talked about it. Not to Coral. Not to anyone. I guess they knew, back at the office, but they didn't get it from me. There was no reason to inflict it on them and I won't inflict it on you either."

I had to be getting close. The shell Mark used to protect himself must be wearing thin. This might be my last opportunity. "You didn't think you owed me an explanation? You were gone when I lost the baby and when I nearly died."

He sat erect with that awful tiredness. "There's nothing you can say to me I haven't said to myself."

I breathed deeply. "All this time I've been thinking you didn't care about me or the baby."

His head whipped toward me. "That isn't true. You know me better than that. Steve, you know that isn't true, don't you?"

"Were you injured?"

He rubbed an eye. "No. Except it's pretty scary to be caught in the middle of a hail of bullets with nothing but a lot of dead bodies protecting you. I've tried to forget it," he ended raggedly.

"Oh, Mark." My eyes filled. "I'm so sorry." I'd been too lost in my personal tragedy to remember that other people could be caught up in tragedies, too, as bad if not worse than mine.

"Love, don't cry." He touched my shoulder. "Damn, I knew better than to lay all that on you. I promised myself I'd never let you know anything about it." He leaned over the console to catch and hold my face in both his hands. "Listen, there's no place in your world for things like this. You ought never to have to deal with any of the dirty things that sometimes happen in life. Can't you see why I didn't want you to know? Can't you tell how it hurts me to see you upset, see you cry?"

"I'm not crying." In truth, the threat of tears had vanished as quickly as it had arisen. When I put my hands on his wrists, his strength flowed through me. "I'm wishing you had told me this a long time ago. It hurts when you shut me out. Please don't shut me out again."

"No." Mark spoke as though with great effort. "This isn't the time now, but later, I'll tell you the rest. I will. Love, from the moment I saw you, I knew you were the sweetest, most wonderful person in the world. I couldn't understand why you fell in love with me, but I promised myself when we married that I'd do anything I could to keep you the way you were when we met. You don't deserve to have to deal with all the raunchy stuff life throws out. You shouldn't have to."

I took his hands, lowered them from my face, caressed them. "Don't put me on a pedestal."

A trace of his old cockiness emerged. "I'll put you anywhere I damned well please. And believe me, a pedestal is the last place I want to put you."

Content seeped over me. I loved the man. I must have been out of my mind, flirting with losing him the way I had the past months. I was a self-centered jerk for hiding my head in the sand for six years, never wondering about his work, never caring how perilous his job could be.

"I wish you'd quit FIFA."

He grinned. "I intend to. One of these days. As soon as I can make enough money on my sculpting. Till then, we can't afford it."

"Coral says the papers had wonderful reviews on Dreaming at the opening."

He brightened. "Did they? Great." He slapped a hand to his forehead. "Oh, hell. Candy was supposed to sit for me Tuesday morning and I forgot to call and cancel. Will she be pissed. Maybe if I offer to pay her double, she'll come back." He frowned. "I've got to finish this Cleopatra model for Dominion. If they like the scale sample, I have a good chance at the commission. God, I hope Candy doesn't refuse to come back."

"She'll be back," I said dryly. "In fact, I'd say you're going to have a hard time getting rid of her."

He gave a questioning glance.

"Ma-ark!" I imitated Candy's flirtatious squeal.

"Come on, you don't think I'd seriously go for an airhead like Candy." He looked amazed and then he howled.

"No," I denied quickly, over his gales of laughter. "Shut up. I overheard her begging to go with you to the Dream Sugar opening when I got back from the lake Saturday. Come to think of it, I didn't notice you working too hard at fending her off."

"Didn't notice me working too hard!" Indignation cut the laughter short. "My dear wife, I fended as hard as I could. Candy's a big girl."

"Then maybe the Cleopatra model will turn out to be just as big, and the Dominion people will love it and let you decorate their new mall."

"Yeah." His eyes glazed at the vision of future projects. "That would be great, wouldn't it?"

I wished I had thought to look for an Atlanta Journal Constitution when we were shopping. "I'd like to read what the papers said about the Dream Sugar opening."

"We'll look at them online when we get home."

There came an awkward pause. Neither of us knew what to say next.

Mark looked at his watch again, then at me. Coming to a decision, he reached over and caught my hand. "Steve, if I've not told you every detail about my life, it's because some of it's too bad to repeat and all I want to do is forget it. I've always wanted to protect you, keep the bad things away from you."

"Maybe I'd rather face them with you than be left out."

He leaned further over, past the console onto my side of the car. I didn't draw back.

"Steve," he murmured, his hand rubbing through my hair. "God, you don't know how much I love you."

"Tell me."

His mouth was an inch from mine, one side black and swollen. "I'm not good at serious discussions."

"Then show me."

No further invitation was necessary. His hand on the back of my neck pulled me to him.

I wrapped my arms around his neck. He wrapped his around me. My heartbeat rang in my ears, dizzying me, or perhaps it was his. He moved his bruised lips away to drag them over my jaw, my throat, my ear. I reached down to his leg, found his knee, traced the hairy muscle of his thigh.

"I want you."

He broke the mood. "I know it sounds callous and unfeeling, but could I possibly beg you to hold the thought?" The roughness in his voice didn't match the crinkles framing his eyes.

I fell back to the safety of my side of the car, satisfied that he was out of breath, too. "I may be out of the mood later on."

"Ah no, please, no," he begged. "Say you'll remember."

"If you don't want me here and now, I can't promise."

"It's just that I don't want the parking lot attendant to call the police," he said meekly. "Your reputation would suffer. Can't you see the headlines? 'Celebrated Sculptor Arrested for Car Sex'. And our photographs plastered on the front page."

"Yes. Although they'd have to add, 'With Wife'. That's not much better, is it? I guess you're right." I looked around and gasped. One of the lot's vans neared, making its round to drop off passengers at their cars.

I slunk down in my seat. What a narrow escape. "Absolutely right. I don't want to be cited for indecent acts in broad daylight."

He laughed. His hand held mine, and it felt right.

For the first time in half a year, I felt like myself again. "Mark."

"Hm?" He put my fingers up to his lips, licking each one, nuzzling each one.

"I don't want a divorce."

"Good." He sucked at my pinkie. "I wasn't going to give you one anyway."

I blinked. "You said you would."

"I said I wanted you to be happy. And I never knew how you could be happy without me. You didn't think I wouldn't put up a fight, did you? I'd have done whatever it took, given up FIFA, given up sculpting if I'd had to, to keep you."

He was back to his normal self. Calm, controlled, smug.

"Given up all that?" My conscience stabbed me. "I didn't mean that, what I said about you giving up sculpting."

He turned my palm up and tickled it with his tongue. "I couldn't work in the studio every day without knowing I'd see you when I got through every night."

I couldn't let him see how touched I was, but there was no danger of him letting me become too sentimental.

"Do you think you can make it home or should we stop at a motel after we meet Abner?" he murmured, his free hand exploring under my skirt.

He needed taking down a notch. "You're going to have to shape up. I'm tired of being a good little helpmate, blind and deaf and dumb." I took his questing hand and put it in his lap.

He started all over again on my fingers. "You're not dumb. I'd never have married a dumb woman."

I thought of Coral, intelligent, gorgeous, and still in love with him. "Why did you marry me?"

"Because I couldn't live without you."

Good enough for me.

CHAPTER SEVENTEEN

AS MARK AND I waited and watched for the illustrious Abner Crowley, several cars entered the shuttle lot. Most of them were midsized or small, carrying single passengers or couples. We speculated about the people inside.

"Woman on a business trip."

"Picking up her husband."

"Man seeing his daughter off."

"Bet he's divorced and she's been visiting for spring break."

"Mother and daughter going to Europe together."

"Or maybe a wedding out of town."

"Salesman going to his next city."

"Or computer geek headed for an assignment."

"Ooh, a limo. George Clooney."

"Why not Angelina Jolie?"

"Too early for a prom tonight, I guess."

"Must be a politician."

So we sat and watched all the traffic go by, making sure no brown pickup drove into sight.

When the shuttle bus from the airport pulled in, it stopped in the unloading zone at the entry office, and people started piling out.

"There's Abner." Mark gathered up the package of Hoo's papers and opened his door.

I craned my neck to see my nemesis.

The smooth telephone voice I had come to loathe over the past six years belonged to a short, balding man dressed in a shabby suit, holding a pipe in one hand and a briefcase in the other. His features were indistinct, but his chubby figure moved away from the bus with a shambling uncertain gait.

More aggressive passengers shouldered by him to grab their bags and climb onto the van taking them to cars parked over the capacious lot.

Abner Crowley meekly shrank aside.

Poor soul. This man didn't seem half so forbidding or threatening as the ogre of my wild imagination. I had the strangest urge to go take his elbow and lead him to where he ought to be.

Maybe he was the wrong man. "That short man there in the baggy suit? That's Abner Crowley?"

"In person." Mark grinned at me as if he knew what I was thinking. "Be right back."

"I'll be darned," I muttered as the door slammed. "Talk about imagination working overtime." I'd pictured him over six feet tall with movie star looks and wearing a blazer.

When the flurry of unloading and reloading finished, and the other riders had gone, Abner remained by the cashier's office. He set his briefcase down. A pipe went into his mouth as he searched fruitlessly through coat and pants pockets for matches.

I couldn't get over how ordinary the despised Abner Crowley looked. He might have been a salesman or businessman waiting for a ride.

No unfeeling monster after all. Mark's boss turned out to be simply a middle-aged, absentminded man.

I was almost sorry Mark didn't smoke, that he didn't have a light to lend Abner.

By this time, Mark's lanky form, purposeful in new khaki shorts and polo shirt, had advanced to the end of the first row of cars. His underarm grip protected the manila envelope containing Hoo's precious papers.

About a hundred yards separated him from the gate office and his unprepossessing boss.

Abner knelt down to rummage through his briefcase.

Still looking for matches.

He hadn't spotted Mark, and I, intent on Mark's progress, barely noticed the black limousine as it glided up.

Not until Mark's door burst open.

A pistol muzzle pointed at me.

A very large and very deadly-looking pistol.

The face above was badly bruised with a prominent nose.

Crooked Nose smirked. He seemed disturbingly unconcerned as to whether or not he might have to use the gun.

I sat paralyzed.

"Mrs. Early, you will see I am better prepared today." He waved the black pistol in a frighteningly careless way. "You will please step out. Do not call out. Do not move suddenly. We would have to shoot you and enough people have been hurt as it is."

Someone rapped at my window. My stiff neck turned.

Another man, mustached and perspiring, gestured through the window at the lock.

"Please, Mrs. Early, cooperate." Crooked Nose had an accented voice as composed as Mark's. Without lowering his pistol, he used the automatic switch to release my door lock. "Go ahead and get out," he continued as the second man opened my door and grabbed my arm. "We prefer there be no violence."

There was no choice.

The mustached man holding me had a gun every bit as nasty as the one Crooked Nose brandished.

I stumbled getting out. Mustache yanked me upright, and I yipped.

"Now, now, Georgio. Don't hurt Mrs. Early," Crooked Nose chided as he hobbled round the car.

With me sandwiched between them, we traced Mark's footsteps toward the parking lot office and Abner.

"It's all right if you want to call out to your husband." Crooked Nose sounded solicitous. "Go ahead."

I couldn't speak, but it didn't matter.

Mark glanced around, took in the scene, and whirled to sprint back.

"Ah. Your husband must be telepathic," Crooked Nose joked before he pushed the muzzle of his gun under my left breast.

Mustache pulled my elbow back behind me.

Hard.

He brought me to a standstill between them.

Except for his bruises, Mark's face was dead white. I had never seen anyone so white.

The pistol dug into my ribs, but all I could focus on was Mark's set mouth and glittering eyes and tensed shoulders. There was no fear and hardly any pain from my twisted arm. Only lightheadedness.

I floated, disembodied, out of touch.

"Stop right there," my captor said when Mark got to within five yards.

Mark stopped obediently, abruptly. He didn't open his mouth. No jokes, no grin, no typical light mockery.

Only naked fear.

One more facet of my husband never before seen.

Crooked Nose said, "We've discussed this before. You know what we want, Mr. Early."

Over the noise of speeding cars and impatient horns from the busy thoroughfare beyond, Mark nodded. "Here." He held out the package. "It's yours. Don't hurt her."

"We don't intend to. Put it down and back off."

"Mark, don't. Don't give it to them."

I couldn't form the words. They came out as a mumble.

Hoo had died to keep his papers from these men, and Mark and I had gone through too much to recover them. Mark couldn't lose them because I wasn't brave. My voice strengthened. "Don't give it to them, Mark!"

No one listened to me, Mark least of all.

He laid the package down.

In the distance, stooping beside the cashier's office, Abner Crowley closed his briefcase and straightened. He triumphantly held up matches to light his pipe. Behind him rose the tall sign marking the car lot. Behind the sign the setting sun hung, a red ball in the sky, turning the clouds various shades of pink. Silhouetted by the rosy beams, a large bird which looked like a seagull but was probably a pigeon, dipped, wheeled, soared.

A car came into the parking lot, stopped in front of the office and obscured Abner. The van ferrying people to their parked cars crawled up one row and turned down the next. Traffic on the avenue beside the lot ignored the speed limits and whizzed by. A diesel fuel smell permeated the air and settled in my lungs like thick syrup.

Life went on.

Except for us.

We stood suspended.

Why couldn't Abner see us? He was the one who wanted the package. He was the one who had given Hoo the assignment. It was his fault this was happening to Mark and me. He ought not be standing around like a disinterested spectator.

"Mark," I said before my voice broke.

My husband, face to us, backed away from Hoo's package. "There it is. Let her go." He did not sound calm.

The tremor in his voice penetrated my stupor. I would remember the timbre of each syllable always. They betrayed the way his celebrated composure had deserted him because of his terror for my safety.

Strangely, realizing his fear quieted mine.

Mustache advanced and picked up the envelope.

Mark watched from his post yards away, jaw set, face chalky. For a second, Hoo's features overlaid my husband's. I remembered how pleading Hoo had been, how desperate when he'd begged me: *Tell Emily . . . Don't give them . . .*

A peculiar calm emerged and suspended me somewhere between outrage and caution.

Some part of my consciousness warned I ought to be frightened. I wasn't. Perhaps my fears had been used up.

When Mustache returned to where we stood, Mark said again, "You have what you want. Let my wife go."

Crooked Nose kept his gun jammed against my rib cage.

I'd nurse bruises tomorrow, but what did it matter?

Crooked Nose said, "Of course we will let her go. We are not murderers."

I spoke up. "You murdered Hoo."

"Not intentionally." His gaze never left Mark, his pistol never wavered from beneath my left breast. "The man responsible is in the hospital under arrest and another is dead. It balances out." He spoke to Mark, "We are professional men, are we not, Mr. Early? We understand these things happen and hold no grudges. And now, Mrs. Early will escort us to our car and will remain undamaged. So long as everyone cooperates. You can collect her once we leave."

I wanted to lunge for freedom, but a cold voice in my head told me, No, not now.

Mark, fists at his sides, face still chalky, watched us walk away.

Before we made the last turn toward the limousine, Abner, briefcase at his feet, leisurely gestured with his pipe as he talked to someone out of sight inside the office.

The idiot. Why didn't he look for us?

The men dragged me along.

I hoped Mark would stay out of immediate danger. I hoped Abner would see what was happening. I hoped he would call for help. I hoped help would come.

In my racing mind, one thought surfaced and remained.

It was wrong that these men could steal Hoo's notes.

Utterly, absolutely, intolerably wrong.

Mustache put his gun inside his shirt to better hold the package. His grip on my arm relaxed.

Crooked Nose still held on with a tight fist, his gun digging into my side. When one of his legs started to drag, he leaned on me to take some of the weight off.

I obliged by slowing to a snail's pace.

If I could push him down, I might be able to take the package from his partner.

No, not yet.

We reached the hood of the limousine.

Crooked Nose released me and took a faltering step before giving a sardonic half-bow. "A pleasure seeing you again, Mrs. Early. Stand away from the car, please." The gun disappeared into his coat as he limped toward the driver's side.

Mustache's hands fell away, too. He thrust me aside.

To open the passenger door, he had to transfer the bulky envelope to the hand nearest me. He caught it by one corner.

The limousine's engine sprang to life.

Now!

I didn't plan it.

Pent-up anger channeled into adrenaline and I burst forward. Before the startled thief could react, I'd grabbed the package.

He didn't let go.

My body turned to auto-pilot. A move from a college self-defense class took command.

With him holding on, I pulled the manila envelope toward me. At the same time, I kicked his knee and wrested the package away.

He stumbled and fell to the concrete.

Cradling the precious package in both arms, I started toward Mark.

I had to try. For Hoo.

My feet slapped the asphalt, as sluggish as feet bogged down by water.

Mustache behind me had hopped up to give chase. I could hear him shouting imprecations.

Mark raced toward me, hair flying, shouting something I couldn't hear.

Far across the lot, Abner, finally seeing us and realizing something was wrong, lumbered along, too.

It took an eternity to bolt across the pavement—my legs couldn't move fast enough to keep up with my mind—but no more than ten seconds must have passed from the moment I pushed Mustache down to the time I raced past the first row of cars.

By then, I'd nearly reached Mark.

I don't know what I hoped to achieve. I realized, somewhere in the back of my mind, that my life was at stake, but I'm not sure I believed either of the men would shoot.

Instinct led me on.

If I could reach a postal box or the shuttle lot's office, I'd cache the package. If the thieves couldn't get to it, Hoo wouldn't have died in vain.

Foolish when I look back. But then I was desperate.

It didn't matter. Mustache caught me.

Grabbing me by the elbow, he spun me around.

I kicked out.

He dodged and snatched the package from my arms, then shoved viciously.

I went sprawling.

Pain seared my chin and knees and elbows and forearms and palms. Black asphalt slipped by inches from my eyes as my body skidded across it.

I came to rest several feet away against a wire fence, stunned. Too many parts burned too much to move.

I couldn't breathe. Tears welled hot.

From behind me, a car door slammed. Feet pounded nearby. An engine started. As Mark knelt down beside me, a car, long and dark, streaked past.

"Steve, oh God, Steve."

I tried to pull myself up, couldn't, caught my breath. "He g-got it back."

"Steve, you idiot. Why the hell did you do that?"

The tears brimmed over. Past his shoulder, the black limousine paused at the cashier's booth.

Abner's chubby figure had reversed its direction to dash back toward the gate. Too late.

"He's g-getting away."

Mark disregarded everything except me. "Steve, my God, Steve," he repeated over and over as he propped me so that I sat upright. "Are you all right? What in hell possessed you? Where are you hurt? Is anything broken?"

My knees and arms and chin and shoulder stung, but pain wasn't the biggest reason I cried. I tried to get to my feet, but Mark held me down.

"Mark, they're leaving with Hoo's papers." My incensed objection came out as a pitiable wail.

"Damn Hoo's papers."

The limousine escaped into traffic before Abner Crowley reached the gate. I saw his short form stop and turn back, defeated.

Hoo's work. Lost.

Don't give them . . . Hoo had told me.

I collapsed into Mark's arms as fresh tears flowed and he called my name over and over.

"Steve, Steve. God, what an idiot you are. You scared the bejesus out of me." He held me to him. "Why the hell did you do that? What made you think you could take on those two bastards? Thank God you're alive. Steve, Steve."

By the time Abner Crowley made his way to us, I had my snuffling under control and didn't embarrass myself or Mark too much.

Like his figure, Abner's face was round, with plump, attractive features, not at all like the hawkish countenance I had envisioned. His eyes, too, were round and looked as if, under normal conditions, they would be jolly.

No, Abner wasn't an ogre at all. He was too inept to be an ogre.

"You must be Steve."

Save for his panting after the unexpected race, this could have been a conventional first meeting. He sounded as unflappable as Mark.

Except that Mark still sounded like someone else.

Mark didn't sound calm and collected as he cradled my head against his chest. He gave me no chance to draw away as decency mandated. He sounded scared and thankful and enraged and glad and truculent.

"This was totally uncalled for, Abner," he all but shouted.

I had never heard Mark raise his voice.

As I listened with interest, he continued to raise it. "Someone ought to be fired for this. Steve was nearly killed. What the hell were you thinking?"

Abner raised an apologetic hand. "Yes, I know. Bad planning all the way around." And to me, "I'm Abner Crowley. Sorry to meet you under these circumstances. My word, look at those knees. And elbows." He leaned over. "And your chin's messed up, too. We need to get something done for those scrapes."

He threw a glance back toward the office. "Can we leave, Mark? I suspect the cashier's telephoning the police." Taking a pipe out of one of his coat pockets, he ran a plump little hand over the bowl as though the day was an ordinary one on all accounts. "If we can, I'd like to give them a miss." He added by way of apologetic explanation, "I'd like to make my flight out."

* * * *

WE WERE ABLE to avoid the police, but Abner couldn't catch his flight back to Virginia. Mark refused to take him to the airport till we found an immediate care center.

Abner didn't seem upset. "As long as I'm here, I may as well speak to Bob." The unlit pipe in his mouth wagged. "I have some things I've been meaning to discuss with him at the field office anyway. Rather than waste the trip, I guess this is a good time to do it."

What things, I wondered. Maybe the leak that had led Crooked Nose to us time and again was on the agenda.

Mark may have wondered, too, but he didn't ask. In fact, Mark didn't say much of anything during the ride. While he drove, his right hand held my forearm. The heel of my raw hand bled, but he clutched my arm tightly as if afraid to let go.

I was glad. I couldn't believe what I'd done.

Foolish. Idiotic. I could have been killed.

If Crooked Nose or Mustache had fired . . .

I imagined a pistol report reverberating through the parking lot. The bullet would tear through clothes and flesh and muscle and bone.

Safe in the SUV, nausea threatened.

At the medical center, we sat thirty minutes until a harried nurse led me back to an examining cell. Mark went with me, and Abner waited in the lobby. A sympathetic doctor dispensed antibiotics, topical anesthetic, and painkillers.

By the time we started toward the field office, the scrapes and cuts were cleaned, the pain numbed. Only my muscles ached.

The adrenaline rush had long gone.

How had Crooked Nose discovered our whereabouts? Mark and I were the only people who knew which parking lot we'd chosen as a meeting place. Abner himself hadn't learned where we were waiting until after he arrived at the airport and received Mark's message.

Coral. But Mark hadn't told her the site of the meeting.

She'd known that Abner was flying in though. Had she alerted the thieves so they could watch and see what shuttle Abner got on at the airport? Had Abner led them to us?

Hadn't the limousine entered the lot about the same time as the shuttle? Yes, Coral's tipping them off might explain it.

Mark might trust Coral but how else would the men have known where we were?

When we pulled up to the field office near Lenox, Abner, who had been chewing on his pipe stem and simultaneously attempting small talk during the ride without much help from Mark or me, took the empty pipe from his mouth.

"Come inside," he said, curtailing my mental ramblings. "I want to talk to you both."

The field office had once been a private residence. Its front yard served as a parking lot. An oak, its base surrounded by bedraggled pansies, shaded the frame cottage.

Inside, the former living room had become a beige and brown reception area. The air smelled stale from old paper files and cigarette smoke.

An elderly lady with bright eyes and unnaturally pink cheeks manned a desk by the door. She jumped up to greet us.

Mark and Abner were already acquainted with Flo, but I had to be introduced.

Without asking questions, she clucked over my bandages and offered us coffee. "Bob had to take his son to the orthodontist this afternoon and hadn't planned on coming back to the office, but I reached him when you called, Abner. He ought to be back shortly. I waited to leave so I could let you in."

Abner and Mark exchanged looks.

Did they suspect Bob of setting those men on us? If so, they said nothing in front of Flo.

Still prattling, she gathered up a purse and lunch bag. "Can I get you anything before I go?"

Abner assured her we were fine and waved her out the door.

"All right. If there's nothing else, I'll go on then. Now y'all be sure and turn the coffee pot off when you leave."

We promised we would. Once the door locked shut behind her, we got our coffee and sat down at the utilitarian kitchen table.

Abner brought out a pouch of tobacco from the pocket of his worn suit coat and filled his pipe. "I'm terribly sorry about all this." He tamped the bowl. Despite his vague air, his movements were spare and efficient.

Like Mark's. Surprising there could be any similarities between two men so different.

Abner went on, "I'd hoped it would be a simple matter to pick up Hoo's notes and carry them back with me."

"Yes." Mark, his chair pulled close and his knee pressed against an undamaged side of my leg, showed no interest in Abner's apologies. His natural reserve had returned. "It should have been a simple matter."

Should have been.

Abner searched his pocket for matches, found a pack and lit his pipe. As he drew on the stem, the sweet smell of rich tobacco permeated the room. "You've had a rough year." Mark's apathy didn't disconcert Abner. "That business in Africa and now this. There's a contract in Canada we're about to get. I planned to assign it to you but if you like, I'll put it off on someone else. Give you another month or so at home."

"Yes. That'll be good." Again Mark sounded indifferent.

Abner, brows knitted, drew on his pipe and shot a surreptitious glance toward my husband.

Mark remained distant.

It was left to me to ask, "What do we do now?"

"Now?" Abner echoed, transferring his attention to me. His face with its benign features and bushy brows, cleared. White teeth clenched the pipe stem. His dark eyes reminded me of Mark's, deceptively mild, hiding intelligence and awareness.

Among other things.

I glanced at my husband, but his cup of coffee engrossed him.

"What do you mean, my dear?" Abner prompted, anxious to settle any worries I might have.

Why had I disliked him so? This man's concern about Mark's present withdrawal was as sincere as it had been about my injuries.

I warmed a bit.

Mark's reticence had colored my entire view of life, including Abner Crowley. If I'd broached my fears, about Abner, about us, in the beginning, would Mark have tried harder to confide in me? Would our marriage have been stronger, closer?

Maybe.

I'd think about that later. "Hoo's papers. What do you do now that they're gone?"

Abner made a comforting noise, his teeth retaining their hold on the pipe. "We'll retrace his steps, redo the audit questionnaires. Things like this happen sometimes. We'll deal with it."

"Two men killed?" I trailed my fingertips along Mark's arm for reassurance, remembering Hoo and the unknown man swept away by the river. "Something that happens?" The death of my dog and a ransacked cottage and a fear of the dark that would never go away? "What kind of things normally happen at FIFA?"

"Not this kind, I assure you." At my revulsion, Abner gestured with his pipe. "There'll be an inquiry within FIFA to discover exactly what went on and who was involved, but that needn't affect you." A stray puff of smoke wafted upward. "I want to apologize to you, my dear. This has been a hideous situation for you to have been thrust into. Mark's quite right to be angry."

I had been hoping Mark would ask. When he didn't, I did. "How did those men know where you were meeting us?"

"That's one of the things we'll be looking at in the inquiry." The answer came out smoothly. "And we will find out, never fear."

"Only Mark and I knew where we'd be—" I began.

"Leave it, Steve." Mark touched my shoulder, looking very tired as I knew he must be.

Me, too.

I was suddenly conscious of nothing so much as a desire to go home and go to sleep in my own bed. My eyes would hardly stay open.

Those darned pain pills. I should have waited till I got home to take one.

The pipe smoke became stifling.

Mark got up. "We're exhausted, and Steve's about to go to sleep. There's nothing we can do here. We'll be at the house if you need us."

As I dragged myself to my feet, Abner rose, too. "The main thing I want is to be sure no one talks about this."

I wondered how he could hope to keep all that had occurred quiet. "What about the police? We're seeing them Thursday about our break-in. What do we tell them?"

"What you've already told them," Abner said, choosing a portion of my arm that wasn't bruised or scraped or bandaged. He patted it carefully. "Your statements ought to be the end of it. If necessary, I'll have Bob fill the authorities in on the rest and you shouldn't be bothered anymore."

He turned his head toward Mark, at least a foot and a half taller. Abner had to look up at him, but that didn't undermine his air of command. "Silly to tell you not to talk about this. You know how FIFA operates. But your wife doesn't."

"Steve doesn't gossip."

Abner's sympathetic eyes were hooded. "I'm sure she doesn't, but I had to mention it."

"Who would believe me?" I asked.

Looking like a benevolent college professor, Abner drew on his pipe and did not answer.

As Mark and I were going out the door, Abner came up to me. "I never had a chance to tell you personally, Steve, how sorry I was about your baby."

"Thank you. I got the flowers." I acknowledged his sympathy and remembered that period of my life without distress. Or guilt, or remorse, or anger. Only a deep permanent sadness that had at long last begun to be bearable.

Mark had known. All the time I had been intent on destroying everything that mattered, he had known I would come back to myself.

"I sent a note to the office thanking FIFA," I told Abner, "and another to you."

"Yes." As he squeezed my uninjured shoulder, a veil of melancholy covered him. "You might not know, but my wife and I lost an infant grandchild." I could almost feel his pain.

So during one meeting with Abner Crowley, my image of him changed. As did my images of my husband and our life together and indeed my own self.

I had prevailed over my grief and I would resume living.

CHAPTER EIGHTEEN

AS WE LEFT FIFA's field office, a compact car, indistinct beneath the street lights, turned into the driveway of the renovated house. Bob Colverton stuck his head out the window and waved.

Mark held up an acknowledging hand but didn't stop.

I was glad. I might be bone-tired, but there were still questions needing answers.

"Why didn't you want me to ask Abner about the leak?" I asked as he wheeled the SUV into traffic.

Dusk had fallen, and the street lamps threw an artificial reddish glow over the car and caused long shadows to graze the dashboard and exaggerate its numerous knobs and cavities.

The LED lights winked. Mark's face in the gloom was barely distinguishable.

Maybe Coral wasn't the reason he had stopped me from questioning Abner.

"Because." He kept driving.

I sighed. I'd have to begin all over again.

Would this struggle go on every day of our marriage? I had to convince my husband to confide in me despite what he feared might be proffered in place of understanding. Maybe my reluctance to dig into his secrets had caused his anxieties to mushroom as much as mine.

Oncoming car lights flickered over his stern profile.

He will tell me or I will ask, I promised myself. And keep asking.

Thus was my new resolve. Thanks to Coral.

But Mark finally continued without prodding. "Only the three of us knew where we were meeting."

"I've thought about that. The limousine pulled in right before the shuttle bus arrived with Abner. Someone must have known he would be at the airport and would lead them to the package. They waited at the airport, saw the name on the bus he took, and hurried over to the lot before it arrived."

He couldn't argue with my reasoning. And that would lead him to the one logical, inescapable conclusion: Coral had told them where we'd be.

His profile remained unbending. "Nobody knew Abner was coming into the airport."

I hated to say her name, but I had to.

Not because I was jealous but because I wanted him to admit the truth. "Coral knew. You said in front of her that Abner was flying in. And that brown pickup came to her hotel as soon as we left her."

He grunted then smiled in a strange bittersweet way that made me want to hold him and comfort him as he had held me. "Okay. Coral knew. Maybe I'm wrong, maybe she's the leak. FIFA will sort it out, Steve. I'm not sure I care anymore. Let's leave it, can we?"

He loved me, and not Coral.

I knew he loved me.

I had seen it in his face, heard it in his voice, watched him give up Hoo's package without a murmur to keep me safe. If ever I had harbored doubts about his love, this day had dispersed them.

He loved me, yet he refused to believe Coral could betray him.

I was curiously deflated.

* * * *

WE ARRIVED HOME exhausted.

Mark insisted I take a shower before falling into bed. "I don't know how well they cleaned your scrapes at the clinic, but antibiotics nowadays can't be trusted to kill all the germs," he said as he sat down to listen to the messages on the answering machine. "Soap and water's the best way to head off infection."

Candy's voice rang out from the box, plaintive, almost querulous. "I got there at nine like you said and nobody was home. Ma-ark, where are you? Call me."

"Ma-ark," I parroted.

He pointed a finger at me. "For that you'll have to chaperon me every single second she's sitting so you'd better get some thick books to read. Go bathe. And use that germicidal soap the doctor gave me when I cut my hand."

As he ran the rest of the tape, containing several more urgent messages from Candy, I took my prescribed shower. Afterward, I allowed him, again at his insistence, to spray me all over with an antibacterial disinfectant.

The cold mist made me shiver. "You may be killing the germs, but have you thought about the good bacteria you're killing as well?"

"Fiona called, wants you to call her back," he informed me as he ignored my complaints and sprayed happily away. "Shit, that guy did a job on you, didn't he? I wonder who he is." He scowled at the skinned place on the front of one shoulder.

"I don't care who he is, and neither do you," I said with alarm.

"If we're lucky, we'll never see him again. Ouch! That stuff burns. I don't care what the label says. Aren't you through yet?"

"No. One more spritz on your knees and that ankle. There. If I do see him again, he's going to be sorry."

"You won't see him."

He wasn't convinced.

"And even if you do, you'd better ignore him."

He offered me the receiver. "Want to call Fee and see what she needs before I start returning my calls?"

"Not till tomorrow. She's just wondering if I'm still thinking about divorce and wants to tell me again I'm out of my mind, giving up a super guy like you."

"Did she say that? I always knew I liked the woman." He took my upper arms carefully and kissed my cheek and the unbruised shoulder.

"I don't know how I'll explain everything to her."

"Ask her why she can't take a joke," he advised between kisses.

I was too tired to do more than wriggle under his caresses. "On the other hand, she may be wanting to trade me Dan for you."

"Tell her artists are notoriously unstable and that you refuse to let her make the sacrifice." He pulled back, looking worried. "Besides, Dan's an ex-jock and you know they all develop beer guts when they get a little age on them. You don't want Dan."

"No," I whispered. "I don't want Dan."

He gave me one last careful kiss on the lips. "Go to bed, love. You look like the wicked witch."

"Why should I take criticism from a man who looks like he met the wrong end of a shovel?"

After making a mental note to talk to Abner and beg him to ensure Crooked Nose never came anywhere near Mark's vicinity ever again, I went to bed. While Mark rescheduled Candy, I fell asleep.

I didn't hear him come to bed, though every time I woke up during the night, and those times were frequent due to virtually every movement setting off new aches and pains, he lay quiet and unmoving, his breathing constant. Asleep.

But he lay on his back. Mark never slept on his back.

Toward dawn, I made another mental note to ask him in the morning why he couldn't sleep.

* * * *

THE DAY AFTER losing Hoo's package dawned bright and clear.

By the time I woke up, Mark lay with a careful hand resting on my waist, sleeping a sound exhausted sleep. Though his shoulder and chest didn't quite touch my sore back, I could feel the gentle rise and fall of his breathing.

His hand at my waist was a sculptor's hand. It curved from fingertips to wrist with promised strength and capability.

Desire stirred, but my various scrapes and bruises were beginning to ache in earnest. In the end, pain overrode passion.

Time for a pill.

When I crept out of bed, Mark didn't stir. I dug into the very back of my closet for a particular robe to wear.

Downstairs in the kitchen, I took a pain pill and slathered on some more ointment. Then I brewed coffee. The aroma would rise to the bedroom and wake Mark.

Before too long, I sat at the table drinking a cup and rejoicing at the subsided pain. Soon I heard the shower, and then Mark's impatient footsteps on the stairs. He burst into the kitchen without shoes and an island shirt in bright reds and yellows drooping from one hand. Damp hair fell to his shoulders in rippling chestnut waves.

He stopped at the sight of me. "Good morning."

"Good morning."

He looked striking, standing in the morning sunshine with his torso bare to the navel and the low-slung jeans clutching narrow hips. Despite the discolored jaw and cut over the eye, he looked fine. Awfully fine.

His face brightened as though I looked every bit as fine to him. "A very good morning." Coming over, he bent down to kiss me. Gingerly, so as to avoid my wounds, he fingered the top of the silk robe I had chosen. "Hey, that's a neat kimono you have on there."

"Why, thank you, sir," I said demurely. I tilted my head to look up into his eyes. "It was a gift from the man I love."

His fingers found my breast beneath the gown and traced the nipple with great gentleness. "Is that right? Really the man you love?"

"Yes."

"He loves you, too. But you're sure of that, now, too, aren't you?"

"Maybe. I think so."

"You'd better be. I can prove he loves you. Wanna go upstairs and let me show you?" He summoned his hopeful leer.

"Maybe. Later. When I see how my bumps and bruises feel. Have some coffee first." I lifted his hand and moved it away, but not impatiently.

"Okay. If you're sure it has to be later." He slipped on the loud tropical shirt but left it unbuttoned and loose so that the middle of his chest remained bared to his navel. The lines of his flat stomach tightened and flexed under his arm movements.

Maybe I ought to rethink my position on going upstairs.

He forestalled me by heading to the coffee pot. "That coffee does smell good, now that you mention it."

Later.

We had toast and pineapple juice for breakfast, smiling at each other across the table as we used to do. He put out his hand as we ate, mingled his fingers with mine so that they didn't brush the scraped heel. Sunshine filled the kitchen.

Finally, I pushed my plate away. "Abner didn't look at all like I thought he'd look."

Mark lounged back in his chair. "No? What did you expect?"

"Someone big. Someone tall and sinister and grim. Not someone who looks like a koala bear."

"A koala bear?" Mark scowled, used the tip of his tongue to clear away a bread crumb in the corner of his mouth. "Believe me, love, Abner's no koala bear. He's a hard-nosed bastard with a heart of stone. I'd have been happier if you'd never met him." He smiled to take the edge off his words.

Abner Crowley was the last thing I wanted to discuss. "I want to stay married to you, Mark. Whether we can make it work or not depends on you. Do you want to finish telling me about Africa?"

The aura of content faded. He removed his fingers from my hand. Though he had another piece of toast left, he pushed his chair back from the table as though he'd lost his appetite. "I've never wanted you involved in my job. Most of the time what I do is pretty boring. Occasionally, it's unpleasant."

"Like what happened to Hoo."

"That was not normal. It was unusual, a freak coincidence that should never have happened. No, most of the time any rough patches in this business have to do with exposing embezzlers or tracing criminal connections. Things like that which very rarely affect me or any of the other auditors directly."

"I'm not sure you're telling me everything."

He sighed. "All right, sometimes people get annoyed at what we find and make some wild threats. But nothing's ever come of them. And there's never been anything like this."

He got up, paced a few steps to and fro, turned his chair around, and swung a leg over the seat to sit in it backward. Wrapping his arms around the back, he lowered his head and rested his chin on the top and stared at the floor. "I never saw any need to upset you with that part of my job."

"Did you think I couldn't handle it?"

"No." His face lifted in dismay. "That wasn't it at all. I didn't want you disturbed or shocked. Or disappointed."

In him? "I hope I'm stronger than you believe."

"Maybe you are at that." He returned to his survey of the floor.

After a few minutes, I reminded him that I was waiting. "Can you tell me now?"

I would keep digging. As Coral had advised.

"Mark?"

He surrendered. "Oh, hell. I really didn't want you to know about Africa."

"And I really want to know about everything that concerns you."

"It would only have worried you. And you already had enough on you with losing the baby and all."

"I was hurting then. But I'm all right now. Tell me."

He started, haltingly at first, and then the words poured out as if he relived the events each day. He might have been waiting all along, needing all along, to put words to what he had witnessed.

He told me about the people dying around him during the beginning of the coup, about the shrieks and the whack of the bullets against flesh, about the thuds when the bodies hit the street and the hideous wails when death wasn't immediate.

"Men and women and children. Some of them were people I'd worked with, Steve. One man I'd eaten lunch with the day before. The back of his head was gone. It was like being trapped in hell."

He never looked at me the whole time he spoke. The morning sun streamed in, kissed his hair to an auburn burnish. He put up a hand to shield his eyes against the rays. Or to shield his face from me.

"How long were you there?" I wanted to touch him, comfort him, but I couldn't. Not yet.

"All that day and the next." Emotionless, he recited how he and a woman had hidden in a dumpster and listened to the firing squads in the next block. How the following night, most of the rioting soldiers had fallen into drunken stupors. How the woman, a native of the country, had led him through piles of corpses and burning buildings out of the city.

He described the desolation of the city, with its main parts ravaged and the bodies stacked like cordwood. He told how he and his companion had sheltered in an outlying house as opposition forces swept past.

Remembering his escape had to be almost as traumatic as living it.

"Then, the freakiest thing." He seemed bemused. "I came across one of FIFA's local people who'd made it through. I can't tell you how great he was. I hooked up with him and he led me to the border. He even found a guide to take me across."

The guide had started out all right.

"Until we ran across some soldiers right at the line. They may have been looking for me. The guide got surly. I caught him trying to get my briefcase so I ditched him." He looked at me. "Actually, I hit him on the head and tied him up and left him. Then I sneaked across the border and hitched a ride to the nearest town."

Still carrying the records he'd picked up from the palace, Mark caught a plane out from the neighboring capital to Khartoum. There, in one of fate's caprices, he just missed a connection.

"By twenty lousy minutes. The one other plane leaving that day went to Karachi, and I took it. I was desperate to get home to see about you and the baby."

Love and compassion mingled, threatened to overflow and sink us both. I put my fingertips together to keep from reaching out to him.

He brushed his hair back with one hand absently, hesitated like debating whether to go on.

He swallowed. "It turned out for the best that I didn't make the connection."

The plane he'd missed at Khartoum had exploded over the Mediterranean.

Horror convulsed him as he told that part. He jumped up, swept up his cup and plate, and carried them to the sink.

"You might remember it." He had his back turned to me. "It made headlines throughout the world."

After losing the baby, I had gone for weeks without caring what happened in the outside world. But he didn't need reminding why I hadn't kept up with the news. "No. I didn't hear."

Still turned away, he rinsed his dishes. He scrubbed with short, determined strokes. The muscles in his shoulders tensed and strained under the loose shirt. "A hundred and twenty-three people died. Four infants and six children under twelve were on the plane. Everyone on it died."

I inhaled shakily. "How horrible. You could have been killed. I'm so thankful you did miss the plane."

"Yes." He cut the water off, turned toward me with his amiable expression that hid so much. He looked the same outwardly. Unruffled and assured. "But all those people died because of me. Because somebody knew those records would sink their drug operation. The bomb was set to destroy the files I carried out."

Pity rose, soared.

He looked the same, but I saw for the first time the grief behind his smiling mask, understood for the first time how he had suffered and continued to suffer.

"You can't know that."

"I do know." The rebuke was gentle, the smile equally gentle. A rebuke nonetheless. "They never found who was responsible, never found any tangible proof. But I know, Steve. If I'd given up the files, those people would still be alive."

"You couldn't have done that. Some other man maybe, but not you."

Poor consolation, but it was all I had.

I understood his feeling responsible for people dying so senselessly. But he could have been among the dead.

Thank God he'd escaped. I wanted to go to him, stroke his hair, hold him. But not yet.

"No." He walked back to the table, eyes blank. "No, I didn't give them up. I ended up flying home by way of Tokyo. I caught a flight from there to Anchorage and then to New York."

He revealed such agony that he might never again reveal, even to me. "You'd lost the baby by that time. The office told me what had happened, that you'd nearly died. That the baby was dead. A courier met me when I changed planes in New York and took the records. I came on home."

With a kimono and roses for me.

My heart bled for him, for us. He had faulted himself for circumstances he couldn't help. And in my misery, I had faulted him, too. Shifting guilt for my own shortcomings, I'd found it easier to blame Mark for his absence than to take the trouble to find out why he'd stayed away.

One failure of many that had nearly doomed our marriage.

It was a while before I could speak. "Thank you for telling me. I wish you had told me before now."

"You've been living with your own heartbreak." He stopped, took a deep breath, and tried to project his old devil-may-care attitude. He couldn't quite pull it off. "No use in crying over what's done. Nothing changes things in the past."

So that was where Mark had been when I needed him.

And when he'd come home needing me, I had remained sunken in my morass of self-pity and disdained his overtures.

I went to him then, framing his face with my fingertips and kissing him on the mouth. I winced as he brushed my elbows.

"Steve."

"Hush." I pushed him down into the empty chair. "Sit down, babe. The backs of my legs are all right." I curled up on his lap and held him to me and comforted him as I should have done months before.

CHAPTER NINETEEN

THAT APRIL CHANGED everything.

Mark and I recovered. Our marriage was still on. We were closer than ever, bound in an intimacy I'd always longed for. The nightmares of that spring receded into the past where they belonged.

Still, there remained a few unsettled ends.

In the days and weeks following the loss of Hoo's package, we continued to adjust to small changes.

I insisted on a night light in the hall. Mark threw out everything in the lake cottage and bought all new furnishings including dishes and linen. We agreed that for the time being, we wanted a cat instead of a puppy.

Another dog might remind us too much of Sweet Rowdy.

And sometimes after we went to sleep, I would awaken to find Mark flat on his back as he had been that first night when Hoo's reports were stolen.

He would lie quietly, perfectly still except for his regular breathing. But awake, always awake.

I knew about those nighttime vigils, and I also knew that sooner or later I would have to confront him.

One night, as I lay on my stomach, curled up against him as close as I could get, I roused to find him on his back, his far hand flung across his chest and resting against my arm. His breathing was measured, but I could see the shine of his eyes reflected in the moonlight as he stared at the ceiling.

My heart sank, but I had learned—give Coral grudging due for the education—to ask. If I didn't, Mark wouldn't tell.

"Mark? What are you doing?"

He turned his head, kissed my forehead. "Thinking how much I like lying here with you like this. Go back to sleep, love."

My injuries had healed to the point where I could nestle against him without discomfort.

I shifted to set my head on his shoulder and push my face against his neck. He smelled piney from day-old aftershave and earthy from the modeling clay and musky from his body oils.

"I don't want to be protected. We've been over that."

"Sorry, I forgot. You're a big girl." He stroked my hair.

The warmth in his voice was for me.

That knowledge added to the content of having him beside me, of being able to stretch out during the night and touch him and know he belonged to me.

I hugged his chest. "Tell me what's wrong. You haven't been sleeping nights."

"I tried not to disturb you."

"I know, but I could tell something's bothering you. Please. Tell me."

He gave a short, dissatisfied sigh and moved me off him. "I've kept going over everything that happened with Hoo. Everything's all wrong." He threw back the sheet and swung his feet off the side of the bed to sit up. "Nothing adds up."

I rubbed his back, afraid he blamed himself for the loss of Hoo's papers. "There was nothing you could do, Mark." Not with the gun aimed at me.

"No." The remoteness had returned. No longer aware of me, he was lost in the puzzle that haunted his nights.

I lay back.

Mark would never be the type of man to blurt out every thought that crossed his mind, and I couldn't change him. I didn't want to change him. I'd have to ask. "What is it that doesn't add up?"

He shrugged. The muscles of his back turned to me rippled in the white moonlight. A mole on his right shoulder blade looked like a fat bug. "Abner and you and I were the only people who knew where we were meeting that afternoon. How did those people know?"

I fingered the mole, leery of opening that can again. "You said FIFA would go into that."

"Yeah, I know what I said, but they haven't. I don't think they're going to."

Perhaps this anticlimactic post mortem was Mark's way of saying he could face the truth about Coral. I kept my voice impartial. "Well, then, going back to my theory, could Coral have told them we'd be at the airport?"

"No." The dark ponytail moved impatiently. "Coral didn't tell."

"How do you know?"

"I asked her."

Why was he so blind when it came to Coral? The only logical explanation led back to her.

Dammit, he ought to be able to see that.

"Babe," I began, careful not to accuse, "the only people who knew Abner was flying in, were you and me and Coral. You and I didn't talk to anyone about it. So isn't Coral the only one left?"

"Abner knew."

"Yes, but Abner wouldn't have set those men on us."

"Wouldn't he?"

I stared at the back of his head. This new direction would absolve Coral. "You think Abner told someone. That doesn't make sense, Mark."

"It doesn't, does it?"

How could he suspect Abner?

To keep from finding Coral guilty. "No, it doesn't. Why would Abner tell anyone? It seems more likely to me that . . ." I wouldn't risk blaming Coral. "You really prefer believing that Abner was the leak rather than Coral, don't you?"

Mark turned around, opened his mouth to speak, closed it again.

The old fears came tumbling back. He loved me but continued to keep things from me.

I seized his arm and shook it. "Mark, is it going to be like this all the time? Am I going to have to pull everything out of you inch by inch?"

He sighed, leaned over the bed on one elbow to trace my lip with his finger. "I'm trying to do better. Really I am. I can't help it if I'm the strong silent type."

"Don't flatter yourself, I've seen you at parties. Really, Mark, is it so hard to admit Coral might be the leak?"

"Look, love, I know Coral. I know how it hurts you whenever I tell you I know her that well. But I do. I can't change the past. And I know she's solid."

"Mark—"

He pressed my lips together with tender thumb and forefinger to keep me from speaking. "No, listen to me. I fell in love with you the moment I saw you. There's never been, never will be, anyone else for me. If I have to quit FIFA, quit sculpting, quit anything else you want me to do to prove it, I damn well will. But Coral's a friend. And I won't make her a villain to satisfy you that she's nothing but a friend."

I was humiliated.

If he hadn't been so absolutely, positively, damnably on the mark as to why I disliked Coral, I wouldn't have been nearly as humiliated.

"No, I don't want you to," I mumbled.

He was kind. "I know you don't. So if Coral's out of the picture, Abner's left."

"Not Abner." Not the plump little man I'd met.

"Yes, Abner. I know, I know. The sweet little koala. Believe me, he's no cuddly koala." He gave an ironic laugh. "No, love, Abner's a devious, manipulative bastard, totally dedicated to FIFA. I've worked for him a long time and I know the lengths he'd go to for FIFA."

I tried to readjust to this unflattering view of Abner Crowley. "That doesn't mean he's to blame for those men finding us."

His hand curled into a fist next to my cheek. "I realize what I've been thinking seems pretty crazy." He exhaled. "But everything leads back to Abner. Abner assigns jobs to us. He knew Hoo's audit could be risky, he couldn't help but know. And Hoo wasn't the world's sharpest guy. If anyone would have handed those worksheets over without asking embarrassing questions, it would have been Hoo. I think Abner chose him for that very reason."

He saw my confusion. He stretched out and rolled toward me, on top of the sheets so that the crisp cotton remained a barrier between his lower half and mine. The smooth skin of his chest spread its warmth through my thin top.

His arm wrapped around my cotton-swathed waist. My arm moved round his bare shoulder.

"I guess what I'm asking, Steve, is what if Abner, Abner meaning FIFA, intended all along to give those men Hoo's audit results?"

I paused to take in his meaning. "That doesn't make sense. Why would he?"

The moon's ivory glow illuminated his face next to mine, changing its outline and bone structure, giving him shadowed sockets for eyes, painting him as some inscrutable night creature. "I told you I was thinking some pretty weird stuff, but this is all I can come up with that explains everything."

He remained beside me but talked to himself. "I never was satisfied that Abner would have assigned Hoo something so important. Hoo was a nice guy. Methodical, plodding, unambitious. He did his job but couldn't look beyond it. FIFA generally gave him uncomplicated, straightforward audits of small government agencies. This audit was anything but straightforward. That paperwork we had was complicated, intertwined with too much other stuff for someone like Hoo to be working on it."

Restless, he removed his arm and plopped onto his back to stare up at the ceiling as he had been doing when I awoke. "Hoo was a little slow on the uptake, but he knew his shortcomings and made up for them with hard work. And one thing about him, he had a very sharp moral compass. He wouldn't deviate from what he thought was right. I'm not sure Abner realized that."

I pushed the sheet back, holding onto his arm. My hand slid across his stomach, felt the flesh smooth and taut over the muscles. I was tired of FIFA, tired of Coral, tired of their intrusions in our life.

Mark didn't notice my hand. "This particular audit was strange. Not normal at all."

Resigned, I laid my head on his chest and struggled to follow the ideas churning in his head. "So Abner assigned the audit to Hoo deliberately."

"Go back to that. What if FIFA chose Hoo for that job because they figured he'd be an easy mark for the oil industries or whoever those people were working for?"

Despite the lack of inflection, I sensed excitement. Somewhere beneath the cool exterior, my husband had worked his way to a threshold of certainty where he refused to look back. He no longer sought other solutions because he wouldn't even admit they existed.

"Why would FIFA want Hoo's worksheets to be stolen? Why not just give them to whoever wanted them?"

His heartbeat filled my ear. "It wouldn't be FIFA, per se, Steve. It would be FIFA's employer."

"That sub-agency of the Energy Department?" I propped myself up on one elbow, found his belly button. "The Office of Renewable Energy Alternatives or whatever? Why would they want to leak Hoo's worksheets?"

"I don't know." He threw up an open hand. "You're right. It's crazy. I'm crazy. The whole thing's been crazy from the beginning. Abner's always such a close-mouthed, sneaky son of a bitch. I can't help but think he knew all along what was happening. But he'll never tell and we'll never know. I wonder about this stuff and it bugs hell out of me."

"Okay." Having gone through so much to get us to the point where my husband would open up, I wasn't about to agree that he was crazy. If he was determined to blame FIFA for Hoo's death, I would help. I racked my brain for an explanation. Any explanation.

"There're rumors of a new underground cartel, an alliance of foreign and American oil companies. Maybe the audits were leaked so, so—" Inspiration struck. "So they can see the government can manufacture its own fuel. If they cut supplies, the government cranks up synthetic production until we don't need their oil any more. How about that?"

"Hmmm. Maybe. They raise prices, we move to the synthetic stuff and do away with their crude altogether, huh? But we're already working on getting out of crude. Even if it may take years to get to that point. Why leak this information now?"

I went back to circling his navel with my thumb. "Well, if you're right, and FIFA's client wanted their reports stolen, there had to be a purpose."

"Uh huh. The leak, if it was intentional, had to be to get information to someone. The someone must have been the oil interests. Why that information, I don't know. Maybe you're right. Maybe that's what it was about. The government shows them they have other options if oil prices go up."

My hand might have been a washrag for all the attention he paid it. "Or if the oil industry raises prices drastically. Don't forget that. If they, say, double prices, the government could start ramping up production. We're already using a lot of ethanol and electric cars. If the government filtered in this new stuff, it could drive prices down."

He looked at me oddly. "Filtering in what new stuff?"

"From the experimental factory we went to. If it works, you know they'll be setting up more."

"Setting up more factories like that one?" Mark threw off my hand and sat up in bed. He ended up cross-legged on top of the covers, as still as one of his statues.

He'd left me again. What had I said? "Mark?"

When he spoke, he was controlled, deliberate. "Lord, you're bright, love. I don't know how you ever got mixed up with such a dumb sculptor."

"Mark, stop." I wasn't about to let him lose me, risk losing him back to his absurd evasions. "What is it?"

He didn't answer. The facts were still turning, finally meshing into . . .

I plucked at his arm. "I'm tired of begging."

He turned his head, but I doubted he saw me. His excitement palpitated. "It's all there. All the pieces. They just needed arranging in the right order."

"I still don't understand."

He put out a hand to my cheek. "Prices, love, like you said. Let's do a scenario. Say our government gets wind that the oil industry is about to jack prices in the near future."

I laughed. "People complain that they do it now. Every time there's a cold snap, the oil people say fuel oil's to blame for the hike. Every summer, they say people are traveling more so gas costs more."

"Right." The words tumbled out so fast I could hardly follow them. "And if prices rise too much, we have an energy crisis on our hands. That'll lead to sky high inflation, unemployment, gas and heating bills out of sight. The economy's so-so now but an oil crunch would put an end to that. We'd have worried business owners and angry taxpayers."

His profile was silhouetted in the moonlight. "What would you do if it was your responsibility to deal with a crisis like that?"

He was in a strange mood.

"I've never been in politics."

Still sitting cross-legged, he took my hand in both his, kissed each knuckle and the palm. "Neither have I, thank God, but it's the dirtiest business there is."

Then his suspicions came spilling out. "That site where the factory was supposed to be located? Nothing was there except an empty building." He spoke too fast to be coherent. His hands unconsciously tightened on my arm. "It had been used recently. I'd guess they had people working there when Hoo did his deskwork, so it would look like a viable concern, but it was deserted when I saw it."

"Look viable? It wasn't?" I frowned. "You mean there was no experimental factory? They were pretending to work on a synthetic fuel for Hoo's benefit?"

He let one of my hands loose, stretched out his legs, and lay back on his elbows.

"It's the only explanation. Abner would never have let everything drop and come down for Hoo's papers unless something big was going on. The whole thing was a bluff. A giant bluff. That audit was set up on a fake business with a fake set of books, intended to be leaked from the beginning."

"What?"

"Obviously, Hoo didn't know that. When it came time to turn over his final figures to the oil interests, he suspected something was wrong and he balked."

"Mark, no. That's . . . that's horrible."

"I think you were right all along."

He didn't hear me. He drove his fists into the mattress, unaware he was doing it.

"My guess is that the client set it up, put in numbers comping out about where they want the price of crude to settle, and then contracted with FIFA for the audit with the understanding the report would be leaked. If our thieves were working for the oil industry, those reports will spoon-feed them the figures. They'll know how high the price of oil can go before the government begins producing synthetic fuel big-time and cuts them out altogether."

He couldn't be still. He swung his feet around and sat on the edge of the bed for the second time. "By producing our non-existent synthetic fuel."

His rancor frightened me. "Mark."

"So oil creeps up to a specified level, and we're going to grumble but we can afford to pay it. The oil companies will make their share without hurting the economy too much and everyone's going to be happy. Damn FIFA. And damn Abner Crowley. He knew about it. He had to."

A sweeping, violent gesture of his arm sent the figurines on the headboard crashing against each other and the mirror before landing on the floor.

I was afraid, of him and for him.

Mark was such a tightly controlled individual. His giving way like this would destroy him.

I massaged his back in a desperate attempt to call him back. "Babe, this is only a theory. You don't know it's true. People don't do things like that. Not in real life."

He picked up a statue from the headboard, a druid, the lone survivor still on its surface after his vicious onslaught. He clenched it tightly. For a moment, I feared he might dash it against the wall.

"Mark."

The flat of my palm felt the anger drain out of his back, dissipating as suddenly as it had formed.

"Sometimes they do." He sounded dispirited.

Mark had never sounded dispirited, and again I was afraid for him.

He went on, "Sometimes people think they know better than anyone else what's right, and they bend all the facts so that everyone goes along. Everyone except people like Hoo."

What if he was right? He seemed certain that he was. And he was so angry . . .

His anger convinced me. Mark knew the people involved as I did not.

I trusted his judgment.

Besides, his reasoning was sound. Abner had known every step we took. Coral had talked to him when she found out about the pen, in time for him to send the men to cut us off at the dam.

Mark himself had told him we were at Coral's hotel, before the brown pickup showed up minutes later. Coral had never called anyone; I had been with her the whole time.

Abner, not Coral or Bob, had known what Hoo was working on.

It hurt to say, "Then Hoo and Sweet Rowdy died for nothing."

"Oh, no, love. Not for nothing. To keep the oil rolling. To keep the economy going."

There was such desolation about him that I clambered up and across the few inches of mattress to hold him in my arms.

His body was unnaturally tense, fixed with outrage but also sorrow. I rocked him in my arms, there on the edge of the bed, wanting to comfort him, wanting him not to care so much that he fell apart. "It's over. You can't do anything, Mark. You can't change anything."

"I know that." His voice sounded strange, ragged. "My head does know that. But it hurts inside. It hurts the same way losing the baby hurt."

I smoothed his hair that had escaped its band and buried my face in its coarse curls. The ache at mention of our baby was that of an old fading scar. I no longer blamed him or myself. His philosophy was right, and I told him so. "You have to accept what's happened and go on. That's what you told me. What's done is done, and we only have the future. That's what you said and it's true."

He turned suddenly, to envelop me in a great shuddering clasp. My eyes brimmed when I felt his wet face against mine, but I didn't cry. I held him tighter so that I would not lose him, nor he me.

* * * *

THE GEORGIA AUTUMN sun beat down on the fading zinnias and petunias and marigolds as I crossed the backyard separating house and studio.

It was time to remind Mark about his appointment with a representative of a group developing the huge shopping mall in Texas.

Possible seven figure commissions are not to be sneered at, no matter that half the money would go to Mark's agent and the IRS. Nor are appointments forgotten with those who could steer seven figure commissions our way.

Mark needed the project. His contract with FIFA would elapse next month, and he had officially notified Abner he would not be renewing it.

None of his models was with him this week.

He worked alone except for our new cat, a refugee from the humane society.

Hunter (Mark had named her Mighty Hunter when on his loosing her in the yard for the first time, she had immediately brought him a small trembling ground squirrel) lay in a pool of sunlight, eyes closed, chin resting on one bent leg.

She was ostensibly oblivious to everything. However, the pricking of one ear when I entered, along with a tiny flick of her tail, gave her away.

Mark, humming along with the *Evita* soundtrack, shaped some intricate points on a clay model at least three feet high.

I stood in the doorway and watched his hands, quick and capable as they smoothed the clay and molded each section until the original lumpy substance became the exact image he saw in his mind. As he worked, perspiration darkened the old athletic shirt and turned the curves of his arms and shoulders into gleaming hunks of muscle that caught and reflected the light each time he shifted postures.

Absorbed in his task, he took several minutes longer than Hunter to sense my presence.

He whirled, recognized me. Dark eyes lightened. "Lunch time?"

I put my hands in my jeans band that was getting a little tight. I wanted to put them on him but didn't care to appear too forward. "Thought you might want to knock off early. You're meeting the Dominion Falls people at two. Egyptian-themed shopping mall. Five atriums needing lots of statuary. And one giant sculptured fountain for a three story food court. Remember?"

He made a face, but wiped his hands on his grungy shorts and went over to the sink to wash. "And I was making such good progress here."

"We need the commission. This cat likes to eat. And so do I." I scratched Hunter's ear before strolling over toward Mark's workbench to view the current project.

A kick in the gut.

The model had been taking shape for the past couple of weeks, but it had been merely a molded blob of clay with no indications as to what the finished work would be. Now, nearing completion, the bow of a small boat shot out plainly, along with its half-raised sail.

There was no mistaking the sailor.

The man's head was thrown back in a joyous attitude of challenge, his hair frizzed out in a halo and his hands holding the lines. I knew without asking that if the marble could come to life, the hair would be red and the face would have freckles.

This was the way Hoo Ogden should have looked, would have looked had he lived.

Mark came over to stand beside me, drying his hands. "It's pretty good, I think."

He'd said nearly those same words when I had come across the marble statue of the baby.

They didn't cut to the quick today. I had finally learned what I should have realized all along. My husband would never intentionally wound me or anyone else. Not with actions and not with words.

And never with his work.

My mouth was dry. "I don't know what to say. Yes, it's marvelous. I never saw him except that one time, but I recognized him at once."

"Did you?" That pleased him. He waited expectantly.

"He . . ." I paused for the lump in my throat to shrink, "he looks like he was meant to sail."

"Oh, yeah, Hoo was a fine sailor. We used to go out on the Chesapeake together when we were training at FIFA and then later when we worked out of the Institute."

"Was he—? Hoo was a good friend of yours, wasn't he?"

Though I'd tried, I had never been able to understand how Mark had remained so calm when he'd learned of Hoo's death, how he had taken the senseless act in stride. Perhaps if I dug, that last secret spot within my husband might be opened.

"Hoo and I got along. We were real close at one time." The mobile eyebrows drew close together as he pondered. "He was a good guy. Totally solid." He put out a hand to touch the wet clay lovingly. "I wish we'd made more of an effort to keep in touch."

I chose my words, trying to understand how he could take a personal tragedy and use it so. "Are you making this as a sort of memorial to him?"

"A memorial?" His frown deepened. Still stroking the damp clay, he considered. "No, I don't think so. It's just how I see him. How I'll always see him."

He pointed to a small, unshaped place in the hold of the boat. "I thought I might put Sweet Rowdy there. What do you think? She liked boating, too, and it seems right to have her and Hoo together."

In one blinding instant, I understood.

Standing with him in the bright sunshine, watching his hand stroke the clay and hearing him speak of his friend and my darling Rowdy, I understood everything about Mark.

His emotions were every bit as volatile and passionate as mine. But unlike me, he kept them tucked away, hidden beneath the casual attitude he showed me and everyone else.

He used his art as a replacement.

In his art he could allow hopes, fears, even grief, to surface without fear of exposing how much he cared. This sculpture was his way of grieving for his friend and Sweet Rowdy.

As the marble baby was his way of grieving for our lost child.

I had been wrong to brood over the past. Those April days had shown me just how wrong.

Mark had never made that mistake. He had taken his sorrow for whatever couldn't be changed and had submerged it in his art.

Instead of the battered, dying man I had seen, he had visualized the vital person Hoo had been, and that vision had given birth to this figure in clay.

A living man was what Mark chose to remember, chose to make into a sculpture, chose to present to the world.

For our baby, he had done the same thing. Instead of

memorializing the sad little dab of flesh never given a chance at life, he'd imagined our child as being healthy and happy as he had wanted. As we had wanted.

Mark watched me intently, waiting for my reaction.

He's stronger than I am.

Stronger but no less caring.

His levity masked how deeply he cared. In my narcissism, I had been too blind to see beyond his mask to the man underneath.

And I understood something else, too. Communication between two people means more than one person expressing himself. Another person has to open herself up in order to listen.

I had failed my part in the past. I wouldn't in the future. "Are you going to do it in marble?"

"Marble?"

"Like the one over there." I motioned toward the corner that I had, until today, avoided looking at, avoided mentioning. "The one you did of our baby."

I could say the words "our baby" without the rending pain. I would always have the regret, that stinging loss, but the reproaches to Mark and to myself were over and done with.

Mark was right. Life was no place to lament what might have been.

"Hm." He stepped up to the clay figure, tossing his towel on the bench as his eyes wrinkled in thought. "No, I think maybe granite. Pink granite because it seems warmer. I ordered some that's supposed to be delivered next week."

"That will be beautiful."

He covered the boat, looking sideways at me. "Do you think so?" He looked pleased, but I could tell he was uneasy.

"Yes," I said firmly. "I think if you don't sell it, it should go outside. Beside the azaleas at the lake cottage. There's a spot up there that needs something on it. I've thought so ever since I first saw it."

He grinned slowly, the caution disappearing. "I don't mind. But if we keep it, it could take away a paycheck. Since I've quit FIFA, we may go hungry."

"I can support you. And this Dominion Falls job could set us up for life."

"Sure." He looked at me, the crinkles around his eyes deepening. "If they like the model I've done. And if I get the commission. There are three of us begging for this job, love." He continued to look at me.

I stepped up to him.

"You'll get it. I have faith in you, babe."

He put his hands on my hips and pulled me toward him, rolling me over him in a deliciously decadent fashion. His voice thickened. "Do you now."

It wasn't a question but I answered anyway. "I do. When you show them that model of Candy as Cleopatra you finished last month, they won't look at anybody else. Nobody does sex as well as you."

"Nobody?" His hold tightened.

"Nobody." I was absolutely uncompromising.

"Well, I'll bet I've got somebody in hand, er, in mind that does. Want to see if I'm right?"

The point wasn't worth arguing about.

Other Fiction

by

Cheryl B. Dale

Romantic Suspense

Intimate Portraits
Set Up

Paranormal/Gothic Romance

Treacherous Beauties
The Warwicks of Slumber Mountain

Light Mystery

Taxed to the Max
Overtaxed and Underappreciated

Vintage Mystery

Losing David

Thank you for reading this book. If you enjoyed it, please consider leaving a review to help others discover it. Among sites that offer places for reader reviews are:

http://www.amazon.com

and

http://www.goodreads.com

If you do have the time and take the effort to leave a review, please accept my sincere appreciation and thanks.

www.cherylbdale.com
cherylbdale.blogspot.com
cherylbdale@hotmail.com

Made in United States
North Haven, CT
02 January 2024

46914545R00133